HIS SPIRITED LADY

ENTERPRISING WOMEN, BOOK 2

Peri Maxwell

ARE YOU SIGNED UP FOR DRAGONBLADE'S BLOG?

You'll get the latest news and information on exclusive giveaways, exclusive excerpts, coming releases, sales, free books, cover reveals and more.

Check out our complete list of authors, too!

No spam, no junk. That's a promise!

Sign Up Here

www.dragonbladepublishing.com

Dearest Reader;

Thank you for your support of a small press. At Dragonblade Publishing, we strive to bring you the highest quality Historical Romance from some of the best authors in the business. Without your support, there is no 'us', so we sincerely hope you adore these stories and find some new favorite authors along the way.

Happy Reading!

CEO, Dragonblade Publishing

*For Terri, the boss who became my friend—
who indulges my love of good bourbon.*

CHAPTER ONE

Norfolk, England
October, 1847

A MELIA CHITESTER WAS bored.

She was well-bred enough to feel guilty about it. After all, it was a lovely fall day. The sky was a blue so bright that it stung to stare too long. Wisps of pure white clouds drifted across it, casting shadows on the ground below. Birdsong floated on a breeze sweetened by rain the day before, the same gentle storm that had gilded the early fall colors on the leaves. This was everything she'd missed in London.

Almost.

Amelia filled her lungs as much as her corset would allow, using the country air to dispel the grayness that had settled in her chest during her, thankfully, interrupted Season. The sunshine warming her through her riding habit helped, as did the feel of her beloved gray mare, Molly, beneath her. Still, there was a spot that couldn't be reached. Amelia tightened her knee around the pommel and wriggled in the saddle, hoping to loosen her laces.

"Would you like to rest a moment, Miss Chitester?"

She turned to her riding companion and smiled. "No, Mr. Raymond, thank you. I'm quite well."

"It would be understandable if you wished to turn back," he insisted. "We've been riding longer than most ladies do this time of year."

He was right. Had they been in London, a few turns in the park counted as a ride, even though horses and carriages were so crowded that it could scarce be called riding. However, *going to stand in the park* did not have the same appeal. Not that it mattered. The purpose of a ride in London was to be seen.

Amelia had seen Ethan Raymond often during the summer in London, and even during her abbreviated fall visit. He drew attention for his impeccable fashion as much as for his height and his excellent seat on a massive white gelding. He must have considered tailoring and horsemanship to be intertwined, for here he was in the countryside, in a hat polished to a sheen that matched his tall riding boots, a jacquard waistcoat the color of wheat at harvest, and a teal blue coat. Who was he dressing for out here? The squirrels?

Wry humor at her own joke gave way to guilt over her nastiness. Amelia knew full well why Ethan was riding next to her in rustic Norfolk rather than in Hyde Park. She also knew all the women in London were stretching their necks to search for him in a crowd, fluttering their fans to hide their stares.

They would have been reveling in his undivided attention, not grousing over having to wear a too-heavy habit on an unusually warm morning. Perhaps her parents were right, and she did spend too much time alone.

"It is a relief to be out in the air after being penned in yesterday," Amelia said, purposefully brightening her smile. It wasn't Ethan's fault that she wished to be somewhere else entirely.

Nor was he to blame that they'd quit the house so that Doctor Anderson could visit with her father again. The doctor had visited every day upon their return from London a fortnight ago, though Father had stopped him upon Ethan's arrival. He'd said he didn't want to dampen the visit, but Amelia knew better. Her father didn't want to be seen as weak in front of someone he considered a suitor.

"I rather enjoyed yesterday," Ethan said. "Rain is always more pleasant in the country, and you made the day entertaining."

Hot coals heaped on Amelia's head. She'd used every trick she knew to keep Ethan occupied, because if he was thinking of moves in chess or backgammon, he couldn't formulate how to propose. If his hands were busy, he wouldn't be reaching for hers. And if they were in the library, her favorite chair for reading was only big enough for her.

"And I dare say," Ethan leaned closer to whisper. "Your chaperone would be much happier *not* on a horse."

His quiet, good-natured laugh was paired with a smile that most young women would envy—both that he had it and that he gave it to Amelia so willingly. But his words had her turning to check on Miss Graves, who had been her governess before being promoted to chaperone. The woman was shooing a fly from her nose while keeping a death grip on the reins of the family's oldest and most sedate horse.

"Are you all right, Miss Graves?" Amelia called.

"Fine, miss." Graves paused from shooing flies to wave her handkerchief at Amelia.

"That looks like a flag of surrender," Ethan joked in a whisper. "Should we stop to give her respite?"

It probably was surrender. Graves was so thin that there was little padding between her and the saddle. She much preferred carriages to horseback, and she'd been quick to suggest they take the landau this morning. Amelia had been just as quick to reject the carriage and its seat wide enough for two.

However, relieving Graves would mean either returning to the house or dismounting here. It was too soon for the doctor to have finished his visit, and dismounting would mean accepting Ethan's help. Amelia didn't want to encourage that intimate contact and the impression that might make.

Ethan Raymond was a nice man, with the promise of a fine

inheritance and a title. He would make some lucky girl a fine husband. But she would not be that girl.

"Let's go to the top of the hill and then turn back," Amelia suggested. "You can see the entire valley from there."

If Ethan was disappointed in her answer, he didn't show it. Though she might have heard a loud sigh from her stalwart companion. Amelia ignored Miss Graves and urged Molly forward at a slower pace than either would have preferred.

They reached their goal, and Amelia pulled Molly's reins. The horse shook her head and sidestepped, arguing to continue down the familiar path. She quieted as Amelia stroked her neck as a wordless promise for next time. It was a promise to them both.

"I say, this is lovely." Ethan's gaze swept across the valley, assessing the neat patchwork of fields stitched together by hedgerows and broken here and there by farmhouses and forests. Amelia was more interested in the small plot to their left, and the neat, new building that sat surrounded by a stand of TK-kind trees.

"How far does your father's estate stretch?" Ethan asked.

"On this side of the property, it stops here." Amelia called on years of training to keep from snapping her answer. Oakdale was not the largest estate in the county, but it was one of the prettiest. Even their neighbors said so.

"I suppose it is difficult to expand if you are competing with the Duke of Rushford," Ethan said.

"There is no competition," Amelia said. "This estate provides a more than adequate income, and Father keeps it small so that he can relax when away from London. And," she added in defense of her friends, "the Duke and Duchess of Rushford are excellent neighbors. They have done a great deal for…the village."

"Rushford's interest in trade has become well-known," Ethan said with a slight frown. "It's odd."

"I think it's admirable." Amelia drew her spine straight. "Why shouldn't people use their talents, regardless of birth or rank?

Why should they be forced to idleness if that isn't their preference?"

Ethan's frown deepened. "Most would find the duties of title and family sufficient to prevent idleness. And most would be respectful of their neighbors so as not to allow business to encroach on boundaries." He swept his hand to the small building that had garnered Amelia's attention. "I'm assuming that's one of his concerns."

"It is not." Amelia bit her tongue and drew a deep breath to keep her temper from running away with her. "Eamon Brewer rents it from my family."

"The distiller of the whiskey your father and I drank last evening?" Ethan asked, his disapproval waning slightly. "I assumed that it was bottled closer to the northern border."

"The water here is better for—"

"No wonder your father is so fond of it," Ethan mused.

He was fond of it because it was flavorful, smooth, and easy to drink. All things a lady shouldn't know.

"Do you think we could visit?" Ethan asked even as his horse stepped forward. "I would like to take a few bottles back to London."

Molly made to follow down the hill, approving the plan as much as Amelia would have liked to have done. However, it would be difficult to explain how the mare knew her way to the stable at the back of the building, how there was hay waiting, and how the young men working there knew Amelia by sight. Not to mention, Miss Graves would swallow her tongue if Amelia set foot in a distillery.

"I'll ask Father to send a few bottles from his next order. Shall we return to the house, Mr. Raymond?" Amelia turned a reluctant Molly toward home. She met her chaperone's relieved sigh with an encouraging smile.

Ethan came along side, and they began the plodding trek back.

"Miss Chitester—Amelia," he began after a long while. "Before we reach the house, I wanted to tell you again how much I have enjoyed our time together this week, as well as in London, and it is my hope—"

Amelia resisted the urge to knee Molly's ribs for an easy escape, but the horse sensed her panic and danced to the side anyway, making Ethan choose between shouting his proposal and silence. To Amelia's relief, he chose silence. Though it would be short-lived without further distraction.

She found it in a lone rider at the gate, a man atop a gleaming sorrel horse. He spied them at the same time, raised his hand as if to wave, but then stopped. Instead, he cantered toward them at an enviable pace.

As he neared, details emerged. He was a newcomer to the village because Amelia would have remembered someone with eyes that blue. The wrinkles in his clothes combined with the shadows under his eyes hinted that he'd been traveling some distance. His clothes, however, were finely tailored and fashionable for the Season. Where Ethan had chosen wheat and teal, the newcomer had chosen gray and navy, which highlighted both his arresting eyes and the shadow of stubble across his jaw. When he removed his hat and bowed, his short hair was a crown of wavy curls most women would envy. There was something about them Amelia recognized.

"I beg your pardon," he said in a deep, pleasant voice. "I seem to be lost. Could you direct me to Felton House?"

Felton House…that curly black hair. "You're Simon's uncle Richard, aren't you?" Amelia asked, smiling.

The stranger's smile was wide and friendly as he dipped his head. "Richard Ferrand…Miss?"

"He speaks of you so often, and looks a great deal like you," she continued. "It's a pleasure. I am Amelia—"

"This is Miss Amelia Chitester." Ethan spoke over her. "Her father is Baron Kilverstone, and this is his estate. I am Ethan Raymond, heir to the Earl of Barnsley. And this is Miss Chitester's chaperone, Miss Graves. The Rushford estate is over the next rise."

"That isn't entirely correct," Amelia said, tilting her chin in defiance of the silence and deference expected of her. "It's several rises." She urged Molly forward. "Oli—the duke and duchess are family friends, and I would never forgive myself if you got lost again on the way. We'll take you ourselves."

"Amelia—"

"Miss—"

Amelia ignored her companions. She knew better than to hope they'd stay behind, but at least Ethan wouldn't propose in front of another man. "Shall we, Mr. Ferrand?"

RICHARD BIT THE side of the cheek to quell his smile as the odd party joined him on the road.

The red-faced chaperone looked ready to cry, which was understandable given both her velvet riding habit and her thin frame. What of her wasn't melting was most likely being ground to dust by the saddle. Raymond, on the other hand, was red-faced for another reason, given the set to his jaw as he drew alongside. His determination was matched by the otherwise dainty Amelia, who flanked Raymond. They all trooped down the road in silence.

"It's kind of all of you to show me the way," Richard joked. The mood stubbornly refused to be lightened, so he turned his attention to the countryside and inhaled deeply. If he couldn't have good company, at least he could have clean air and a view. Though the rolling fields reminded him of his too-recent rough crossing and revived a bit of queasiness.

"How are you related to His Grace the duke?" Raymond asked. "As his son's uncle, are you a younger brother?"

Raymond must either be visiting or daft. Perhaps both. Oliver had led him to believe everyone in the county knew his story.

"He is my brother-in-law."

"The duchess's brother then." Raymond surmised with a nod.

The assumption that Oliver's life had been limited to these shores, that all relations were tied to his new wife, rankled. "No. His first wife was my sister."

"First wife?" Raymond asked, curiosity threading through the words. Like a town gossip in church pew fishing for a hint of scandal.

"She died."

Two short syllables that could never be softened, their impact always fresh. Julia had died and left him and Oliver alone to raise Simon. And then Oliver had taken Simon to England for a visit that was doomed never to end. And then Oliver had married someone else.

"Have you just arrived from Canada, Mr. Ferrand?" Amelia asked. "Mr. Raymond, the duke and Mr. Ferrand run a successful timber enterprise in Quebec province."

"Timber?" Raymond asked as he swept his gaze up and down Richard's suit, clearly shocked by meeting a businessman rather than a roughened lumberjack. "So you are in trade as well?"

Richard ignored the man's frank curiosity, choosing instead to lean forward to address Amelia. Her eyes were shaded by her hat, but he guessed they matched the dark blue of her riding habit. Most society mothers chose colors to highlight eyes. His tailor had encouraged him to do the same. His sister, Julia, had insisted on a red jacket, claiming brown was too drab, and black, which matched her hair, was only suitable for funerals.

How prophetic.

"From France," he answered. "Family business called me over."

"I'm certain—"

"Paris?" Raymond asked. His tone was conversational as he cut through Amelia's question. And as he asked, he looked toward her. He must have smiled because she gave him one in return. It wasn't friendly, though. Julia had given both Richard and Oliver similar ones over the years.

"North of Paris, on the coast," Richard said. It was still odd to explain why he'd been in France and the outcome of his visit, and strangers—even polite ones—didn't need the details.

"Bad luck that you couldn't make it into the city," Raymond said, not sounding sympathetic at all. "I was there in August, and it was the best distraction. The tailors do help set the style. London always seems a season behind."

Richard cast an eye over the other man's form-fitting coat. If the gelding took off at a gallop, Raymond would come apart at the seams. His leather gloves would likely be shredded if he so much as touched a tree.

"Which Mr. Raymond will only say because he can't be over-heard or judged harshly in the country," Amelia said. "Where fashion is always behind and the only seasons that matter are planting, harvesting, and hunting."

Her brief laugh and wide smile made Richard wonder if he'd imagined the cut in her words. However, they also hinted at Raymond's status.

"You're down from London then?" Richard asked him.

The other man nodded. "I've come to visit because the ball-rooms aren't the same without Miss Chitester." His glance slid to her. "I'm due to return this afternoon, though I have a matter I hope to settle before I go."

A gasp from behind them had Richard turning to make sure the chaperone hadn't fainted. She was still upright, and smiling so widely her thin face threatened to split in half.

"Make this next right, at that knotted tree," Amelia said.

Her command was much too measured for a young woman who had all but been proposed to. In Richard's experience, society women tended to burst into blushing giggles at the thought of a man getting them punch at a dance, much less following them into the countryside and declaring their inten-tions in front of strangers.

Of course, he also knew women who played hard-to-get.

The lane they turned into was narrower, making it impossible to continue three abreast.

"We'll leave you here," Raymond said.

"We will not be so unneighborly," Amelia retorted. "The duke and duchess—"

"He has made his way across an ocean, at least part of France, and from the coast to here," Raymond argued. "Surely he can make his way up a road."

Richard was inclined to agree, if simply because he felt as though he were a pawn in a larger game.

"If you are in a hurry to return and pack, Graves and I can make our way home." Amelia and her mare nudged Raymond and his mount aside. "Come along, Mr. Ferrand."

"Miss—"

"Don't be silly, Graves," Amelia said. "I know the way better than either of you." She glanced over her shoulder and flashed another bright smile. "And I doubt Mr. Ferrand will attempt to abduct me in broad daylight in strange surroundings on an unfamiliar horse."

Richard gave way to his smile as he joined her at the front of the parade. "Little wonder he misses you in London," he murmured, careful to be quiet because Raymond had drawn up behind them.

"I could list a dozen things Ethan misses in London," she replied just as quietly. "Just as I'm sure you have many things you miss in Quebec."

"Of course." Richard's response was automatic, but when her silence prodded him to produce something, he was hard-pressed to do it. "Not the weather. It rains half the month this time of year."

"Your home, certainly?" Amelia scanned the hills laid out in front of them. "I dreamt of Thetford while we were in London."

He missed sleeping in his own bed, but that likely wasn't the proper thing to say to a lady. "I have been so busy that I am rarely at home for long periods of time."

"With the duke here, your load there must be doubled."

"Yes." It was the easiest answer. How else to explain that it was easier to deal with work when there wasn't a youngster at home to entertain, that there weren't mealtimes to meet, and bedtimes to negotiate, but more difficult at the same time? "It was unusual to have nothing to do but read."

It hadn't begun that way. There had been plenty of diversions aboard ship, including his fellow travelers. But by the end, he'd exiled himself to his cabin to avoid a persistent young woman bent on being more than a diversion.

"Or look out over the ocean," Amelia sighed. "Father and I have spent hours at the bow guessing whether shadows on the horizon were our destination or just another wave."

Ahead of them, shadows of clouds skated along the surface of green hills, and behind those hills were others of darker green, and then others that were a lighter blue. They continued until they were phantom shapes. "I missed having landmarks."

"Like trees?"

The teasing lilt of her question drew Richard's attention. For the first time, he could see her well. Her eyes were indeed a dark blue, almost the color of a sea during stormy weather. Her nose was a perfect point over lips that formed a delightful bow even when she smiled. Delicate and fair, she resembled a forest sprite in the stories Simon had loved. Richard had the intense desire to push off her hat to see if her ears were pointed.

"Yes, Miss Chitester. Like trees."

"Never fear." She smiled and pointed ahead of them. "You'll have your fill over the next rise."

"Is that a fire ahead?" Raymond asked. "Should we turn—"

"It's the engine at the mill," Richard assured him, grinning from ear to ear as a plume of white steam rose into the horizon. It was a sight as familiar as his own reflection. And, as if on cue, axe blows echoed in the distance.

They crested the hill and, to their left, a wide expanse lay beneath them, dotted with tenant farms and houses, crossed by narrow cart paths and rock walls to mark property lines. The mill lay to the left, nearest the forest. For the first time since he'd boarded the ship in Quebec, the world was stable on its axis.

Amelia drew her horse to a stop in front of an entrance flanked by massive stone and brick gateposts. The iron gates were staked open, and the path was wide and well-maintained. "This is where we leave you. Felton House is at the other end."

"Thank you for your hospitality," Richard said. Unable to resist, he tilted his head toward his stubborn guide. "Are you certain I won't get lost between here and the door?" he whispered.

Her lips twitched. "Unfortunately, yes. Wish me luck upon the return trip." She straightened and turned her horse to face Raymond. "Let's cut across country and save time. I'll ride with Graves to ensure she stays in the saddle."

Richard lifted his hat to Raymond and the chaperone, and then watched as they crossed into a field. If he wasn't mistaken, the outlines of the manor where they began the journey were visible in the gray distance. They could have taken this shortcut and left plenty of time for a proposal.

Cheeky wench. Ethan Raymond would have his hands full with Amelia.

Richard urged his horse forward, through the gates and on toward the house. A short way down, on his left, was a cottage surrounded by a large garden, both nestled against tall stands of hardwood trees. An elderly woman stood at the gate, shading her eyes to stare at him. Clad all in black, she reminded him of a raven on a high tree branch.

When she didn't return his greeting, dread surged in Richard's chest. He'd written that he was coming, but there was a chance he had outpaced the delivery. There was also a chance that Oliver wanted to turn his back on Canada and the sadness he'd left behind.

The dread multiplied when he rounded a bend and Felton House came into view. Their home in Quebec would fit in one wing, and the garden had an honest-to-God maze. Bright flowers bobbed in the sunshine. Butterflies drifted on the breeze. The cold, muddy streets of Quebec could become a memory quickly.

Another woman walked from the back of the house, a basket on her arm and a dark green cloak over her shoulders. Her copper hair glowed in the sun. She shaded her eyes with her hand for a moment before walking toward him.

"May I help you?"

"I am looking for your…master?" What did one call a duke when addressing his servants?

"Master?" Her lips twitched.

Apparently, he'd guessed wrong. Perhaps all of England would be laughing at him by the end of this trip. He dismounted, eager to stretch his legs and get firm ground under his feet. "The Duke of Rushford. I wrote of coming, but—"

The woman's smile broke wide as she extended her hands. "Richard! We've been expecting you." Her grip was warm and strong. "I'm Thea. Come in for tea."

CHAPTER TWO

RICHARD FOLLOWED THE Duchess of Rushford around the back of the house, past a lush kitchen garden, and through the back door. She talked the entire way.

"Oliver will be irritated he wasn't here to greet you." She grinned over her shoulder. "More precisely that I was right—that he didn't have time to go back to the mill and finish his ledgers."

"He is committed to finishing his day with numbers before he forgets." Richard wiped his shoes on the carpet laid over the threshold before entering a kitchen large enough to house most of the first floor of their Quebec home. Light poured through large windows across oak workbenches and bounced from cream-colored pottery and black iron pots. A modern stove sprawled across one wall, perpendicular to a stone fireplace he could have stood inside without stooping, if not for the low fire there. The room smelled of bread and sugar.

She went to the hearth and returned with the kettle, placing it on a trivet in the middle of the table next to the makings for tea. Richard dragged a chair from the table, the legs bumping along the stone floor as the wood, polished by years of care, warmed against his palm.

"Julia always said..." His gaze flew to his hostess, or to her back since she was retrieving something from the stove top. How would she react to the mention of his sister, the woman Oliver had married instead of her?

Thea placed a plate of cookies on the table before sitting opposite him. Her smile was gentle. "Don't stop the story, please."

"She always teased Oliver that he saw his day in numbers rather than words," Richard said as he spooned tea leaves, sugar, and milk into his cup, which was large enough to hold a proper drink. "She called his ledgers his diary."

Julia had kept a journal all her life, and she'd warned him and Oliver against reading them. It had taken them over a year after her death to dig into the crate. One night, they'd put Simon to bed, opened a bottle of whiskey, and sat on the floor with the box between them. Richard had expected revelations. Instead, he'd read the mundane details of their lives from her perspective, laughing and tearing up in equal measure.

He had left the later ones for Oliver to read alone.

While his tea was steeping, Richard bit into a cookie and let it melt on his tongue. Warm cinnamon and sugar loosened his muscles. Oliver had written about his new wife's skill in the kitchen. He hadn't overstated it.

Richard wasn't sure about the rest. Oliver had always described his childhood home as a hive of activity reigned over by his queen bee of a mother. To all appearances, Thea was here alone. "Is the house always this quiet?"

Her eyes danced as she sipped her tea. "If Hazel were home, we would be banished to the front parlor and forced to use china. The maids would tiptoe around rather than focusing on their work, and Lionel would be fussing about entertaining on short notice. They all mean well, but they still aren't accustomed to entertaining family like family."

From outside came barking and yipping, followed by a deep whoop Richard remembered from years in the wilderness.

"No fair, Papa." The boyish shout was sprinkled with a giggle. "The garden is off limits."

A heavy slap against the door timed with the thud of boots on the steps. Seconds later, lighter steps and a lighter tap sounded. "You cheated," the little boy scolded, still giggling.

The door opened. "And you sent that beast of a dog in my path. I lost a good five seconds untangling from him," Oliver teased. "I had to take a shortcut to compensate."

Both arrivals paused inside the kitchen door, eyes wide and smiles wide.

"*Oncle* Richard!" Simon launched at him, and Richard caught in him in a tight embrace.

The almost-four-year-old he'd last seen waving wildly from a ship's stern had become a gangly six-year-old. As Richard buried his nose in the boy's hair, smelling sweat and fresh air, Simon wound his arms around his neck. Tears stung Richard's eyes, and his ears heated with embarrassment. He hadn't forgotten.

Oliver strode toward him with a wide grin and open arms. "It's about bloody time."

Richard stood, bringing Simon up with him, but straining under the weight and relishing that his nephew clung tighter. The boy's feet grazed his thighs. Richard managed a lopsided half-bow. "Your Grace," he chuckled.

"You arse," Oliver said as he gave him a back-slapping hug. They all listed dangerously when paws the size of saucers landed on Oliver's shoulders and a furry muzzle shoved past his head.

"Down, Brownie," Oliver ordered as he backed away.

Thea's laughter bounced from the walls. Still seated, she was wiping her fingers under her eyes. "Now all of you are covered in dirt."

"It'll wash," the men said in unison, which resulted in more laughter.

Oliver backed away and went to her, taking her in his arms and resting his forehead to hers. Their hushed conversation was punctuated by touches and strokes.

Giving them their privacy, Richard focused on putting Simon back on firm ground, something his back thanked him for immediately. Brownie, a shaggy gray Wolfhound whose shoulders reached Simon's ears, lumbered forward, sniffing and lowering his head for a pet. Richard obliged.

"He's a great dog. We got him when we went to get our pig, Pinky. He lives in the stable with my pony, Spot the Larger." Simon tugged his hand. "Come see."

"Tomorrow, Simon," Oliver said as he left his wife and plucked a biscuit from the tray. "Let Richard rest after his trip."

"Carys is sleeping upstairs with Mrs. Palmer." Thea kissed him on the cheek. "I'm going to the cottage to cut herbs and give you three some time on your own. Be sure to clean your shoes, or Hazel will get the broom after you." She winked at Simon as she picked up her basket. "And I need to see who's been in my garden. I'll be home for dinner."

"Bye, Mama."

The word went through Richard's heart like a sharp saw blade. Oliver wouldn't meet his eyes, but Thea's soft smile hinted that she understood.

"Wish your mother well," Oliver said as he joined her at the door. "Start walking home well before dark, Mrs. Hawkins."

Their kiss sent Richard back to petting the dog, staring into his large brown eyes until Simon shoved a cookie into his line of vision. Richard snatched it before the dog could reach it. "Thank you, Si."

Oliver joined them, picked up the tray, and carried it out of the kitchen. "Come see the rest of the house."

Following Oliver down the servants' hall and into the entry-way, Richard understood why they preferred the kitchen. The space was a polished cavern full of blond oak and marble. Though he couldn't see anyone, he could feel eyes on him. An older man dressed in a black suit pressed to sharp creases appeared at the bottom of the stairs. "Welcome home, la—" He spotted Richard. "Your Grace."

Oliver's shoulders heaved in a deep sigh. "It's fine, Lionel. This is my brother-in-law, Richard Ferrand."

"Oh yes." The butler's smile widened. "Welcome! We've put

your things in the room next to Master Simon's. He insisted."

"Thank you, sir." Richard imagined the very proper butler's reaction to unpacking his limited wardrobe.

Oliver kept going, stopping at a door to the left of the stairs. "Could you ask a maid to sweep the kitchen floor before Hazel and Fred return, please? And could you please make sure Simon gets upstairs to Mrs. Palmer for a proper bath?"

"But Papa."

"But Simon," Oliver said around a mouthful of biscuit. "You know the rules. Bath before dinner."

The routine had been the same for as long as Richard remembered. Breakfast, work, snacks, bath, dinner, story, bed. Despite the presence of a nurse, the rhythm was comforting.

"Can *Oncle* Richard come?"

"Your uncle and I want to talk about grown-up things," Oliver said. "But he can tell you a story before bed tonight."

Simon scuffed his feet up each stair, turning halfway to look back at Richard in a plea for solidarity. It was never clear whether the boy hated baths or being exiled.

"I'll be next to you at dinner, Si," Richard promised. "Just like we used to."

Once they were alone, Oliver led him into a study. Painted a deep blue and accented with white trim, the room was dominated by a dark walnut desk stacked with account books. The room was lined with bookshelves, with a large watercolor of a garden occupying the one open wall.

"I'm sorry, I should have warned you Si calls Thea that," Oliver said as he put the tray on the desk and opened the whiskey decanter. "It was just easier when Carys came along."

They'd known the topic of mothers would come up as Simon aged. Richard took the glass he offered. "Does he know?"

"As much as he can understand, but he knows Thea loves him." Oliver dropped into a chair, slung one arm across the back, and sipped his drink. "She really does, Richard. And he adores her."

He had seen Oliver in every mood possible, from miserable new arrival to determined negotiator. He'd seen him grieve Julia's death and beam over Simon's first steps. The man across from him was at ease in a way Richard had never seen before.

"This place suits you." Richard sipped his drink and raised his eyebrows at the warm flavor spreading over his tongue. "And this is damned fine whiskey."

"It's a local distiller, Eamon Brewer. He's just over the ridge between us and the Chitesters."

"I met their daughter this afternoon. She's a handful." Poor choice of words, because now all he could think of was her on that horse as she rode away. Her riding habit had been perfectly tailored to showcase every curve. "Her beau will find her a challenge."

"Beau?" Oliver raised an eyebrow. "Are you certain?"

"Some dandy from London made it pretty clear he was here to propose." So the intriguing Miss Chitester was off the market. For anyone who would be *in* the market.

Which wasn't him.

"Hmm. We'll see…" Oliver plucked another biscuit from the tray and grinned. "I halfway thought you'd arrive with a wife."

Julia had teased him about that often, telling him she didn't want him to be lonely. That she wanted him to be as happy as she and Oliver were with one another. His sister had wanted many things. "I haven't the time for a wife, especially now."

Oliver hovered on the edge of speaking, but closed his mouth into a frown, reconsidering. The skill must have come with his new title, because he'd never been careful with his words. "How was Rosnay?" he finally asked.

It had been surreal to get to a small village in France and hear everyone talk of another Richard Ferrand, this one his uncle, his black sheep father's older brother, to read *the death of Richard Ferrand* in the local papers, and to learn his own, now dead, *Oncle* Richard had followed his success in Quebec.

"I own a bloody winery, Ol."

A slow smile spread over his brother-in-law's face. "How convenient."

"A fondness for wine isn't the same as a head for the business," Richard said. It was a lesson his uncle had apparently ignored. "It's like the difference between visiting a brothel and seeing to the laundry."

Oliver choked on his biscuit, but eventually, his cough dissolved into laughter. "Probably not the best sales pitch."

"Likely not." Richard grinned. "But that's about all I know of it. I'd be happier milling the barrel staves."

Oliver grunted in agreement as he refilled their glasses. "I know someone who may be able to help."

❧

AMELIA WAVED GOODBYE to Ethan, smiling until her lips stiffened and her cheeks ached. At last, his coach made the bend in the lane and disappeared from view. If she hurried, she'd have just enough time to change and—

"He's a pleasant man," Mother said. As they turned back toward the house, she looped her arm through Amelia's and slowed their steps. "Wouldn't you agree?"

Amelia nodded. She couldn't argue with Ethan's agreeableness. He was like every well-bred man in the *ton*. He could ride well and play cards skillfully. He didn't talk too much, yet he wasn't surly. He drank and spent in moderation, and he knew all the best tailors, gentlemen's clubs, and party hostesses. He also knew exactly what to expect from his lady wife.

Emphasis on *lady*.

"I'm so glad for the weather today. It makes up for the rain, and it gave you a chance for a ride," Mother continued. "Though I do wish you'd have taken the landau instead of the horses. Poor Graves won't be able to sit for a week."

"I know, and I'll make my apologies to her." Graves deserved a war medal for today. "But you can't see the prettiest parts of the estate from a carriage, and walking wasn't practical."

"You were out for quite a while. You must have shown him the whole county." Mother gave her a sideways glance. "Or was there another reason for the delay?"

Her coy tone, combined with the sly look, renewed Amelia's guilt. Her mother had liked Ethan from the beginning of the Season, and it was clear she was hoping for a proposal. Perhaps he had already spoken to her and Father about it.

"We had a lovely time out, and we came across the Duke of Rushford's brother-in-law, Mr. Ferrand, who'd become confused in reaching Felton House. We guided him the rest of the way. It seemed the proper thing to do."

"Ah. Well, yes. I suppose it was." Mother's disappointment was evident, but she wouldn't begrudge the kindness to a family she considered friends. "And afterward? Did Mr. Raymond say anything?"

He hadn't needed to. His behavior on the ride had made his position plain. Ethan saw it as his responsibility to protect her from unfamiliar men and shelter her from unexpected events. To speak for her. Answer for her. Decide for her.

Mother would never understand how that chafed. As the second Lady Chitester, she'd married a man already secure in his place and his future. She'd played her part in furthering his influence by being a charming hostess and a wonderful mother to a child she'd inherited and loved as her own. She never expressed opinions in public, and she never asked questions where anyone could overhear.

Marian Chitester and *scandal* didn't belong in the same sentence, much less under the same roof.

"We were in such a hurry to get back so he could keep his schedule to return to London," Amelia said. "His sister's ball promises to be a lavish event."

"We still have the invitation." Mother's eyebrows went up as her smile widened. "And your father could do without us for a few days. We could make arrangements."

Panic clutched at Amelia's lungs just as her foot touched the entryway's marble floor. They needed a new topic of conversation. "How is he after Doctor Anderson's visit?"

"He's resting now, and I'm sure he'll want to talk with you after he wakes. But I'm confident he'll be fine alone if we go to London."

Of course Father would be fine. He'd reveled in having the house to himself when they'd gone shopping in Paris.

She, however, would *not* be fine in London. Ethan's pursuit of her into the country would be fodder for gossip. His sister would see to that. If Amelia returned to London for the party, they'd be as good as engaged before the supper dance. She wouldn't even have the option of choosing her own partner.

"It would be far too much effort for one party." Amelia freed herself from her mother's well-intentioned tether. "And the last few days have left me exhausted. I think I'll rest upstairs until dinner."

Her mother's smile wobbled. "If you're certain."

Amelia kissed her cheek as a consolation prize. "I am, Mother. Thank you."

The care it took not to run up the stairs and down the hall made Amelia's bones ache.

Graves was waiting in the hallway, her lips set in a smile, though her eyes were clouded. "Is he gone then?" Amelia's nod drew an answering sigh. "Amelia, you will not be able to avoid this for much longer."

"I wasn't avoiding anything." Despite the words, Amelia couldn't look her chaperone in the eye.

"You have been a terrible liar since the nursery," Graves said as she walked to Amelia's door, her slight limp a rueful reminder of their over-long ride. "It is one of the reasons I love you. You used horses to escape a proposal from a young man that is perfectly suitable for you, not to mention your behavior with Mr. Ferrand. I taught you better than that."

She had. Between Amelia's first mother and her second, Lillian Graves had swept into the house with an armful of books and a globe. She'd made family trips a chance for cultural immersion, teaching everything from history and geography to dances, language, and customary foods. Cook had grumbled to no end, the music master had developed an unrequited attachment, and the dressmaker…well, she'd run several of them off for not knowing the difference between French and Italian patterns. One had left in an uproar after being asked to make a sarong for a trip to India.

But Graves had always insisted Amelia be a proper lady.

"I know that you didn't like the way he spoke over you." Graves took Amelia's hand in hers and squeezed. "But sometimes, that protection is a good thing, especially with strangers."

"Mr. Ferrand was forthright about his family connection, whom we all know and respect. He would never—"

"You don't know that, Amelia. People—men—can be deceitful." She held up a hand to stop Amelia's argument. "If nothing else, they can be easily led. A lady's behavior cues them to the treatment they will expect. If you are forward, they will be so in return." Graves cocked an eyebrow. "Likewise, if you are flirtatious or standoffish. Do not lead Mr. Raymond—or any man—down a path you do not wish to travel."

She had done everything possible to push Ethan from her path, but he seemed determined to follow. She hadn't even invited him to visit. "Of course not."

Graves's soft smile returned. "I know you wouldn't do anything untoward intentionally, but I would hate for your…enthusiasm to trap you into a situation not of your own making." She turned toward her room. "I believe I'll rest before supper."

"Let me ask Rose to draw you a hot bath," Amelia offered. "A good soak will help with the aches from the ride."

Graves usually refused such a request, claiming servants shouldn't be serving *her*. This time, her shoulders heaved in a sigh. "That sounds wonderful, Amelia. Thank you."

CHAPTER THREE

AMELIA OPENED HER door and gently clicked it closed behind her. Then she flew into action. Dropping to her knees next to her bed, she reached for the box stored underneath. She tossed the lid aside and pulled the clothing free. The afternoon was escaping her.

The riding habit was easy to escape on her own, but it took precious seconds to fold the clothing with care and respect.

"Amelia, just because you are finished with something, you cannot toss it aside and expect others to clean up behind you. Our staff has other responsibilities. And if you cannot treat your belongings with respect, I have other things on which to spend my money."

Her father had given her that lecture at seven years old, in his library while she was sitting on his knee. It had been her favorite thing, reviewing their day—him at work and her in school—in the cool shadowy room that smelled of books and leather. His tobacco-scented wool coat always caught her curls and dragged them into disarray, which had frustrated her nurse to no end.

The old woman would suffer a fit if she saw Amelia now. Dragging a shirt over her head brought fine strands into her eyes, and the loose linen was certainly not the height of fashion. Not to mention the drab gray skirt, which was *split*. Amelia grinned as she wrestled the black braces up her arms and let them snap against her shoulders.

Ethan Raymond would have run screaming back to London the moment he saw these clothes. Especially her boots, which were made for work rather than dancing, but were easily her most comfortable shoes in recent memory.

Maybe she should have greeted him like this.

Amelia tip-toed to her bed and arranged the pillows under the coverlet until they resembled a sleeping miss. Then she shoved a straw hat on her head and pushed her messy hair back under the brim and into the crown. After drawing the drapes, she left the room and hurried to the back stairs.

Halfway down, she met her maid, Rose. The young woman dropped a quick curtsey, her eyes wide. "Miss. Are you…going out?"

"I'll be back well before dinner," Amelia whispered. "Would you please draw a bath for Miss Graves?"

"Yes, miss, but are you certain—"

"I'm not leaving our property. I'm perfectly safe." The extra money Amelia paid for the maid's silence couldn't buy confidence in her decisions.

It also couldn't buy Amelia more time. She stepped into the servant's hall, and strode toward the rear door. She'd learned long ago that skulking drew more attention than acting as though she belonged somewhere. In the courtyard, chickens scattered, squawking and scolding, and half-dry laundry slapped in the lavender-scented breeze.

Once in the stable, Amelia buttoned her gloves before tying her hat under her chin. A groom waited with Molly's reins in hand.

"Thank you, Henry." Amelia stepped up and looped her knee around the pommel.

A twitch of the reins urged the horse at a sedate pace with a toss of her head. Her large ribs heaved in what could have been a sigh. Amelia stroked her neck as they reached the paddock. "Just a bit longer, girl. I promise."

On the other side of the paddock, Amelia urged Molly into a

trot. After they crested the rise behind the house, Amelia shifted in the saddle, swinging her leg over so that she was astride. She leaned forward, Molly's mane coarse against her cheek, and pressed her heels into the horse's ribs. "Let's run."

There wasn't a need to ask twice. Molly's hooves thudded against the ground, and her mane whipped across Amelia's face, bringing the scent of sweet hay and sunshine. The wind pushed Amelia's hat until it tumbled down her back and freed her hair to the warmth of the sun.

They reached the distillery far too soon for Amelia. Molly agreed, given how she pranced in the rough-hewn corral. However, the promise of fresh oats and cool water helped calm her. Amelia dismounted and looped the reins through a ring at the front of the trough. An orange tabby wobbled against her ankles.

"Drunk again, Caspar?" She bent to scratch between his ears. "Someone needs to mop up better."

The distillery door swung open. "You're late, *Eamon*."

Drake Fletcher was leaning against the threshold, arms crossed over an intricately patterned waistcoat of black and gold. The black matched his shirt, which matched his trousers, which matched his hair, a shock of which dropped over his eyes. Every time Amelia saw him, she imagined him fading into shadows with nothing visible but those eyes, like a wolf in the woods.

Except for the smirk on his face.

"Who knew society earls could be so tenacious?" she said as she brushed past him and entered the distillery.

"Probably every young woman in London." Drake followed her.

Their steps echoed from the stone floor and walls of the barrel room. The musty smell of cold rock blended with the sweet smoky scent of unused barrels and the freshly cut pine shelves, most of which sat waiting for stock to fill them.

"Thank you for watching things here while I was away," Amelia said.

"That's why you pay me," Drake replied. "But you're welcome."

It had been one of the luckiest days in her life when the Duke of Rushford had introduced her to Drake Fletcher in the barnyard at The Galloping Goat. The man was brilliant, loyal, and trustworthy. He used his brain, but he never shied from getting his hands dirty.

Through another door was the bottling room. A long table stood in the middle of the well-lit space, a group of empty honey-colored bottles at one end. A box of corks and mallets were in the middle.

Two desks sat on the opposite wall. "It's good to see they've arrived," she said.

"It took all the boys to bring them in, but Sara appreciates them," Drake said. He pointed to the gas lanterns resting on the desktops. "Especially those. Her writing is already better."

Amelia plucked a neatly printed label from the box on the nearest end of the table. *Fine whiskey made and bottled by Eamon Brewer in Norfolk.*

A shiver of pride shot down Amelia's spine.

"And Florence?" She'd sent the village girl to Drake after Reverend Carson had mentioned her affinity for mathematics.

"Carson was right. She's quick with numbers. She's very shy. I had to have Sara in the room with us before Florence would speak to me in more than one word sentences." Drake chuckled as he produced a ledger. "But that just means she'll be discreet."

The figures were straight and even, and the mechanics weren't visible on the page—something Amelia had never managed. But the balances were dwindling.

Amelia fought the urge to rationalize. She was a young woman who wasn't supposed to make her own money. Therefore, any number larger than zero at the bottom of the column was a success. It should be enough.

But it wasn't. What good was making the best whiskey in Norfolk if you were stuck with small batches that disappeared in a week? How did it help to employ the young men *and* women in Thetford if they didn't have dependable income? Why do this at all if she couldn't support herself?

Amelia placed the ledger next to the labels and turned her back on the table, walking toward the opposite door. "Good. I believe her family needs the funds."

The third room was dominated by two copper pot stills, their bulbous bellies topped by graceful swan necks, tethered to condenser columns. The hot, humid air was so full of flavor that it coated Amelia's tongue.

"The boys pulled the wheat out of the drying room this morning and started the mash," Drake said as he pointed to one large tub. "Though they turned their noses up at the figs. What made you think of them for flavor?"

"We had a fig sherbet at the Gerards' ball before we left for London," Amelia said. "I kept thinking it would taste wonderful with barley."

"Far be it from me to second-guess your palate." Drake ushered her to the opposite still. "This should be ready to distill tomorrow."

Distilling would take all day, and she'd likely walk away with a case, maybe two. "It won't be enough, will it?"

"It will be another small batch," he said. "But done in succession, those batches; white whiskey is helping fill the coffers while the other ages."

Help. Not fill them. Not since the business had expanded beyond her working alone in an abandoned shed with a still the size of a pumpkin. Not since she had a loan to repay to the London Ladies Charity Circle, who had advanced the funds for the desks, the payroll, the additional bottles and ingredients. The building. Everything but the barrels, which still needed to be sourced.

The ladies would review her ledgers in a month and find her a poor investment. Especially since her first aged whiskey would be bottled in the same week as the circle meeting.

The challenge of transitioning from white whiskey to aged spirits had intrigued Amelia, reminding her of why she'd begun distilling in the first place. Now she stood in this room, equally pleased by the business she controlled and terrified of failure. If she tapped those barrels in a month only to find scum or—worse—poison, it would be humiliating. She'd lose the inheritance from her first mother, the only money she could call her own.

She'd lose the ability to make her own future.

"I need more options, Drake."

He was quiet for several seconds, his hands clasped behind his back. His waistcoat strained across his chest as he stared at his boots, which reflected the light in the room. His brow furrowed as his chin shifted from side to side, contorting his mouth and his jaws. She'd never seen anyone think so visibly yet remain quiet.

He looked to her and nodded. Finally. "Leave it to me."

RICHARD TUGGED AT the knot in his cravat. At home, he only wore it to society dinners and the theatre—if he couldn't escape an invitation. While he'd packed his evening suit, he'd hoped to avoid wearing it. Especially in Norfolk, where Oliver had assured him daily life was much like theirs in Quebec. That apparently didn't extend to supper with neighbors.

Across the coach, Oliver ran a finger between his collar and his neck.

"You two," Thea sighed. "You'd think they were nooses."

Oliver cast an obvious eye at her fashionably low neckline.

His wife smacked him on the shoulder. "I will trade you a corset for a cravat any day." Despite her grumbling, she smiled. It deepened when Oliver took her hand.

It is just like Quebec, Richard thought. A couple, very much in love, out for the evening. Their tagalong brother in their wake, sharing the joke.

Though he wasn't anyone's brother now, not really. And Julia had loved parties, while Thea seemed to share Oliver's dread. And their love seemed older, more settled, than the newlyweds they were. It was as though it had never lessened, never been interrupted by anyone else.

Richard wished he had chosen to ride alongside the carriage. The fall chill would have been a welcome distraction.

"You'll like Augustus Chitester," Oliver said. "He's not one to stand on ceremony, despite his relation to the Marquess of Ramsbury, who is the most insufferable man I've ever met."

"Even worse than Moneybags Malone?" Richard asked. Malone had been the first banker to back them, but he'd pulled out after Julia's death because they'd brought a colicky Simon to a business meeting.

"No one is worse than Malone," Oliver said. "Closed-minded curmudgeon."

"What about the Earl of Lambourn?" Thea asked. "Or the Duke of Shrewsbury?" She winked at Richard. "Or the—"

"Fine. I take your point." Oliver pointed his finger at his wife, his smile wide. "But just because I complain doesn't mean it isn't true, Your Grace."

"Mainly because they disagree with you in lords." Thea pushed his finger into his lap, laughing. Something Julia would have done.

His sister would have made an excellent duchess.

"What is the disagreement?" Richard asked.

"I'm pushing for child labor laws," Oliver said. "Politicians want to change them to *regulations*—rules for using children rather than not using them at all. Shrewsbury doesn't have the heart of his predecessor, and Lambourn will go whichever way his father, Ramsbury, wishes. They are in lock-step when it comes to protecting the status quo. It's amazing Augustus is related."

"He's the duke's second son," Thea explained. Her eyes were kind. "All the names confuse me when we're in town."

It reminded Richard of when Julia had been Oliver's interpreter those early days in Quebec. As a new arrival with a mediocre grasp of French, Oliver had struggled to grasp how things worked in a city that was a country in itself, especially in social situations.

"Especially when they all go with grizzled chins, red noses, and rheumy eyes," Oliver said. "Add the wigs, and I can't tell anyone apart. Except Althorne. You'd like him, Richard. He's half French."

"Perhaps you'll find an ally when Mr. Warren succeeds Lambourn." Thea pushed the curtain aside, letting in a breath of chill air. "We're almost to the Manor."

Oliver squared his waistcoat and ran a hand over his hair. "I don't hold much hope for Warren. He seems content being idle until the sun sets." He sighed. "I don't relish him as a neighbor, Thee."

Once again, Thea looked to Richard. "Mr. Warren is Augustus Chitester's heir. At some point, Oakdale and the property will be his."

"Except for the distillery," Oliver said as the carriage slowed. "That belongs to Amelia."

Thea's gaze shot to Oliver, her eyebrows arched even as she touched his knee. "The land does."

Oliver blinked and then, once again, thought about what he was going to say. "Of course."

A footman opened the door, and Richard exited first, followed by Oliver.

"How does Miss Chitester own land?" Richard asked as he surveyed the front of the house and the grounds. Even in the dark, he could tell the gardens were sizable, and the fresh smell of turned earth hung on the fall air. The house was smaller than he'd expected, but still much grander than anything in Canada.

"She inherited it from her mother." Oliver handed Thea down from the carriage. "So it escapes the entail. It's not a large parcel, but having the distillery as a tenant gives her a small independent income."

They went up the short, wide steps to the door, which was already held open by a butler who reminded Richard of a tree.

"We are so glad you could come on short notice," the man crowed. "I've had enough of *ton* society." He greeted Thea with a bow that was little more than a bob of his head and an impish smile. His wife embraced her.

"Welcome home, Augustus." Oliver extended his hand first to his host and then to his hostess. "Marian." He bowed. "It is lovely to see you again. May I present my brother-in-law, Richard Ferrand."

"Lord Kilverstone." Richard bowed deeply to the husband and then the wife. "My lady."

"Enough of that. We're Augustus and Marian at home among friends, if you please." The baron shook Richard's hand with unaffected zeal, adding an honest tone to the request. "It's good to meet you, though I believe you met your daughter yesterday."

It was easy to see the connection between him and Amelia. They shared the same open manner, and their eyes sparkled in much the same way. "She was kind enough to extend her ride with Mr. Raymond to act as my guide."

"I'm sure she was." Augustus's laughter filled the front hall, which was lined with golden maple.

A large Aubusson carpet lay over the stone floor, its color and pattern hinting at the roses that were likely in the gardens. The staircase was tucked along the back wall, rather than dominating the room. It didn't dictate that you separate either right or left or force you to enter another room. Instead, it encouraged you to linger near one of the fireplaces or view the eclectic mix of paintings that hung like windows into other places and times.

"Amelia is always happy to ride." Marian Chitester's smile was warm, but her eyes were guarded. "Most days, it's difficult to keep her in the house."

Especially when she's trying to avoid a suitor. "I was glad for the company," Richard said. "If I hadn't stumbled upon the group, I might still be wandering the countryside."

The object of their discussion was on the stairs, and Richard saw more benefits to the hall's design. First, the upper floors and hallways were concealed from view, keeping them private. Second, the staircase allowed him to watch Amelia in profile as she descended at a sedate pace in a berry-blue gown that, if he recalled correctly, exactly matched her eyes.

If he didn't know better, he would've assumed such an arrival was meant to draw attention. But he'd seen her ride. This pace was likely making her toes twitch.

Sure enough, the moment her feet touched the stones, she doubled her pace to reach them. She greeted Oliver and Thea first with a quick curtsey, though she grasped both Thea's hands once she rose. Then she turned to Richard.

"It is nice to see you again, Mr. Ferrand."

The gown indeed matched her eyes, and the gold lace complemented her hair. Not for the first time, Richard wondered if dressmakers and their clients understood how a high waist and a perfectly placed bow made it impossible for men to ignore a low neckline. All but the most small-breasted young women benefited from the design.

"Miss Chitester." Richard dipped his head. Other than the color, the dress was simple. This wasn't a ball gown meant to be seen and admired. She, like her parents, was dressed for an evening at home.

Amelia wasn't small-breasted, something her riding habit had concealed. She was also shorter than he'd expected, given her parents' heights. Her head stopped a few inches below his shoulder, which gave him a chance to admire her braids as he escorted her into dinner. She smelled of apples and cinnamon.

Dinner was laid out on the sideboard, allowing them to help themselves. Footmen helped them into their chairs and then retreated.

"Father can't bear the fuss," Amelia whispered as she placed her napkin in her lap. "He says it gives him indigestion when people watch him eat."

No wonder Augustus and Oliver were good friends. "I'm sure the servants don't mind escaping. I wouldn't want to watch someone eat mutton and then go below for cold ham." At least, that's what he'd overheard aboard ship.

"Our *staff* has the same meal we do," Amelia said. "Unless there's a party, which, thankfully, we rarely do at home."

"You don't enjoy parties?" Didn't all young women long for the Season in London and the social whirl? The ladies in Quebec were forever trying to recreate it.

"Why would anyone enjoy a mass of people traipsing about their home spilling punch on the carpet while judging their decorating choices?" She paused with her spoon in her soup. "My apologies. Of course I didn't mean this evening; this is—"

"No offense taken." Richard used his napkin to hide his smile. He enjoyed the decorations at Oakdale Manor, especially the lively one beside him. "I loathe punch. Unless it's liberally mixed with whiskey, of course."

"Whiskey makes everything better." Amelia paused again. "At least that's what Father says."

The pause made Richard wonder if her knowledge wasn't more firsthand, but one didn't ask a young lady if she drank when no one was looking. In his experience, the only women who drank whiskey didn't care if they were seen doing so.

"No Mr. Raymond today?" he asked, willing to change the subject to something she might find more agreeable.

"He left yesterday, back to London." Her sigh sounded more satisfied than regretful.

"You didn't enjoy his visit?"

"Have you ever had a puppy follow you home?" She looked up at him, and a pretty blush stained her cheeks. "That's unfair. He is pleasant company, but we didn't expect him to visit and we had…things to do."

Richard was set to ask what she did when she wasn't entertaining unwanted guests, but laughter caught his attention. Oliver was regaling Augustus with a tale of a childhood adventure, one he'd apparently undertaken with Thea given her objections to the retelling.

"I remember them like that," Amelia murmured. "When they were younger."

"They are difficult to ignore." Not that their behavior was inappropriate, or even rude. It was just so clear that they were happy together. That they had *always* been happy together. Oliver even seemed younger.

"Gossip dogged them everywhere, especially after Oliver sailed for Canada."

And found a wife there.

"It's difficult, isn't it?" Amelia's hand closed over his, her gentle touch contrasting with his tight grip on his soup spoon. "*Moving forward* sounds better than it feels." She smiled when Richard met her gaze. "I remember when Father brought Mother home. I enjoyed hearing him laugh again, but part of me was angry that he was going to replace my first mother, as though she'd never been there or hadn't been important."

Richard looked from the young woman next to him to her mother—stepmother—at the end of the table. "What changed?"

"It got easier with time."

Richard grasped her fingers as they slid from his. Squeezed. "Thank you."

"You're welcome." She freed her fingers as her mother went to the sideboard for the main course. "Now, would you tell me about Canada? We always intend to travel there, but the Season prevents us from going until fall, which Father has heard is a poor time to visit."

CHAPTER FOUR

"I T'S GOOD TO be home," Father said to no one in particular.

Amelia marked her page and looked across the library. "It is, and it was good to see the duke and duchess."

Their custom of dining early when in the country was one of the traditions she had always enjoyed. Inviting friends with whom she had much in common, even in secret, was a welcome addition. Combine those with reading in the library, enjoying sherry and sweets while the fire crackled, and Amelia was in heaven.

Other girls could enjoy the chaos of London's late, noisy dinners and dancing. Girls who hadn't spent the day bent over a tap, distilling apple-flavored white whiskey into as many bottles as she could fill.

It never seemed enough. Too few bottles, too little profit, too little time. Amelia shifted in her chair in the hopes of easing the twinge in her back. "What are you reading, Father?"

"The Dumas novel about the chap who escapes from prison. It seems apt," he chuckled. "Are you rereading your favorite?" When she nodded, he shook his head and gave her a wide smile. "You should be able to quote it from memory by now."

Amelia likely could, but she enjoyed the tale of two sisters learning to balance romance and manners. She could imagine her mothers playing opposite one another. She always cast herself as the youngest sister, eager to make her mark in the world. This time, she was focused on how their father's death had irrevocably changed each woman in the story.

It was a bit too close to home.

Years ago, Father had read her to sleep every evening and then carried her to bed himself. He'd seemed like a giant then. Even as a grown woman, she considered him larger than life and twice as strong. Barrel-chested, ruddy-faced, and boisterous, the only thing he hadn't been able to control was his hair line. His fine blond hair had made the baldness more pronounced.

Now he sat across the room, the cigar smoke circling him before it drifted out the window Mother insisted he open when he smoked, and his glass of whiskey gleaming under his reading lamp, the surface almost silver in the light. The shadows in the library made it possible to believe his color had returned over the last few weeks, and his smoking jacket bulged around him in the chair, making him broader than he was when standing.

"How are you feeling after such a busy week?"

He waved off her question. He always did.

"Fine. Fine. Anderson is a worrier." He drew deeply on his cigar. "But I agree with you. Having Raymond descend on us so soon after returning from London was exhausting."

"Augustus," Mother chided from her chaise lounge, smiling as she swatted his knee. She always sat near enough that they could touch, which they did often. "Mr. Raymond was missing Amelia's company. It was kind of him to come make sure we'd arrived safely."

"As though I couldn't get my family home," Father grumbled.

He'd done his best to direct everything about their hurried departure between coughing fits that had bent him double.

"And I believe he thought we'd be bored to tears, pining away for parties," Father continued. "He could have written about a visit before appearing on our doorstep with his trunks and a valet."

"It actually set me to thinking about hosting a house party for the hunting season," Mother said. "Don't glare at me like that, Augustus. It would just be a small group. A few could come up from town, and more local young ladies could attend the events." She looked between them. "Not for long. Maybe four days? It was nice having more young people in the house."

A knowing look passed between her parents, and Amelia scrambled for a sensible reason to avoid spending four days cooped up like a turkey being fattened for Christmas Eve with the likes of Margaret Gerard. Her schedule had been interrupted enough.

"Mother—"

"If we invite the local young ladies, we should invite Mr. Ferrand. I enjoyed his company this evening," Father said. "Didn't you, Amelia?"

"Yes I did, but Father—"

"I've caught a chill," Mother said as she unfolded herself from the lounge. "I'll just go fetch a wrap."

"I can close the window, Marian."

"Nonsense. You haven't finished your cigar. I won't be but a moment. You two discuss other guests while I'm gone."

The door clicked closed behind her, and Father's book fell closed with a muffled thump.

"Does she appear well, Amelia?"

Amelia thought back over the last few weeks. "She seemed gay in London, but the Season is exhausting." If they hadn't been attending parties, they'd been preparing for them. Days were spent at the modiste for fittings or the milliner for hats. "It seemed like we were forever calling on ladies or being called on. Perhaps she is just tired."

Every time Amelia had awakened on the carriage ride home, Mother had been awake and alert, adjusting Father's blanket or soothing him while coughs shook through him.

"She frets over me worse than Anderson."

Since the doctor's name had come up more than once, it

seemed a good time to broach the subject. "How was your visit today?"

"Fine." Father exchanged his cigar for his whiskey. "He believes the country air has helped my lungs, though God knows why he doesn't want me out in it. I've walked and ridden these fields all my life." He looked over the rim of his glass. "Something you seem to be doing frequently these days."

How much had Mother told him of Ethan's visit? "I've enjoyed being home." That wasn't a lie. She loved Oakdale and the freedom it offered her. Since returning from London, she couldn't get her fill of it. "And I thought Mr. Raymond would enjoy seeing the estate." That *was* a lie. She'd reveled in the display of her father's management skills borne by a love of this place. It was something she shared, and she was proud that she'd been able to step in as his health had wavered.

"Tempting him with a prize he can't win," Father said. His wry grin implied much more. She had never been able to fool him.

"He's not for me," she replied, hoping it would end the matter. When she married, she should be able to choose her own husband. She should have the freedom to decide if she married at all.

"There's nothing wrong with him, Amelia."

There wasn't anything right with him either. When she thought of his visit, all she remembered was hours of dread, thankfully broken by the arrival of Richard Ferrand.

After a week of Ethan's banal attention, Richard had been refreshing. He'd spoken little, but the empty spaces in his conversation had said a great deal. He'd spoken to her like she had a brain in her head. By the end of their ride, he'd made her a conspirator in his humor. That had continued this evening over dinner.

He reminded her of Drake and Oliver, which was probably why she'd felt so comfortable with him.

"You will have to marry, Amelia."

Her father's flat statement snapped her out of her thoughts. "What?"

"Before I die, you need to be settled in a home of your own."

The plain practicality of his statement stole her breath. Father had often remarked in passing about his death, but it had been a future event, like when they planned for a journey abroad. Their winter in Italy had begun as *one day we'll go*. After they'd set a date to travel, it had changed to *when we go*. As the date neared, it had become *before we leave*.

Tears welled. "Father."

"None of that. There's not a certain date, but plans need to be made, and we need to be realistic. Oakdale will fall to Warren, with the exception of the property you inherited from Elizabeth."

Jasper Warren, a distant cousin, would inherit her home simply because he was male. And he was the only male in her generation. All her other cousins were female. And married. They were managing homes that belonged to their husbands, bearing children to those husbands, handing them off to nurses so they could continue to entertain in support of their husbands' careers.

Amelia thanked God she had the distillery. "I have my own money, Father."

"Your inheritance and the rent from Brewer aren't adequate. Marian will be generous with her income. Probably too generous. I don't want either of you to struggle."

So she'd have to leave her home, and her business, for a life moving between someone else's estate, someone else's family, and London parties. Her business would be her husband's reputation.

"We have a bargaining position now." Ever the businessman, her father. "We should use it. A house party is a good idea."

It was the worst idea Amelia had ever heard, worse even than when the former duchess had tried to force her and Oliver into a match.

"You spend too much time alone, Amelia. A party will be good for you." He rose from the chair. Not too long ago, her father had been a giant bear of a man. Now, his clothes hung awkwardly in places, like when a modiste placed fabric over a frame in preparation for cutting a dress.

"I'm going up to bed. Work with your mother on the guest list. She already has a list of eligible young men, but invite the young women you like—don't overlook the Gerard girl."

Amelia blinked rapidly to keep the tears at bay until she was alone. "Yes, Father."

RICHARD BLESSED THE shade provided by the buildings surrounding Thetford's square. It had been months since he'd been awake and moving this early.

"If Simon repeats that poem about bollocks covered in weeds at school today, I'll put you on the front pew at church on Sunday. You'll bear the brunt of the vicar's next sermon alone," Oliver said. Despite his grousing, he had a grin on his face.

Thetford's market bustled around them, full of the farm smells brought by fresh produce and the sweet scent of fresh bread. Richard suspected that if he plucked an egg from a basket, it would still be warm.

"It wouldn't be the first time I've withstood a vicar," he replied.

"You didn't have Thea beside you trying not to laugh," Oliver said as they walked over cobblestones worn flat after decades of travel and use.

He stopped at a stall tended by a neatly dressed woman not much older than them, her hair covered by a plain, clean linen scarf. "Good morning, Mrs. Bell."

Her curtsey was as quick as her smile. "Good morning, Your Grace." She reached out to ruffle Brownie's shaggy head. "Good morning, wee lad. You're getting to be as big as a pony."

"Don't put that association in Simon's head, or he'll be asking to ride the beast to school," Oliver said. "May I introduce my brother-in-law, Richard Ferrand."

"A pleasure, Mrs. Bell." Richard stretched out his hand. After a moment's pause, Mrs. Bell took it in a strong, callused grip and gave him a business-like nod. Her smile never wavered.

"Hazel says the pig is coming along," Oliver continued. "Thank you again for letting us keep it there to fatten."

"It's a pleasure to see her stop by, but if she keeps bringing pies, the children will be as fat as the pig," Mrs. Bell teased. Another customer queued up to the stall, and she dropped another curtsey as a quick dismissal. "Good day, Your Grace. Mr. Ferrand."

They ambled away, the dog between them much like Simon had been on the streets of Quebec. Richard couldn't help but make the comparison between the crowded streets of the city and this simple square in the morning sunshine. Windows sparkled and new shingles freckled across worn roofs. Freshly painted signs swayed in the cool breeze.

"You have a pig, but she keeps one for you as well?" Richard asked. "Is that an entitlement as a landlord?"

"It's a favor she does me so I don't have to explain to Simon how Pinky ran away from home while we eat bacon with breakfast. The Bremen Town Musicians will only work for so long."

The more things changed… "Surely, one of the boys at school will mention where bacon comes from." Not to mention eggs, roast beef, and babies.

"They might." Oliver nodded hello to another villager. "But we'll fell that tree when we reach it."

Richard opened his mouth to argue. As much as he'd liked watching Simon giggle as he fed apples and kitchen scraps to a grizzled, snuffling hog, he didn't want the boy thinking bacon grew on trees or sprouted like carrots.

"Good morning, gentlemen."

The bright greeting interrupted his argument. Amelia

Chitester was approaching them. In a yellow dress, with a wide smile and her white-blonde curls spilling from under a wide-brimmed straw hat, she looked like a daisy in the middle of a wood.

"Good morning, Miss Chitester." Richard looked to her ever-present shadow. "Miss Graves."

The older woman looked much more certain on foot than on a horse, but no less wary. "Mr. Ferrand." She dropped a curtsey. "Your Grace."

"I was—we were on our way to the train depot. Will you join us?"

"We shall," Oliver said. "I need to visit with Drake myself." He offered his arm to the chaperone. "May I escort you, Miss Graves?"

With no option, Richard did the same for Amelia. She took it, her tightly patterned white lace glove contrasting with his black wool coat. Looking down, all he could see was her hat brim. "Are you expecting something on the train?"

"No." She paused for so long that he thought that was all he'd get. After a moment, she continued. "I'm always excited to see what arrives, to know that we don't always have to go to London for fine goods." She glanced up at him, and the shadow cast by her hat made her eyes darker. "You must think me horribly dull."

"Not at all. There's a spot that overlooks the port at home. I like to stand there and wonder where the ships are from and what they're carrying. Where it will end up."

It was something he'd begun doing after Oliver and Simon had left.

"But those ships come from all over the world. This train comes from Norwich. For all I know, there's nothing in those boxes but gooseberries and wool knickers."

Her chaperone coughed sharply, and Amelia's cheeks tinted pink before she refocused on the train. "Unmentionables. My apologies."

Richard was seized with the impulse to tease her about how

itchy wool knickers would be, and how inconvenient that would be at parties. He resisted, but he also decided chaperones were the most inconvenient women ever created.

"But you don't actually *know*, so that's the mystery." Richard tilted his head to whisper, so close that the flowers on her hat tickled his cheek. "Isn't it?"

Amelia looked up quickly, and the change in position put them almost nose to nose. "That's it. Exactly."

Her eyes had brown circles around the blue, giving them a depth he always thought his own lacked. A man could drown in them—after he'd shipwrecked on her smile.

Richard straightened and resumed their walk. The depot laid ahead, its new wood gleaming. Steam from the train rose like fog from a river. As they passed, several villagers stared openly, though they smiled and nodded a greeting.

"Do they always stare like this?" he asked. "Or is it Oliver?"

"They're accustomed to Oliver in his work clothes, though it took a while." Amelia tightened her grip on his arm and leaned closer. "It's you."

"Because I'm walking with you." Had they seen her with Raymond last week? Maybe another man before that? Did anyone else know she smelled like fruit and flowers, as though she'd been walking in an orchard before her trip to town?

And why was that so bothersome?

"No. It's *you*. You're new and you're rather overdressed for market day." Laughter tinged her words.

Oliver had said the same thing over breakfast. "I wasn't sure how to dress in the company of a duke with his tenants. But we had to get Simon to school, so there wasn't time to change."

Though Oliver had insisted Richard leave his hat in the cart they'd brought to town. Richard hoped it hadn't become a toy for squirrels.

"Just be yourself," she said. "They'll not give you a second glance after a few weeks." She looked up at him. "I'm assuming you're staying for a long visit after all this time."

He hadn't really made a plan, but it made sense to stay close to France for a bit longer. Not to mention how much time he'd already missed with Simon, and Oliver wanted his opinion on the mill's operation. As though he needed it. The two of them had perfected starting a new location three sites ago.

Plus, he was walking with one of the most intriguing women he'd met in years.

They'd reached the depot. A giant of man came out to greet them. "Hello...Mr. Hawkins."

Oliver took his outstretched hand. "Thank you, Hamish. I'm sick to death of titles today. Meet my brother-in-law, Richard Ferrand."

The young man greeted him with a hearty handshake. After Raymond's curiosity, Richard hadn't been sure what to expect in the village. But no one questioned how he and Oliver were related.

"How are things?" Oliver asked.

"Going well," Hamish said. "The new hoist made short work of Brewer's new stills. Wish we'd had it when your steam engine arrived."

"Too right," Oliver laughed. "Is Drake around?"

"In the office, looking over the books and staring into space like he does when he's counting." Hamish opened the door and nodded toward Amelia. "We have a few chairs if you ladies would like to wait."

"Thank you so much," Amelia said, but once they entered the building, only Miss Graves took a seat.

"Mr. Fletcher," Amelia called as she walked down the hallway as though she were at home. "Are you available for visitors?"

"Of course. Come back."

The deep rumble suggested a tall man, but there was no way to predict the well-dressed bean pole standing in the middle of the room waiting on them. "Miss Chitester. What a pleasure to see you this morning. And Oliver as well. How are things at the mill?"

His greeting was warm and easy. Familiar.

"We're on our way there now to check the shipment before the men bring it over. Let me introduce my brother-in-law—"

"Mr. Ferrand." He took Richard's hand in a strong grip. "Drake Fletcher. Thea said you had arrived. I trust you're enjoying your stay so far."

When had he spoken with Thea? It would have been this morning when she'd gone for a walk. Richard looked to Oliver, who seemed to take everything in stride. "I am. Thank you."

"And you, Miss Chitester." Fletcher's smile widened. "Out for a stroll in the sunshine?"

There was something about his tone, or maybe his arched brow, that gave the impression he was laughing. And, rather than being perturbed, Oliver and Amelia appeared comfortable. Perhaps they were in on the joke.

"I was checking with a few of Father's tenants, since we couldn't see them last week," Amelia said. "Did you know Mr. Butler has an abundance of pears? I thought Mr. Brewer might be interested in acquiring them."

Richard's interest was piqued. "The distiller?"

Fletcher nodded once, a quick dip of his chin. "I manage the distillery's accounts and keep a watchful eye when Eamon is traveling."

"Which seems to be more frequent as of late," Oliver said. "You'd do well to buy a house in the village rather than staying at The Goat."

Richard had passed The Galloping Goat on his way to the village. The inn had a large front garden, a newly painted red door, and smoke curling out of the chimney.

"I like The Goat," Fletcher said. "And I believe Jenny is finally growing accustomed to me." He turned to Amelia. "I'll check with Butler about the pears. Eamon has been searching for a good supply."

"We won't keep you," Oliver said. "We need to get to the mill. Come for supper tonight so we can have a longer visit.

Richard can tell you about his—"

"About my visit to France." *Winery* sounded like he was trying too hard. Besides, it led to a lot of embarrassing questions.

"Thank you for the invitation." Fletcher ushered them to the door. "I'll come 'round at the usual time."

They left the building and headed back up the hill to the village. Richard wanted to know why Amelia was checking on her father's tenants, how she even knew where to start. Most society ladies he knew spent their days avoiding farmers or anything that would dirty their skirts.

"I enjoyed dinner last evening," he said instead.

"I should have said something." Amelia sighed. "Graves will have my ears if she discovers I forgot to say something like *you were delightful company*." Her steps faltered. "Drat. That sounds like you weren't and I'm just being polite."

Richard's laughter built under his ribs and climbed upward. "Thank you, I think."

"I'm sorry," she sighed. "It's just that my mother is planning a house party."

And Amelia hated parties. "I see. Can I assume that Mr. Raymond will be returning?"

"She's sure to invite him." She didn't seem the least bit excited. "Which will cause all sorts of problems."

Richard looked down at her hat, waiting in vain for her to speak. It was as though she'd forgotten he was attached to her, or that they had been in a conversation. He didn't mind the silence.

When they reached Oliver's cart, Richard unwound himself from Amelia. The air smelled of trees and earth, and his forearm cooled.

"I would like to hear more about France," she said. "I hope you will be a guest at the party."

"How forward of you." Her quick blush had him regretting the tease. "My apologies, Miss Chitester. I just..." *What? Am at ease with you in a way I've not felt with a ton girl? I like hearing you laugh?* He needed to come to his senses. She was destined for

London and he was destined for Quebec. "Why don't you come to dinner?"

The spark in her eyes died quickly as she glanced to her chaperone. "Dinner would be an ordeal. It's always a group affair."

Richard nodded. It was one of the reasons he avoided society girls.

"Perhaps another time," Amelia said. She had the most appealing quirk to her smile.

"Perhaps at your party."

CHAPTER FIVE

I T HAD BEEN one of the best days in Richard's recent memory. His muscles were tired from the exertion, his lungs were full of clean air, and if he concentrated, he could still smell the damp of the forest.

When he closed his eyes, he could imagine all those nights, years ago when he and Oliver stumbled home from the mill with Simon bundled against them. Just the three of them in a house that had been meant to hold a gaggle of children, loving parents, and a doting uncle.

With eyes open, he couldn't pretend any longer. Oliver was there, though the plump, happy baby in his arms had red hair. Simon was there, but now he cheerfully recounted every funny story from school, and everything his friends said, and everything he'd learned. They also weren't alone any longer.

"Jenny and John are doing well with The Goat," Thea said, handing a ledger back to Fletcher. "Though I didn't expect otherwise. He mentioned a new barn when I was there today. The location is far enough from the inn so as to not bother the guests."

"And it will save funds in the long run," Fletcher said. "They need more livestock, and definitely more chickens. Jenny has resorted to buying eggs, which she hates to do."

The businessman was across from him in a matching wing-back chair near the fire in an almost identical pose—his feet propped on an ottoman and a whiskey glass in his free hand. Though his boots gleamed in the firelight while Richard's well-used work boots soaked in the heat. He had to admit one benefit of having a staff. The sitting room was warmer, given that there were people in the house all day to stoke fires.

"Which is why I told them to go ahead," Thea said. "We have more than sufficient funds." She looked to Oliver. "John will come see you tomorrow about the lumber, and I expect a bill."

"Maybe I'll charge you double since you're reaping the benefits of increased trade in the village." Oliver's tease ended in a laugh as Thea punched his shoulder.

After Oliver's return, he'd written of Thea, who he'd found again as a local innkeeper, but Richard hadn't paid much attention. He'd focused on the talk of the new mill, Simon, and family struggles. She had been featured more prominently in later letters, but the inn was hardly mentioned. This conversation wasn't what Richard had expected from a former innkeeper rescued into the life of a duchess.

"Thea owns The Goat," Drake said without opening his eyes, much like someone would state that Lord Russell was the prime minister.

"You mean Oliver—"

"No," Oliver said, his smile widening. "He means exactly what he said. Thea owns it, and Drake is her man of business."

"*Our* man of business," Thea said. She rose from the sofa with her daughter in her arms and approached Richard. "Carys has been watching you all evening. Would you like to hold her?"

He reached without thinking. While he'd never admit it to anyone but family, he'd enjoyed holding Simon for years. Carys had the same warmth, the same reassuring weight, and the same trusting look in her eyes. As though she could look past the outer trappings and know what was in his heart. Her toothless grin and hearty kick were apparently signs of approval.

"I believe she likes you, *Oncle*," Thea said. She met Richard's surprise with a smile. "Oliver loves you like a brother, and I have never had one of my own. Plus…" She looked to Simon, who was now yawning in Oliver's lap as he listened to a quiet story.

"It's easier," Richard surmised. Though he didn't mind the convenience, especially not when Carys loved the same rowdy bouncing that her brother had at her age.

Rather than returning to Oliver, Thea sat on the ottoman in front of the fire, heedless of his boots. "Just as it was easier, and necessary, for everyone to believe Drake owned The Goat. They still do."

"But all I really do is what she tells me," Drake rumbled. His smirk was the same brotherly one Richard had given Julia years ago.

Thea pushed his feet from the ottoman. "Because I'm always right."

Drake returned his feet to their spot, his smile widening. "Yes, Your Grace."

Across the room, Oliver barked a laugh as he stood, his sleeping son in his arms. "I'm going to carry Simon up so he doesn't witness this brawl."

Richard refocused on Drake, who was still content by the fire. "So you pay him a salary?"

"He earns it," Thea stated flatly. "I wouldn't have survived without his aid when I first started, and I wouldn't have been nearly as successful in the following years."

"He is also awake and right here," Drake drawled. His gaze was too sharp for a man who'd been almost asleep a moment ago.

"Do you manage other businesses?" Richard asked.

Drake nodded. "I have clients here and in London."

"Like Hamish and the freight depot?" An idea was forming in Richard's brain. If Oliver trusted this man…

Drake shook his head. "Hamish and I are partners in the depot, though I currently own the controlling interest. He has the brawn and local knowledge."

"And you have the money and the contacts?"

"I have colleagues in imports and shipping."

Richard was vaguely aware of Thea moving from between them, of her taking Carys from his arms, and of the door clicking closed behind her. Across from him, Fletcher's eyes had sharpened. The whiskey glass was no longer in his hands.

"How can I help you, Mr. Ferrand?"

They were alone. If Fletcher could help a woman own an inn and a farmer start a freight depot, perhaps he could save a winery.

"I have inherited a winery near the French coast." He kept talking to keep Fletcher from the usual congratulations that followed the statement. "My uncle died without heirs, and I was the nearest that could be found."

"Is it productive?"

Richard sipped his whiskey before he shrugged. "There are grapes to pick, and the casks are full. The staff there seems knowledgeable and capable of harvesting it and preparing it. The problem is distribution. My uncle was…fond of his own product."

"I see."

"His bills were left unpaid, and distributors refused to do business with him because of it. The staff confessed to me that they have been doing without in order to save this year's harvest, but next year's will be in jeopardy."

"So you have wine to sell?"

"I have casks that risk turning to vinegar." Not even his uncle could consume that much. They'd have to resort to bathing in it. "Which is a shame, because it's a decent product."

"I'm assuming by *decent* you mean it isn't comparable to other French wines?" Fletcher asked. When Richard nodded, he leaned forward, his elbows on his knees. "So you need someone to get it out of France to a new market and a distributor in that new market?"

"Yes." It was a relief to confess it to someone. Starting the mill in Quebec had not been as nerve-wracking as inheriting a sinking ship with staff still on board.

"I think I have an option."

So quickly? Could anything this easily obtained be honest?

"I represent Eamon Brewer," Drake said. "The distillery has a facility and a small staff for bottling and labeling. Are you available to meet tomorrow afternoon?"

Richard nodded, unable to withhold his smile. "Thank you, Fletcher."

"Don't thank me yet. Eamon is…rather single-minded." The other man extended his hand. "Regardless, you'd best call me Drake. We'll be seeing a lot of each other, Richard."

AMELIA SAT IN her mother's office, in front of her spindle-legged desk in a fine-boned chair, doing her best not to fidget as the moments of her day ticked away. The list of party guests lay before her. "So many?"

"It's only eleven," Mother said. "We can count on a few crying off, given the Season. But if they all accept, we have room for them." She smiled over her chocolate. "Sometimes I forget how much like Augustus you are."

Amelia recognized every name on the list. They'd attended the same parties, the same afternoons in the park. They'd expect the same bright entertainments here, softened by the country, of course. There would have to be fishing, shooting, and at least one dance. There would be tea every afternoon, and they'd dress for dinner every evening.

This was important to her parents.

"It will be twelve with Mr. Ferrand."

"And thirteen with you. Our numbers will be uneven. Perhaps we could find another young lady to invite. Do you have a suggestion?"

Amelia would rather strike off a name than add one. "It might make for more entertainment if the young men couldn't assume they always had a dance partner."

"Or it may make the other men resent him." Mother tapped the feather of her quill against her chin. "I do hope he'll feel comfortable in this set since he's not…from London."

Amelia knew better than to believe Mother to be a snob. More likely, she expected their guests would share Ethan's earlier reaction to someone in trade—and French.

After spending more time with him, Amelia was certain he could hold his own with the *ton*, if he cared enough to worry. Besides that, he had come to Norfolk to visit family, which they weren't, and to do business—not to play cards, dance, and hunt for sport. He might have no intention of spending hours in idle chatter over tea or on a dance floor. Which would be a shame. Having walked with him yesterday, she wondered what it would be like to have his warm arms around her as they waltzed.

On the other hand, it had been far too easy to speak her mind with him. That was warning enough to stay clear.

"Thirteen it is then." Mother took the list. "I'll write up the invitations this afternoon. Have you decided on entertainment? We'll need to tell the ladies what to bring for day wear."

Amelia glanced at the clock standing over her mother's shoulder. It was half past ten. Drake had asked her to come for a meeting at eleven. She'd been awake most of the night planning how to incorporate apples into the barley mash.

"Croquet and shuttlecock, I think. And lawn bowls." The minutes ticked by, thrumming through her chest and down until her toes twitched. "The men will enjoy Father's new billiard table, and shooting. Maybe archery for the ladies." It was a combination of every discussion in every London drawing room.

"Riding, of course." Mother jotted down the list. "And the gardens will be lovely for walks. We'll have to dig out the board games for when the days are too chilly for outdoors."

Games wouldn't be a problem. Father had collected sets from every country they'd visited. They could play checkers on a different set each month for a year, though some of them were so beautiful Amelia feared touching them.

"What about the menu?"

Amelia stood. She really did need to go. "You don't need me to choose food." She kissed her mother's cheek to soften her abruptness. "Father asked me to see to the Baxters' roof. I want to make certain the reeds have arrived."

"Do be careful. We'll talk after dinner this evening, and you can make sure I've included all your favorites." Mother put a hand on hers. It was warm and yielding. "I do want to make sure you enjoy the weekend, dear. This shouldn't be a chore."

Fighting the guilty pull of that hand, and the gravitational force of her chair, Amelia backed away from the desk. "We will. I promise." Her smile was genuine. She knew girls who had no input on their choice of husband, much less the menu for a house party that laid out eligible men like a smorgasbord.

"What of Graves? You shouldn't be out alone." Mother reached for the bell. "We can ask a footman—"

"We're not in London," Amelia said. "And I'm not riding with a man, or in the village where someone could whisk me into an alley." *And Graves would be little help in any situation.* "Please let me be alone. If the house party is a success, I won't have much more time here. I want to store as many memories as possible."

It was a dastardly ploy, playing on her mother's kind heart to get her way. But it worked. Mother left the bell on the desk, and Amelia all but ran from the room.

Once in the hallway, Amelia lengthened her stride to a scandalous pace, down the back stairs and through the courtyard to the stable. Molly was waiting patiently, already saddled. A small pack held Amelia's work clothes and boots, and the groom stood ready.

She was away in a flash, letting the horse have her head until the distillery sheltered them from view. Caspar was an orange pile of fur, snoozing at the bottom of the haystack.

Amelia swept through the back door, then through the barrel and label rooms. The still room's sweet, earthy scent slowed her as it always did. She loved to bask in the copper tinted sunshine, close her eyes, and soak in the warmth while she imagined the scent of her whiskey when it was uncorked, the silky ribbon when it was poured, the color of it in glasses. How the ingredients would meld to smooth the bite of the alcohol.

However, this time, she wasn't alone. A young boy, standing in the shadowy corner, dropped the firewood in his hands and snatched his hat from his head so quickly that his fine blond hair floated in the sunlight.

"May I help you, Miss Chitester?"

"You can, Freddie. Thank you. Did the thatch arrive for your parents' roof?" *There. I'm not lying to my mother.*

"It did, miss. My mam says it's dry as a bone and thick as a wool blanket. Tom and I are going to carry it up this afternoon, when he's done in the fields."

"And when you're finished with school, yes?" She and Drake had made this decision early on. Hiring older children meant fewer questions and fewer temptations to drink the product. It also gave local families additional income. However, they weren't supposed to miss school in favor of money.

Freddie nodded. "I said I'd come stoke the fires on my way. The vicar said I could be late since I'm better at math than most—except Florence. She's better'n everyone."

"And your father is recovering well?"

"Yes, miss. The doctor says he'll be back behind the plow in a few weeks. Which'll be good because he's in a right foul mood." A blush flooded the boy's cheeks. "Pardon me, miss."

"My father's been ill, too. He's in the same mood." Amelia looked around, casting for a reason to be here. Freddie didn't know of her involvement, but a lady visiting a distillery was a topic for conversation. "I've come to see Mr. Fletcher about buying Mr. Butler's apples. Is he about?"

"Yes, miss. He's in his office." Freddie pointed to the door in the corner. "He said something about a meeting this morning. I was supposed to be gone before it started, but I wanted to make sure there was enough wood to keep the stills bubbling."

It was on the tip of her tongue to thank him, but these weren't supposed to be her fires. "You'd best get going then. I'll let him know you've gone on to school."

"Thank you, miss." Freddie clapped his hat over his head as he ran past and out the door, eager to be on his way.

Amelia went to the office and knocked quickly before entering. "I'm sorry to be late, Drake. Breakfast took—"

Richard Ferrand sat across from Drake in the chair she normally occupied, his brows drawn into a frown that deepened the longer she stood in the door. "Miss Chitester."

"Mr. Ferrand." She looked to her man of business. "I've come to talk about Mr. Butler's—"

"Amelia," Drake interrupted with a quiet word and a smile. "Mr. Ferrand is here to discuss how the distillery can help him distribute a large supply of French wine he's inherited."

Wine. His solution was to bring her another alcohol that aged for years?

"It's ready to sell as soon as we get it over the channel and into bottles," Drake said. "Good quality and a fair price. It will go quickly."

"Can we get it over easily?" Lost in details and decisions, she forgot they weren't alone.

"Richard can send word to the winery to deliver the casks to the port. I have a colleague who can bring it over." Drake paused for a moment. "Though bottles will be an issue."

"There are crates of empty bottles in Rosnay." Richard still frowned as he looked between them. "They could bottle it there."

Amelia rubbed the tip of her tongue against the roof of her mouth, imagining how red wine would meld with barley and figs, or apples. "What's the bouquet?"

Richard blinked at her, no doubt shocked by her question. Men expected young ladies to simply drink what was poured for them. "The grapes are mild and sweet, not sugary. More like honey," he said. "And it tastes of oak, but the barrels are lighter than the oak here. It results in a fresher taste. It isn't bad really."

Amelia nodded. "Don't bottle it there. Send the bottles with the barrels. We'll bottle it and split the profits sixty-forty. Out of your sixty, you're responsible for the excise. With my forty, I get your empty barrels." She looked to Drake. "Did I miss anything?"

If she didn't know better, she'd interpret the look in his eyes as pride, like when Father had watched her come down the stairs for her first ball. "I'll want an additional fee to pay the shipper," he said. "Not much above my usual, but it will mean your forty percent won't go as far."

But she'd have an income to help pay her first loan install-ment, and she'd have barrels for her next batch. Barrels already flavored with well-aged wine. "I can live with that."

Richard's eyes widened. "Wait. What is going on? Is this—"

"It is." Drake waved his hand toward Amelia. "Richard, meet Eamon Brewer."

As much as anonymity chafed at times, as much as she want-ed to brag about what she was accomplishing, the secrecy could be comforting. Without its protection, she was exposed to laughter, criticism, and disbelief. Hoping he would respond kindly, she extended her hand. "Do we have a deal, Richard?"

He didn't mock or demand explanations. He simply stood and shook her hand in a strong, solid grip. As a businessman would. "We do, Amelia."

CHAPTER SIX

WHEN THEY HAD visited Morocco, Amelia had ridden a camel in the desert.

Guiding a full whiskey barrel through the distillery was much like riding that camel. Laden with liquid, it wobbled and sloshed as she guided it to the shelves in the barrel room and wrestled it onto the bottom shelf. Caspar lurked nearby, hoping to catch an adventurous mouse or, more likely, to lap up any leaking spirits.

"Pesky bugger." Amelia scratched the cat between his ears and smiled at his squinched eyes and loud purr. "If you ever learn to claw out a bung, I'll be overrun with mice and have nothing to bottle."

She straightened and kept bending, arching her back to loosen muscles that ached in a way riding and dancing didn't inspire. It was a good feeling, compounded by the newest row of full barrels left to quietly age. She had done this. Made it with her own two hands. She was keeping her family's tenants from poverty in her own small way.

No wonder Oliver preferred the sawmill to lords.

With the last of the spirits stored, Amelia went to the loft to see about the grain. Up here, the smells changed from the pungent sugar and fruit of whiskey mash to earthy wheat spread across the drying floor. The heat rising from below made her lightweight work clothes a relief.

Sunlight through the windows left bright squares on the wheat, the wind through the trees creating random patterns. Outside, sparrows chittered away while wrens sang and jays squawked about the noise.

Amelia closed her eyes and soaked in the smells and sounds of home.

Not my home for much longer. If her life didn't change due to marriage, it would change with her father's death. She dreaded either.

"Hello? Amelia?" Richard called up from the first floor.

He had been a frequent visitor over the past two weeks, but always when Drake had been present as an inappropriate chaperone. A moment of panic flitted through Amelia's thoughts as a shadowy cloud over the drying wheat. While she met with Drake all the time, he had acted more as a brother since their introduction. Which was the difference. She trusted Oliver and Thea, and they trusted Drake. However, she had always met Richard in the company of others.

It was one thing to avoid marriage in order to start a business, quite another to be trapped into marriage with one's business partner in order to avoid a scandal.

Amelia shook the thought from her head. This was ridiculous. No businessperson would think twice about holding a meeting. She strode to the top of the stairs and looked down, making sure to smile. "Come up."

He did as she asked, but stopped when he was at eye level. "I saw your horse, but not Drake's."

"He went down to Ipswich to ensure the wine arrived safely and to secure the wagons we'd need for transport." She returned to the drying loft, almost certain he'd follow, and yet delighted when the boards creaked under his feet. If he didn't treat her like a scandalous lady, she needn't think like one.

"Don't you worry about being here alone? What if someone stumbled in and decided to take advantage?"

"I'd bribe them with whiskey until they were properly

sloshed and then make my escape." Amelia handed him a rake. They needed to stir the grain. "Besides, who's going to pass by a distillery and think *I believe I'll see if there's a young lady in there alone?* Other than you."

Oh drat. Richard had gone from laughing at her passable impression of a Norfolk villager to staring at her like she had two heads. And now all she could think of *was* him coming in to take advantage. She went to the far end of the loft and shoved her rake into the grain.

"Your mare is recognizable," Richard said from his post at the opposite end of the floor.

Her whole body tingled as she imagined his arms around her, keeping her against his chest. When they'd shaken hands to seal their agreement, his had been warm and lightly callused. It was easy to think of them cradling her jaw as he kissed her. But that was where her imagination stopped. She'd never been properly kissed. She'd never met anyone who inspired it.

And she was certain business partners didn't consider kissing one another.

"There are dozens of grays in Thetford." She gentled her strokes in the wheat. "Go easy. We're not threshing it, just making sure the damp grain comes to the top."

It was the same instruction she repeated every time she touched a rake, the same that had been grumbled by a good-natured miller who'd given into her pestering without knowing her motives.

"Like this?" Richard asked, pleasing Amelia that he'd asked, yet she worried about being too pushy.

"Yes. Just smooth it flat as you go. Leaving piles leads to mildew." Pushy be hanged. This was her responsibility.

Her thoughts calmed as the grain worked its magic. Her breaths slowed to the beat of the rake as she stepped in time along the wide boards that kept her feet out of the grain. It was like waltzing.

If your partner was a garden implement—or all the way

across the room.

"It's never bothered me being alone," Amelia said. "My first building was so small there was barely room for me and the still. I kept dragging my skirts through the fire."

Richard finished his first row and stepped over to the next. "Why did you begin in the first place?"

Because no well-bred young woman woke in the morning and thought about how to make a living, much less how to be a distiller. "Why did you begin with trees?"

"I like the forest, and I could see a way to keep mine healthy by cutting the largest trees and making room for the younger ones to grow. But I needed to find something to do with the timber, and Quebec was growing. It needed material." He glanced her way and grinned. "Is this your way of telling me you drink your father's whiskey?"

A shudder went through her. "I tried it once because I wanted to see what it was like. He always drank it, but he'd make the most awful face after he'd gulped it down. When I was younger, I thought it was medicine, which he found quite funny."

He'd laughed for days over it, every time he poured a drink. It had been a grand, strong sound. She'd always loved making him happy.

"So you decided to make it because you hate the way it tastes?" Richard asked. "Sound decision."

If he'd been close enough, she'd have smacked him with her rake. "Once the burn subsided, I could taste the flavors underneath, mostly molasses and barley, like good thick bread. And there was a smell that reminded me of autumn, which compounded the warmth it spread through me." She swiped her rake over the wheat, creating streaks of light and dark grain. The dark streaks were finer every day. This would be ready to mash soon. "I thought I could do it better."

Richard had stopped halfway up the row, his hands resting atop his rake. "All I had to do was pick up an axe."

It wasn't true. She knew what it took to start a business.

Months of questions, finding a location, experimenting with product until she'd gotten it right.

"I've always loved to cook," she said as she stepped to a new row. Which was the truth. Since she was small, she'd preferred to be in the kitchen surrounded by flavors and smells, wondering where everything came from, imagining recipes, hiding from a well-meaning Graves. "But proper misses aren't meant for the kitchen."

"But they are meant for house parties." He resumed raking. "Thank you for the invitation."

"You will come, won't you?" After weeks of planning, guests would arrive tomorrow with their valets and maids in tow, not to mention their drivers or horses. The house would be full to the rafters, everyone looking to her for entertainment. "It would be nice to see a friendly face."

"If these people aren't your friends, why are they coming for a party?"

"Because it's the done thing," Amelia sighed. Just like young ladies were expected in town for the Season. It was one thing to attend balls, gossip between dances, and sleep until mid-day while in London. It was quite another when those dancers, gossips, and layabouts were under your roof when you had other things to do.

Which was uncharitable. She was looking forward to seeing a few of the young women she'd met—the ones who spoke of books and lectures rather than just about eligible men and their titles. "There are a few who will be entertaining. And my cousin Jasper is coming as well." She passed her rake through the wheat and watched as the silky grain slid back into place like she'd never touched it. "But you know my secret, and they don't."

"Then tell them." Richard was close enough now that she could see sunshine reflected in his boots.

"That's quite easily said by someone..." She stopped, horrified at how snooty her unguarded thoughts were and at how easily they slipped free when he was near.

"In trade?" he finished, his voice flat.

"Well…yes." There was no point in denying it. "But that's not all of it. You're *allowed* to be in trade because you're a man."

"Allowed?" Richard scoffed. "That's an arguable point, Miss Chitester."

She disliked how bitter her name sounded on his tongue. She hated that he hadn't called her Amelia. "Don't do that. Please. *Ton* people can look down their noses all they like, but many are one poor wager from being there themselves. And the women are twice as vulnerable because they have no say over their husbands' habits and no way to support themselves. The point is, you *get* to be in charge of your own fate, and I don't."

"Society will put up with a lot of eccentricities," Richard said. They were face-to-face now, and his bright blue eyes reminded her of the sky past the windows. "The Duke of Rushford married an innkeeper."

"Oliver married a successful businesswoman who kept this village going in spite of his mother's neglect," Amelia said. "But no one can know that. Just like I can't go up to my guests and say, '*Hello, before we play croquet, let me take you to my still where I've been working through the night to ensure everything was barreled before your arrival.*'"

Richard's lips quirked. "It would make for a much more interesting party."

"It would make me an outcast. It would make my parents laughingstocks and ruin their hopes."

"*Their* hopes?" He raised an eyebrow, revealing a small scar, barely a nick, at its apex. She wondered how he'd gotten it.

"Daughters marry, Richard. Whether they wish to or not." She breathed easier having confessed it to someone else, though she thought it odd that she had to explain it to him at all.

"Then tell the truth, be an outcast, and leave it all behind." Her dumbfounded silence let him continue. "You either want to be on the shelf or you don't."

Spoken like someone who had a choice, who didn't reap repercussions. "Why can't I be on the shelf simply because I wish to be?"

His eyes sparked. "Because beautiful young ladies holding themselves at a distance are a challenge, as your Mr. Raymond has proved. Their only deterrent is a family afraid of a scandal, whether it's a loon in the attic or a broken-hearted miss jilted after...poorly timed anticipation." He waved his hand toward the stairs and the stills below. "Better to just be the loon and have done with it."

She should argue over his interpretation of society, but he was right. She was also too busy thinking. She didn't want to be the loon, truly. What she wanted was to have a life of her own making, which she would never have in the *ton*. So what she needed was a fiancé of her own choosing.

Someone handsome and charming enough to make everyone believe she'd fallen for him in a whirlwind courtship, but rakish enough to imply a scandal at some point. Perhaps someone who could agree to jilt her. Definitely someone who could agree to a temporary arrangement, who understood this as a business relationship.

Richard stood in front of her, waiting for her to agree with him. He ticked every item on her list and, if Oliver was to be believed, was always up for a lark. Better yet, he was leaving after his wine was sold and his visit was concluded. He'd be across an ocean living out his life on a wild continent.

Amelia licked her lips and prepared to do one more thing a well-bred lady would never do. Propose. "Would you be my fiancé?"

"Have you been sampling the barrel?"

It was the only reason logical reason for her question, except the most obvious. However, it was difficult to believe Amelia would use refusing to marry as a ploy *to* marry.

"Not a real one, of course." Amelia paced away from him, giving him a view of the braces crossing just below her shoulder blades and gathering the too-large linen shirt with them. "Just one to make sure I'm scandalous enough to avoid afterward. Someone who won't be around, so it can be assumed…"

She'd most likely snatched the shirt from the servant's laundry, and it had most likely belonged to a field hand given the thick rolls of fabric bouncing against her forearms as she waved away his shock.

"So it can be assumed that I ran away and broke your heart?" A startling idea flitted across his brain, no doubt inspired by her split skirt. Who knew gray wool could sway like that? "Or be accused of ruining you before I ran?"

Oliver would shoot him.

"It wouldn't have to be that way," she said. "I could do something to make you run." Her grin, when she spun, had the same devilish spark as when she'd negotiated about distributing his wine. "That would certainly keep everyone at bay."

Her father would shoot him.

"No." Richard shook his head to emphasize the point. "Absolutely not."

She grew quiet then, and he breathed easier. Every inhale smelled of grassy wheat and fermenting fruit, reminding him that she was already scandalous. No wonder her thoughts went down that road like a log down a sluice.

As did his when her position in front of the window let the sunshine filter though her shirt like a curtain, casting her curves in silhouette. He cast his gaze around the room, searching for another focus, but finding none. Instead, he walked away from the window, hoping she'd follow. When she did, relief and frustration mingled into a dangerous and unfamiliar potion.

"I suppose I could ask someone else," Amelia murmured, her eyes fixed on the grain like she could read a name in it. "It would just be easier if the man knew everything beforehand. I don't have much time."

"Ask Drake then," Richard said. "He is at least familiar to more people, including your parents. It might make it more believable."

The thought of the other man helping with this cockamamie plan stung more than was comfortable.

"I don't believe I can afford him."

Her giggle made Richard uncomfortable for different reasons altogether. He could imagine it at night when they were alone in the dark, which made him realize they were alone here in a shadowy spot. Worse, he could imagine it as her co-conspirator, wreaking havoc on her potential suitors. Wiping the condescension from Ethan Raymond's face was a good reason to reconsider.

"And you think I'm less expensive?"

He'd intended it as a joke, but hope lit her face. "Does that mean you would if—"

He walked to her, the wide scaffold bouncing under his boots. "Do not insult yourself."

"But it is a business arrangement, and I didn't expect you to do it for nothing."

Oh, he had all sorts of ideas about his reward. They doubled when he put his hands on her shoulders. Her heat soaked through the well-worn, almost silky linen shirt, teasing his palms as much as her curves tempted his fingers. Now that he knew how she spent her time, it was easy to identify her scent. She smelled of whiskey mash.

"You haven't thought this through." Richard's fingers surrendered first, curling around Amelia's delicate shoulders. His palms were next, sliding down her arms to her elbows. The contours of her biceps were a reminder that she wasn't a typical society miss, making him imagine how work would have toned the rest of her.

Her cheeks had flushed the most appealing pink, and her wide-eyed gaze held his. The air between them was so still Richard swore he could hear the roof trusses creak in the wind. He had all of Amelia's attention, and one chance to convince her this was foolish.

That's the only reason he didn't release her.

"What happens if your parents push for a short engagement?" he asked. "What happens if your accomplice doesn't leave quickly enough, and you're forced to marry simply to save face? What if, God forbid, your plan to ruin yourself goes horribly wrong and you're forced to marry your scapegoat?" He hated to see the light fade from her eyes, hated more that he was the cause of it. "You will get through this weekend with the same deft ability I saw you use with Mr. Raymond. I will help you as I can." He held up a finger. "In any way that doesn't involve a betrothal."

He forced his other hand from her and ignored the impulse to rub his fingers together. She was a baron's daughter. They were supposed to be soft to the touch.

"I must go." Richard said it for himself as much as for her. It was on the tip of his tongue to ask for another chore, but staying was dangerous. He couldn't be close to her without talking, and the more she talked, the more he wanted to be close to her. More than close, if the twitch in his fingers was any indication. Even if he didn't succumb, just being caught alone in a forbidden space would cause a scandal that would trap them both.

Still, it made him nervous to leave her alone. "You should leave as well."

"I have much more to do, especially since I'll be unable to work for four days." She reached for his rake. "Thank you for your help."

"Amelia, it would—"

"You are my partner, not my employer." She thumped the rakes on the plank, making it shake beneath his feet, and squared her shoulders. "Or my father, or…anything else. I have work to do, which is something you, of all people, should respect."

Despite her height, she reminded Richard of a commander in the middle of a battle. She also reminded him of his sister—especially the tilt of her chin. There would be no winning this argument, even if he was right. "Fine, but I will move your mare into the stable so she can't be seen by anyone passing by."

"As you wish," Amelia snapped. Her cheeks reddened a moment before she smiled. The thin arc of it was evidence of how little she wanted to do so. "Thank you."

Richard went down the ladder first, intending to be there if she lost her footing. Instead, he had a view of how well her split skirt shaped to her arse. He was torn between looking away, as a gentleman would, or protecting her—which meant staring. In the end, she hopped from the last rung unharmed, her boots thudding against the floor.

"Thank you for your help today, Richard." She dusted her hands against her skirt. "I suppose I'll see you tomorrow night at dinner with my other guests."

Amelia's forced cordiality rankled almost as much as being lumped in with the people she was dreading. She could be angry all she wanted. He was right.

"Until then, Amelia." He dipped his head in as much of a bow as he'd give and left her alone.

He put her docile grey mare out of sight, taking time to add a measure of grain to her bucket and replenish the water in her trough. Then he mounted his gelding and sighed as he stroked the horse's chestnut-colored neck. "It's just as well, boy. I have things to do."

At the top of the hill, Richard glanced over his shoulder and cursed the sting of disappointment when she wasn't visible in the freight yard. She was his partner, after all. Just like Oliver. He'd never worried that Oliver couldn't look after himself.

He urged his horse forward, increasing speed until they were galloping toward the trees on the horizon and the steam rising from the engine at the mill. The large gelding responded like he was meant to race, which Richard hadn't expected from a hired horse. The result was that he arrived at the lumber mill quicker than expected with a genuine smile on his face.

Oliver looked up from his work, shading his eyes with a gloved hand. "You look happy."

"Would you consider keeping this mount for me, if I bought

him?" Richard asked as he dismounted. "I dislike the idea of a stable letting him out to anyone with enough coin. I'd be happy to pay for—"

"You don't have to reimburse me," Oliver said as he shucked off one glove and ran his hand over the gelding from neck to flank. "I'd take it in trade for exercising him. Plus, it would give you another reason to visit more often."

Amelia in her work clothes sprang to mind. She would *not* be a reason to visit. She would either be married and hating him for not being a player in her plot, or she'd be here and hating him for making her be realistic and honest.

Of course there was always the possibility that she would be married and happy, surrounded by children, and laughing that she'd once recklessly proposed to a Frenchman in trade.

"Thank you." Richard stripped out of his jacket before rolling up his sleeves. He donned the gloves Oliver offered and plucked a shave knife from the nearby rack. The thick handles felt like home.

Oliver resumed his place on one side of the log. Richard took the other, notched the tool at the correct angle to catch as little wood as possible, and pulled. After months away from work, the strain of his muscles made him smile. The rough, dark bark peeled away, leaving the gleaming white gold of fresh lumber in its wake.

Soon, he and Oliver were racing to see who could get to the end of their side first, laughing as they went. They'd done it since the beginning, when they were the only two in the forest and the work was unending.

Richard had missed this.

"If you're buying the gelding, I assume you enjoyed your ride this morning." Oliver grunted as he struck a knot. "*Mierda.*"

"I did." As he worked to even the wood, Richard took the lead in their race. "I stopped by the distillery on my way back. Fletcher should have my wine delivered in a few days."

"I didn't know Drake was still in town."

"He's not." Richard swung his head to the right to avoid a large chunk of bark as it splintered. "Amelia was there."

"Rich—"

"I kept a rake in my hand and stayed on the other side of the room." *Most of the time.* "And I told her she shouldn't be there alone."

Oliver shot him a glance, his smile wide. "How did she respond to that?"

"I believe she evicted me." The knife hung as Richard misjudged the angle. "*Méprise.*"

Oliver chuckled. "*Erreur, en effet.*"

"I didn't make a mistake, Ol." Not with Amelia anyway. "She shouldn't be alone, and the fact that everyone lets her—"

"No one *lets* Amelia do anything," Oliver said as he took the lead in their race. "And since when has it bothered you when a young lady was alone?"

"You make it sound like I'm some sort of lecher." Richard doubled his effort, refusing to think of Fiona, who he'd met on the sail from France. Or more aptly, the young lady who'd met him. "Every woman in my path is clear on our relationship."

"However fleeting it may be," Oliver teased.

The joke was irritating. "Which is why I don't entangle myself with society misses." Richard slicked the last of the bark from his side a moment before Oliver.

He strode to the head of the log, leaving Oliver at the foot, and together they turned the log to reveal another dark swath. This time, they raced toward the middle. "And I wouldn't be entangled with one now if you had warned me I was going into business with a baron's daughter and a pirate."

"Smuggler." Oliver grunted a laugh. "And if I'd told you, I'd miss all the fun."

CHAPTER SEVEN

"YOU LOOK LOVELY, dear."

Amelia met her mother's gaze in the mirror and smiled. "Thank you."

She was just vain enough to take the compliment. She might not want to have a party, or a husband, but that didn't mean she wanted to have ugly dresses and drab hair.

The dress was meant to make her stand out. In contrast to the coppery gold bodice and skirt, the modiste had used a French silk for the godets and the center of the bodice and skirts. Every time Amelia stepped, gold constellations sparkled against a blue as deep as the night sky. They'd found the silk years ago on their travels. Amelia believed Mother had hoped to use it for nursery curtains. That opportunity had never come.

"It would make a beautiful wedding dress," Graves said from her chair next to the gleaming dressmaker.

Since the fabric couldn't be used to celebrate an heir, it could be used as bait. Amelia shoved the bitter thought away. It wasn't their fault if she had other interests. "It will also be perfect for this weekend's dance." To prove her point, she twirled in a shaft of sunlight so the stars could spark. It made her feel like a girl again.

"With your beauty and that fabric, every man in the room will notice you," the modiste said. "There will be a queue to speak to your father."

Every man except the one she had hoped would do it. Amelia closed her eyes to calm her thoughts, and a vision of Richard at the altar swam in the darkness. Amelia cursed her imagination as she opened her eyes to the harsh sunlight. That wasn't what she'd wanted, though it seemed to be exactly where his skewed logic had taken him. Leave it to a man to believe she wanted to restrict his freedom when all she wanted was her own.

She twisted her hand behind her back to reach the laces. "Should we try the pink one next?"

That gown was equally pretty, if a bit more traditional, and there were gloves to match. That gave Mother the urge to ask for blue gloves for the gold dress, which was draped over the bed, shining in the afternoon light. It was as though a *ton* miss had collapsed on the bed after a successful society evening.

School had been dismissed by now, which meant the distillery was full of noise as the children arrived for work. Amelia had hidden in the office one day to listen, just to make sure she'd selected her employees well. Freddie Baxter was a natural foreman, even if he was only twelve. Sara, her label writer, was a fretful girl, always worried about mistakes or using too much paper—or glue. She didn't like it when it oozed around the edges and dried in globs on the glass. *"Wiping it off when it's wet makes the label crooked,"* she'd told the younger child helping her. *"Wiping it off too late makes the glass cloudy. Here, let me show you again."*

Amelia had increased Sara's wages after that visit. Freddie's, too. She'd seen Sara's mother in the market, her basket laden with necessities. The thatch on the Baxters' roof gleamed gold in the sunshine.

It was prettier than any dress.

"The guests will be arriving soon. I should change."

"Of course." Mother moved to the door. "Miss Gleason, if you'll follow me, I'll see to your payment. Amelia, I'll send Rose in to help."

"I'm happy to do it, my lady." Graves came to Amelia's side.

"I'm sure Rose is seeing to Amelia's wardrobe for the weekend."

"True," Mother sighed. "There's so much to do. Thank you for helping, Graves."

Once they were alone, her chaperone carried the gold dress to the wardrobe. "The blue for this afternoon, I think."

"The brown," Amelia stated.

"Your mother would choose—"

"I'm weary of blue." Truthfully, she was weary of everyone seeing the dress and complimenting her eyes. If she wore yellow, they commented on her hair. Pink drew comparisons to the blush on her cheeks. People always assumed she was blushing due to flattery. They never considered she was furious they never looked past her clothes to notice her head was full of something other than lace. "Besides that, all the ladies will be in traveling clothes."

Graves carried the brown dress to the mirror. The bodice contrasted with an orange skirt. "It suits the season." She nodded. "And it gives a depth to your hair."

Amelia rolled her eyes.

"Don't bristle so," Graves said as undid the laces at Amelia's back. "Of course you are intelligent, and your husband will value that in you." She met Amelia's gaze in the mirror. "But they will only see the obvious at first."

And if she didn't want a husband? "What if he doesn't get past the obvious?" What if she was across the country in a strange home with a man who expected nothing from her but balls and babies?

Graves skimmed the pink silk into a pile on the floor, and Amelia stepped out of it. Despite the fire in the grate, she shivered.

"You will have to trust your father not to choose a man that dim."

Amelia stepped into the brown dress Graves was holding open for her. "I should get to choose myself."

"We aren't the Mosuo." Graves sighed. "Unfortunately."

"Would they adopt me if I became a Buddhist?"

"I don't know." Wry humor twisted Graves's lips. "But your Mandarin is atrocious, and you don't want to move out of the county, so it's likely you would be unhappy in China."

Amelia's laughter died as the bell rang downstairs, announcing an arrival.

She didn't want to move from this room. She didn't want to know who was on the threshold. She didn't want to dance and hear of someone else's home. She wanted to ensure the success of her business and the lives of her family's tenants. She wanted this house filled with laughter and love, not sitting as an empty holding.

But she took the wrap Graves handed her, using it to fight the chill as she descended the stairs to meet the first of her guests. One she recognized as Belinda Martin, a blonde young lady with impeccable taste and a lively wit. She was a fine dancer—and a horrible gossip. Amelia wished she'd paid more attention to her mother's guest list.

She stretched out both hands and forced herself to smile. This was important to her parents. "Belinda. I'm so glad you could come."

"Amelia!" Belinda squealed as though they'd been separated at birth and squeezed her fingers in greeting. But her eyes swept over Amelia's dress, and her smile was too sharp.

Amelia's appraisal was just as quick and just as sharp. She'd been right. Both women were dressed for travel, though with more feathers than she would have chosen.

"I do hope you don't mind, but my cousin arrived after I'd sent my reply. She's just returned from the Continent, and I just couldn't leave her alone in London."

Belinda had once cornered every eligible young lady in the retiring room and tried to convince them to assist her in a scheme to snare a visiting Italian dignitary. She wouldn't think twice about bringing a surprise guest.

"Of course not, you couldn't." At least Mother's numbers would now be even. Amelia turned to the newcomer. She was tall with patrician features and dark hair. "You are more than welcome, Miss…"

"Fiona Allen." Her smile was as insincere as her cousin's. "Thank you, Miss Chitester."

The bell rang again. The party had officially begun.

"Amelia, please. My maid, Rose, is on the landing. She'll show you to your room. You don't mind sharing, I hope." Drat. That made it sound like the house was too small. "At least until we've had time to make up another."

"Our families would insist on us sharing for the weekend," Belinda said. "You needn't make up another at all."

With that, they walked back to the stairs, arm-in-arm. Amelia stared behind them, irritated by the implication that the cousins were sharing a room to protect their virtue. Of course she'd heard tales of parties that had become bacchanalian, but those were usually hosted by bachelors like her cousin. And, honestly, who would send their daughter to a party where they didn't trust the hosts?

"Mr. Raymond," the footman announced.

She drew in a deep breath and schooled her features before she turned. Ethan was already to her, so close he blocked out most of the room.

"Miss Chitester, thank you for the invitation to visit again so soon." He raised her hand to his lips. "You could be Demeter herself in that dress."

"Thank you, Mr. Raymond."

It was going to be a long four days.

"Good evening, Mr. Ferrand. The party is in the drawing room." Oakdale Manor's butler swept his hand to the right of the hall.

The man looked very much like Lionel, Oliver's butler. Richard wondered if they were related, or if Parliament had passed a law as to the necessary characteristics of butlers.

"Thank you…" He kept eye contact as he trailed off in a question, hoping austere man would catch on. He hated not knowing people's names.

"Simms, sir." His nod was quick, his smile quicker. He handed Richard's topcoat and hat to a waiting footman. Conversation floated into the hall, echoing from another room like a river through a forest. One young lady had an unfortunate laugh. It sounded like a heron crying at dusk.

"I don't believe you'll have trouble finding them," Simms said. "But would you like me to introduce you to the room?"

"I'll be fine, Simms." It seemed too pretentious, especially for a group in a drawing room. It also didn't allow Richard a chance to be anonymous and gauge the crowd of strangers, something he'd learned from his father.

"Listen more than you speak, my boy. And watch more than you listen. People's actions will always betray their motives."

It was how Richard had determined Oliver Hawkins, who he'd found moping at an alehouse near the docks, would be a solid business partner and a good friend.

Following his usual practice, Richard slipped into the room and stood at the back, unnoticed. The drawing room was like the rest of the house, and the family in it. The wallpaper was white on white, and the glossy pattern flickered in the twin glow from the lamps and the fire. The group was standing around a table near the windows, arguing playfully over a stack of board games and which set would be used by what pair of competitors.

One man stood at the edge of the cabal, a glass held as though he didn't mind whether it spilled. Tall, broad, and blond, he looked very much like a young Augustus Chitester. The resemblance marked him as Jasper Warren, whom Oliver had said was Augustus's nephew and heir.

Amelia was easy to spot, and not simply because she was in the middle of the fray. Her yellow dress was the same one she'd worn to the market, and it made her look like a beam of sunshine had landed center stage in the shadowy room. It reminded him of how she'd looked in the loft, watching the wheat as she raked it—as though it could predict her future.

Ethan Raymond was standing behind her, close enough that when she snatched an inlaid case, her elbow collided with his gut, bending him slightly as he stepped backward.

"Oh, Mr. Raymond!" Amelia clutched the case to her chest. "I didn't see you there. I'm so sorry. Are you all right?"

Richard covered his laugh. She was no sorrier than he was that Raymond was now clear of her. The man's wordless nod didn't match with the set to his jaw and the color flushing to his face. Amelia wasn't the only one lying.

"Am I too late to choose a team?" Richard asked as he stepped forward.

Every head turned to him, but Amelia's smile was his focus. She left the crowd and came toward him, one hand outstretched as though they were old friends, not simply business partners.

"Mr. Ferrand. I am so happy you could join us." She tucked her fingers into his elbow. "Please come meet the rest of our merry band. Mr. Raymond you've met, but this is my cousin Jasper Warren, and this is…"

The names and titles, so popular in society, meant nothing to him. Amelia carried the same scent of apples and cinnamon that clung to his clothes after he left the distillery. It was as hard to reconcile the distiller with the young lady on his arm as it was to believe she made whiskey in the first place. But she did, and she worked diligently at it.

As diligently as she worked at being a hostess for a party she hadn't wanted to happen. "All, this is Mr. Richard Ferrand, brother-in-law and business partner to the Duke of Rushford." She put her other hand on his bicep, her fingers curving to his arm in a way he found reassuring. "He's visiting his family and has graciously agreed to round out our numbers for the week-end."

Jasper Warren offered him a glass. "Drink, Ferrand?"

Richard took it with a nod. Mint tickled his nose a moment before pear teased his tongue, carried on a whiskey so smooth it might have been water. The warmth spreading through him almost matched what he'd felt when he'd had hands on Amelia in the loft.

Amelia had likely smelled like this a few months earlier.

"Richard?"

He knew that voice. After taking another sip of his whiskey, he turned toward the young lady who had just entered the room. "Hello, Miss Allen. What on earth are you doing in Norfolk?" He placed his hand over Amelia's and squeezed, pleading with her to stay beside him.

She looked up at him, a quirk of a smile across her lips. "You two know each other?"

"We came across the Channel together," Fiona said.

"On the same ship," Richard corrected.

Fiona Allen was a lovely girl, and she had caught his attention the moment they'd boarded the ship to cross the Channel. Her dark eyes and darker hair contrasted with her pale skin, giving her an exotic look, which she enhanced with her richly colored dresses. Her lively conversation had been a welcome respite from wine, debts, and his *oncle's* miserable life.

But her questions about Quebec and Rosnay had become questions about his checkbook. One reckless stolen kiss, inspired by a starry night after a fabulous dinner and too much champagne, had flown to outright hints as to when she would be alone. When he'd ignored them, she had taken to dragging him into passageways. Miss Allen was surprisingly strong.

She was also a walking, talking marriage trap.

"I looked for you when we debarked in Ipswich, and then hoped you'd call at my cousin's home in London." Fiona swept her fan across her neck and chest, much as she had aboard ship, even though the wind had claimed several shawls and a great many hats during the mercifully brief journey. "But there are several Martins in town. It was very confusing."

"It was," Richard said. He could have told her that he'd never looked, had never even remembered she had a cousin much less that cousin's name. Agreeing was just easier.

"And then Belinda received this invitation." Fiona spread her hands wide. "Fate has once again thrown us together."

Amelia slid free and stepped away. "I believe there's a set of checkers remaining. The two of you could play opposite one another." She offered him an ivory box that was slick and cold against his fingers. "Before you both arrived, we'd decided that each group playing checkers would compete, winner against winner, until there was a champion. The same with the chess competitors."

"Miss Chitester and I are playing chess," Ethan Raymond said as he joined them. He offered Amelia his arm. "We should begin if we're to finish before the dinner gong."

"This house isn't nearly large enough for a gong," Margaret Gerard said as she walked past with Annabel Pearce. "My mother says ours is nearly half again as large."

If Richard had been forced to guess, he'd wager Miss Gerard was the young lady with the heron-like laugh—but perhaps that was inspired by the overabundance of feathers in her hair. By contrast, Miss Pearce drew his attention because of her serenity. Rather than gossiping with Margaret, she simply took the seat opposite her and opened the board, motioning for Miss Gerard to select her color of choice.

Richard held Fiona's chair for her before sitting opposite. The set Amelia had given them was ivory and jade, the intricate pieces cool to the touch.

"This is akin to playing with art," Richard said as he set the board.

"It reminds me of Venice." Fiona lined up her pieces. "Art is found in everyday use throughout the city. Have you been?"

"No." Richard waited on her to make the first move. Across the room, Amelia was contemplating the chessboard, tapping one of Raymond's pawns on her chin. "I've always planned to go."

"Father will be returning to Rome in the spring." Fiona made her move. "You recall he represents the Crown's business in Italy?"

"I do." Richard countered, choosing to move his piece by picking it up rather than sliding it over the ivory. To his thought, this set should be set on a shelf to admire. Across the room, Amelia tucked a curl behind her ear as she considered the board.

"How long will you be staying in Norfolk?" Fiona asked.

Richard jumped one of her dove gray pieces and collected it. He glanced up and met Amelia's stare. He refocused on Fiona and smiled. "I've not yet decided."

"Father will be meeting with Parliament in November. If you are in town, perhaps I could arrange a dinner."

"I would be honored to meet your father, Fiona" Richard said, doing his best to be kind. "But I do not believe business will bring me to London." He also didn't believe an English diplomat would welcome a French tradesman at his table unless there were national negotiations at stake.

"I won't give up that easily, Mr. Ferrand." She took two of his pieces in a masterful move.

"Mr. Raymond, I will thank you not to move my pieces." Amelia rapped her closed fan over her opponent's knuckles.

"I was merely trying to help you decide," he said. To Richard, his condescension was obvious.

"I can play my own game," she snapped. It was to her as well.

The bell rang, announcing new arrivals. She stood so quickly her chair rocked backward. "If you'll excuse me."

Raymond swept his hand across the board, scattering pieces. One rolled to Richard's feet. It was a mahogany king, carved to the likeness of Henry VIII. Well done enough that his beard appeared combed.

"Ethan hates to lose," Fiona whispered.

So did Amelia. Richard looked to his partner. "If you'll excuse me, Miss Allen. I believe my family has arrived for dinner. I should go greet them."

"Of course." Her smile was sad. "Thank you for the game."

Richard put the king on Raymond's table on his way out of the room. Relief washed through him as he entered the hall and saw familiar faces. Oliver and Augustus were sharing a laugh as Amelia greeted Thea, the tension in the drawing room forgotten.

As he watched, however, Augustus swayed as though he'd had one whiskey too many. However, Marian's rush to his side, sliding under his arm to support a giant shoulder, told a different story. Oliver rushed to take the other shoulder.

"He's had a bit too much activity today," Marian whispered. "Let's get him to the library."

Amelia hurried across the hall, her skirts lifted. "Simms—"

Richard stepped to her, halting her sprint and offering his arm. "If you act calm, no one will notice." He led her behind her father, vaguely aware of Thea closing the library door behind them. Marian and Oliver placed Augustus on a chaise lounge.

It was another comfortable, shadowy room packed with a hash of colorful collectibles. Leather-bound books crowded shelves and tables, and the warm scent of cigars hung in the air, no doubt rising from the upholstery. Richard could spend an entire day in here.

Amelia draped a blanket over her father's legs and knelt beside him. Her hair was an intricate mass of golden curls and braids, her skirts a golden pool. "Papa."

Augustus patted her hand. "I'm fine, girlie." He was pale, and in the shadows, it was easy to believe his skin was too big for his body. "You need to get back to your party. Raymond will come hunting, or Jasper. I'd prefer—" His sentence ended on a gravelly cough and a strangling wheeze.

She hesitated for a long moment, and Richard knew her well enough to suspect she wanted to argue.

"Amelia," her mother said as she took Augustus's other hand. "He'll be fine in a moment. You really must go."

Her blonde curls bounced as she nodded. Richard dropped his hand into line of vision, and she took it, using him for balance as she stood. Her fingers trembled against his. "We'll see you at dinner."

Richard tucked her hand into his elbow and led her from the room. Once they were in the hall, Amelia pulled him to a stop. He expected her to dissolve into a puddle. Instead, she drew a deep breath and then another, standing taller with each one.

She had her father's grit.

"I'm glad you're here." Amelia kept her voice low. "One can only hear about London parties third-hand for so long without screaming. Margaret Gerard is asking everyone for the names of their dressmakers, and I'm already weary of Miss Allen's references to Italy." She looked to the drawing room. "Papa doesn't want anyone to know he's ill."

"I can respect that," Richard said. He could also understand it. Augustus didn't want his heir appraising his holdings, and he didn't want his presumed son-in-law to have an upper hand in marriage settlement negotiations.

Richard spied the butler near the stairs, his face etched with worry. "He's fine, Simms, but we need to distract the guests if dinner is delayed. Have you any wine?"

"Will champagne do?" Simms was already moving. "I'll have it served. You two wait here until we've carried in the trays. It will let you slip in."

It took just a few minutes for the footman to walk in the far door, holding trays aloft. Richard and Amelia went through the other door, entering the room without being noticed.

Except for the narrowed gaze of Jasper Warren. Ethan Raymond stood with a group of equally tailored young men, his arm propped on the mantle like he was already lord of the manor.

Amelia's hand trembled on Richard's coat. He placed his fingers over hers, looked down at her, and winked. Then he faced the group.

"I'm glad you each already have glasses for a toast." He glanced around the room, ensuring every stare was focused on them. "Amelia and I are betrothed."

CHAPTER EIGHT

"I T WOULD HAVE been nice to know this before we invited your friends from London for the weekend," Father said. He'd recovered most of his color, helped along by dinner and the whiskey he was sipping.

Her whiskey.

"I understand that, and I'm sorry," Amelia said. "But it only happened this afternoon, and—"

"What exactly happened?" Oliver glared at Richard over the rim of his glass.

Filled with her whiskey.

"Nothing like what you're thinking," Richard countered. His knuckles were white around his empty tumbler. He'd downed her whiskey with one quick swallow after he'd joined her on the sofa. He'd squeezed her hand as he'd done so, either in appreciation of her craft or in solidarity of their predicament.

She didn't like the stares directed at him. "I can assure you, Richard has behaved like a gentleman every time we've been together."

"According to Miss Graves, that's been twice, other than church," Mother said. "You can surely understand—"

"We've seen each other more than that." It was important her parents believed this arrangement was real. "He's joined me on rides when I've gone out to see the tenants. We've—"

"Alone?" Mother's eyes were wide. "You've seen him with no chaperone other than your horse? Where was Graves?"

"She hates to ride. You know that," Amelia snapped. "Just as you know that I've ridden and walked these fields alone my whole life."

"Watch your tone, Amelia."

"Why, Father?" Amelia looked to him. "Why is it that I'm free to roam until I hit the magical age of twenty, and then suddenly everyone's terrified I'll hoist my skirts—"

"Amelia!" Mother's hands twitched in her lap as though she wanted to cover her ears. "That is quite enough."

"What's quite enough is five years of house arrest," Amelia cried. "Of doing what everyone else expects, of not—"

Richard's large hand warmed her shoulder. "You're not helping," he whispered.

He moved his hand, no doubt prompted by Oliver's pointed stare from across the room. Behind him, Thea was a portrait of composure...until Amelia caught the laughter dancing in her eyes. At least she had one ally.

"I know the timing is a shock for everyone," Richard said, his gaze sweeping the room. His tone was even, his smile easy.

He threaded his fingers through hers, and while Amelia appreciated the effort, her shoulder was chilled.

"No one is more shocked than I at this development," Richard continued. "And I apologize for not coming to you first, Augustus. Amelia wanted to, but I knew it would be a difficult match for you to accept since our acquaintance has been brief and because of my circumstances. I had hoped I could use the party to improve my chances." He looked at her then, his blue eyes catching the lamplight so that they looked full of stars. "But I walked into that room full of people and realized I didn't want to act like nothing had changed."

Dear God, he was good at this. Amelia sipped her sherry and grimaced. One of these days, she was going to pour herself a proper drink.

He shifted his gaze to her mother. "Marian, your daughter has charmed me with her quick wit and quicker mind. Her smile has bewitched me, and I would gladly lose myself in her eyes. But—forgive my frankness—her skirts have remained firmly on the floor. She is too wise to be seduced by the first Frenchman she sees."

Amelia shook herself free of the spell his words had woven. Their engagement was fake, but their relationship was not, and it wouldn't do for her business partner to think her naive. "You're not the first one I've seen."

Richard's polished smile broke into a laugh as he dropped his head. He'd tamed his curls with pomade, but one at the back of his neck struggled for freedom.

Her father and Oliver chuckled as well. Even Mother relaxed. Thea winked her approval.

"So, how do we move forward?" Her father asked. "Do you expect to marry quickly?"

Richard's head snapped up. "I believe it would be best if we used the next few days to become better acquainted. All you know of me is that I own a sawmill and am related by marriage to a duke."

Amelia came to his rescue, happy to repay his kindness. "We could continue the party as planned and give everyone a chance to get to know Richard."

"But what of Eth—Mr. Raymond and Miss Allen?" Mother asked. "They are quite upset."

Ethan wouldn't leave so long as there were young women to charm, and if Fiona Allen departed in a huff, so be it. "Everyone has said how glad they are to be out of London, and they've already declined invitations to be here. They won't risk being at loose ends by leaving."

If anything, Mother looked more worried. "That isn't the basis for a successful party."

Thea stepped around Oliver's chair, releasing his hand as she went to Mother's side. "Why not use Richard's announcement to encourage the others to find romance themselves? A betrothal is sure to put it at the top of everyone's mind, Marian."

"And sending them home would give the impression that we don't approve of the match," Father said. He cast a look toward them. "Though it is not a foregone conclusion."

"Augustus is right. We have a lot to discuss." Oliver's stare was far too pointed. "We should leave."

"Could I…" Amelia squared her shoulders and lifted her chin. She was practically married, for all they knew. There was no need to beg for time alone with Richard. "I'd like some time alone with my fiancé."

Mother hesitated. "Ten minutes, and Graves will be outside the door."

"I'll knock at five minutes," Oliver said. Despite his stern warning, he smiled as he took Amelia's hand in both of his. "This is probably not the beginning you hoped for, but I am pleased you'll be joining our family."

Thea embraced her. "We'll talk soon."

The door closed behind them. The ticking clock filled the silence as she and Richard stared at one another. The tick grew louder, a reminder of the time they were wasting.

"I wish you'd changed your mind about this earlier," she whispered. "We could have prepared better."

"You're welcome."

The quirk in his eyebrow, his crooked smile, was contagious. Whatever his reason, she was glad he'd changed his mind. "That was quite a performance. You could have a career on the stage. Or in lords."

"Commons." Both eyebrows went up this time. "You're betrothed to a tradesman, remember."

She was learning. One eyebrow was a joke. Two were a question. "I'm betrothed to a successful lumber baron who is now dabbling in wine." She put a hand on his arm. His wool jacket was comforting, but not nearly as much as when his hand had been on her shoulder. "And I'm proud of that." This felt far too real. Amelia dropped her hand and stepped backward, searching for familiar ground. "I couldn't ask for a better partner."

"We may need to amend our contract," Richard said.

He'd said he didn't want payment, but that had been when he wouldn't even consider her plan. His agreement changed things. If they were really to be married, he'd be getting her dowry. She couldn't afford that much, but she would take up a lot of his time. He deserved some sort of compensation.

Amelia looked up. One eyebrow. "You're joking."

"But it was fun watching you calculate terms in your head." He sat on the sofa and pulled her with him. "You're going to have to relax a bit if people are going to believe us. Less thin skin, more devil-may-care. You're marrying down and don't give a damn about it."

"If I have to do that, then you have to be less class conscious," she replied. "According to Oliver, you're wealthy enough to buy your way into the *ton* with or without me. Act like it."

His smile widened as he nodded. "I was planning to just ride over for the events. Does this change things? Will I need to stay?"

She shook her head and then giggled at his obvious relief. "If this were real, I would be offended."

"If this were real, your father would insist I..." Richard cleared his throat. "Never mind. It's just that I'm enjoying my time with the children."

"Well, you *are* here to visit your family," Amelia said. "I appreciate you surrendering some of that time for me."

He rested his elbows on his knees and steepled his fingers, alternately erecting and collapsing them. "It isn't as altruistic as you might believe. Miss Allen and I...I may have kissed her one or two times."

"I expected as much." She pulled her attention from his long, fine fingers with their blunt trimmed nails. "You looked like I'd walloped you with the mallet I use to pound bungs into barrels."

The look in his eyes, the shape of his parted lips, made her aware of all the places her clothing touched her. Everything was too tight and too heavy at the same time.

He stood with a *whoosh* and walked to the hearth. "I just thought you should know."

When he faced her again, his affable expression had returned. He was no less handsome, but somehow, Amelia felt cheated. It was a ridiculous thought. She was getting everything she wanted from their arrangement.

"Thank you for telling me." She joined him in front of the fire. Looking up into his face, its features more angled because of his stern hairstyle, she had the mad impulse to make a mess of him. "But I'm familiar enough with kissing to believe a gentleman would know if he kissed a lady. So I'm assuming you *did* kiss Miss Allen." As he nodded, his gaze fell to her lips, and that too-tight feeling returned. It was too enjoyable to be proper, but Amelia didn't care. "And I'm assuming you don't wish to do it again."

He shook his head, and the denial filled her with a heady, wild sensation.

"Though I'm not sure how you managed to kiss her. She never stops talking."

Richard's laughter began in his eyes before it sputtered from his lips and shook into his shoulders. He rested both hands on her shoulders and pulled her toward him. "You are—"

A sharp rap at the door cut him short. It also ended the contact that had warmed Amelia to a dangerous level, like when her still began to bubble and hiss. "Oliver really meant five minutes, didn't he?"

"Because he knows what can happen in ten," Richard muttered.

That made no sense. People spent hours together in London and nothing happened between them.

Richard kissed her hand, his lips warm through her lace glove, his breath lingering longer than the touch. His eyes twinkled. "And I hope you never find out."

~

"Good morning, Mr. Ferrand," Simms said as he ushered Richard into Oakdale Manor's hall.

Richard checked his hair in the hallway mirror, making sure his ride over hadn't left him a mess. He hated preening, but this crowd was focused on style and he didn't want to give them another reason to mock Amelia. He met the butler's gaze in the mirror. The man was smiling ear-to-ear. "Are you always this happy about visitors, Simms?"

"There is something about a full house," the man said. "But there's a rumor among the staff that you and Lady Amelia are betrothed. I rarely listen to footman's tales, but—"

"We are." It wasn't a lie. But when the term of their agreement expired, Simms would be another disappointed villager.

"Then I congratulate you both on behalf of the entire household." If possible, the man's smile widened. "She is special to all of us, Mr. Ferrand. We've been hoping she would find someone who would value her as much as we do."

He would *not* feel guilty about this. "Thank you, Simms."

Richard handed his hat and coat to a waiting footman, whose name he didn't know and who looked so much like the other one that they could be bookends. Perhaps there was only one of them. How was he supposed to keep everything straight?

He wasn't. This was not his home, and it wasn't going to be. "Has Miss Chitester come down, Simms?"

"Yes, sir." The older man stepped down the hall with a crispness that would have impressed many a Canadian banker. "Most of the guests are down as well." He stopped just short of the dining room. "Though they're not fond of Lady Amelia's early hours," he whispered, still smiling.

Early was a relative term. Had he been home, he'd have been in the woods for several hours already. That was likely too early even for Lady Amelia.

Though she did have a penchant for surprising him.

As she'd done last night. From a tantrum over her lack of freedom to talking of mallets, pounding, and kissing while sitting close enough he could see down her bodice. The temptation would have been too great had talking with her been less fun. By the end of the evening, he'd fallen under her spell.

Who was he kidding? He'd fallen under it long before last night. Hell, when he'd given that speech to her mother he'd half-believed it.

Which was nonsense. He admired Amelia's pluck, and he genuinely liked her parents. To see Raymond playing lord of the manor while Augustus lay in the library struggling for breath had spurred Richard's decision as much as Fiona Allen's appearance.

"Sir?" Simms was still there, holding the dining room door. Scents of coffee, bacon, and fresh scones drifted into the hallway, making Richard's mouth water even if his stomach didn't rumble.

Amelia sat facing the door, though Margaret Gerard had all her attention.

Richard took the chair to Amelia's left and lifted her knuckles to his lips. *"Bonjour, chéri."*

It was something his father had done every morning at breakfast, as though he and his wife hadn't awakened together. Oliver had greeted Julia much the same way. He'd done it with Thea this morning, but in Spanish.

The custom took on a new meaning with Amelia's warm, bare fingers against his. Last night, they'd been covered in lace, and kissing them had made him think of shifts and petticoats. Bare they made him think of things that were inappropriate, especially surrounded by people at breakfast.

Amelia's grip tightened as her wide eyes met his; the coat of her riding habit shifted with her deep breath. *"Bonjour."*

Her blouse was fastened with the tiny pearl buttons that entranced male eyes even as they frustrated fingers.

"I'm glad you're here," she said. "Do you want breakfast?"

If he moved from this chair, the scandal from last night would be long forgotten. "I ate with Simon this morning." He nodded as a footman offered him coffee. "It's something I've missed."

"I'm sure he's saved all sorts of stories for you," Amelia said. "I did that when Father traveled to London without me."

Richard tried to imagine her at Simon's age, in this house with no one but servants. The life he and Oliver had worked so hard to ensure Simon escaped. "How long—"

"Miss Gerard was just asking me how I'm looking forward to living in Quebec." Her gaze swept the room, reminding him of the other people and their penchant for gossip. "I have to admit, I know little about it. I'm completely basing my happiness on you."

Which was exactly why he'd never marry. This game was fine, but happiness was fragile. Too many people lost it. Richard sipped his coffee, considering the best things to reveal about the place he missed the most.

"The city comes up out of the sea and works its way inland, climbing the valleys and butting up against cliffs until it reaches the forest. In the winter, the hills are perfect for sledding in the snow. It seems like all of Quebec is out in the cold."

"Do you do that?" Amelia asked.

"I haven't in years." Truthfully, not since Oliver and Simon had left. He wasn't even sure Simon remembered it as sledding. He'd been bundled in so many blankets that he'd broken into a sweat. "My sister Julia and I loved to sled when we were children. We'd play for hours and then run into the house, sliding along the floors until we reached the fire and the cocoa awaiting us. We left giant puddles in the kitchen, and our mittens shrank over-night as they dried."

Miss Gerard pulled a face. "Cold and wet doesn't sound pleasant. Father took us to Scotland once for Christmas. It was the most boring—"

"Quebec doesn't sound boring at all, Margaret," Amelia said. "It will be a grand adventure in a wilderness."

"Not really a wilderness," Richard said. It always amazed him that people thought lumber men lived amongst their lumber.

"We have a home in the city, on the corner of a quiet street." Oliver had insisted on buying it, and then had insisted that he and Julia move in.

The wallpaper Julia had selected long before she and Oliver had married had begun to fade, especially where the sun came through the windows.

"A large one?" Miss Gerard asked, no doubt looking more favorably on Amelia's impeding situation.

"Not estate-sized, but there's plenty of room." He placed his empty coffee cup in its dainty saucer. Julia had inherited a service like this from their mother. It was still behind glass, waiting on a special occasion, or on a user who didn't tease about the small servings.

"And society?" Miss Gerard said. "What of that? Country life is fine for a short period, but one does need parties."

Richard didn't think anyone needed parties. Beside him, Amelia's eyes twinkled over the edge of her teacup. Apparently, she didn't either. Thank God.

He stopped himself. His lack of a real social life was not going to inconvenience his pretend fiancée.

"There are plenty of entertainments." He decided to take Amelia's advice and be more braggadocios. "And there are frequent parties in my set. Before I sailed, there was a small reception for our new governor so that he could meet the businessmen building the city." He turned to Amelia. "When did you wish to ride, *chéri*? It's getting late."

"Late?" Raymond said as he walked from the sideboard to his chair. "I'm rarely up by this hour. The early to bed rule has never suited."

Richard looked the length of the table. "I've never been one to stay indoors when I could be out with a lovely lady." He placed his hand over Amelia's. "And I do enjoy watching my betrothed on horseback. It was one of the first things that struck me."

"In the interest of keeping my fiancé happy, I'm going to the stables." Amelia stood. "I hope you all will join us. The countryside here is beautiful, and the day promises to be fair. We have a picnic scheduled for luncheon, so you'll need to work up an appetite."

"Some of us will have to work harder than others," Miss Allen whispered as she walked past. "Though I never considered you one of those, Mr. Ferrand."

Amelia took the arm he offered, staring as Fiona left the room. "What did she mean? Because I'm fairly certain it wasn't—"

"It wasn't food." Richard's face heated as he looked into Amelia's earnest stare. "I'll tell you later." It was a lie. If he ever spoke of sex with her, it would be the end of him. If he didn't strangle on the words, her father would shoot him.

"I won't let you forget that." Amelia led him from the dining room and toward the stables. "Don't think you can distract me with pet names." She looked up from under her lashes, a slight quirk to her lips. "*Chéri?*"

"I thought using it would help prove our attachment." He was unaccountably pleased that she'd liked it.

"It's a fine idea. Too bad there isn't an endearment for Richard. I suppose I'll have to stick to the standard ones. Oh! *Mon bûcheron.* That would work, wouldn't it?"

Her lumberjack. In English, it was sweet; in French, not so much. It also wasn't true. He hadn't felled a tree himself since well before Oliver had left Quebec. "It makes me sound like a horse. Why not stick to the standard ones?"

They emerged from the house, and the sunlight caught the dark gold strands in her hair. She secured her hat and slipped on her black kid gloves.

"*Chere* then?" Her smile tilted up at the corners as she stared up at him, shading her eyes with her hand.

He nodded. "I like that just fine."

Dear God, help him. He liked it a little too much.

CHAPTER NINE

"**I** HAD FORGOTTEN how lovely Oakdale is," Cousin Jasper said.

Amelia had selected her favorite spot on the estate for their picnic. Large oaks shaded the riverbank, and soft moss provided a perfect mattress for their blankets. The narrow river bent in front of them, the water gurgling and splashing against boulders it had battled for years while on its way to the village. "You should visit more often," she said.

It seemed the thing to say to family.

Above them on the ridge, under the supervision of two grooms, the party's horses nickered and snuffled against the grass, glad to be rid of their riders. Below them, the water and the smooth river stones beneath it tempted her to wade. If she hadn't been raised here, had only visited, she'd still miss it.

"Grandfather keeps me busy between London and Ramsbury," Jasper said. "Not to mention Father's estate in Lambourn."

Ah yes. It wasn't enough that Jasper would inherit *her* home. Eventually, he'd be a baron, an earl, and a marquess all rolled into one. "However do you manage?" Amelia murmured.

"I'm lucky that Ramsbury and Lambourn are near to one another." Jasper reclined on the blanket, his long legs encased in buff breeches. The sun glinted off his blond hair and his black riding boots. "God only knows what Uncle Augustus thought about inheriting someplace so far flung from his family."

Father had told her the story often as they'd ridden. "He loved coming here as a child, visiting Grandmother's family during the summers." He'd told her he'd welcomed the chance to make his own way, away from under his father's, the old marquess's, influence. "He loves the air here, and the sky."

"I suppose it's because you're nearer to the sea." Her cousin squinted up into the bright, cloudless day. "The tenants are doing well."

She'd been sure to introduce Jasper to every farmer they'd met during their ride, content to let the rest of the group go ahead. It's what Father would have done had he been able to ride today. Besides that, now Jasper could have faces to go with the numbers in ledgers that he'd no doubt review before he left. Father would want him to see the accounts, to brag on what a fine inheritance Jasper would be taking as the smallest jewel in his crown.

"What of the distillery? Is it—"

"The distillery is mine," Amelia snapped. The dangerous truth of her words stunned her for a moment, but she forced an airy smile. "Mr. Brewer is my tenant. Father used part of Mother's dowry to buy that parcel as my inheritance. He intended that I have a home here no matter where I went."

"And you let it to a distiller?" Jasper's lips quirked.

"For a fair price that goes into my own accounts and, when the business outgrows this location, the still can be torn down in favor of a cottage."

"Expansion seems a safe bet," Jasper said. "It's one of the finest whiskeys I've tasted. If it were aged a bit, I suspect it would mellow the flavor even more."

"It's made from local wheat and produce, supporting some of the tenants you met today." Amelia pointed below them. "The water comes from this river, which is filtered through limestone and sandstone as it travels from the sea. And Mr. Brewer has been aging a small batch. It should be ready to bottle soon."

"You certainly know a lot about your tenant," Jasper said, laughing. "I've met stewards not half as astute as you, cousin."

Drat. She'd let her pride run away with her tongue. "I hope you find someone capable to manage Oakdale. It would be painful to see it decline."

"From Quebec?" Jasper asked.

"Richard is a close relation to the Duke of Rushford." Amelia's brain spun as she talked. "As I'm sure Father told you. And they are partners in the lumber business, including the mill just outside the village. I'm certain we'll visit often. Especially when he travels to Rosnay to check on the winery." She invented that last part. She didn't even know Richard's plans past the pending shipment.

She needn't have bothered with the tale. Jasper was looking past her, a sly smile on his face. Amelia glanced up the hill and found Miss Allen wearing a matching expression.

"Not to worry, cousin," Jasper drawled. "I'm sure I can find someone to live at the manor."

"I'm amazed you've kept her at bay for this long," Amelia said. She forced herself to face him, to keep still. It was just as rude to slap his face and storm off as it was to stare.

"They may assume I'm counseling you on your choice of husband," Jasper said in the same lazy tone. "Are you certain of this, Amelia? Moving to Canada with a lumberjack?"

Canada, with its wild sea and winters on sleds. Richard, with his dry wit and ready laugh. And his hands weren't so callused as to believe he wielded an axe every day. "Richard could buy and sell most families here. The life he's built has required a determination most in the *ton* never aspire to unless they are chasing party invitations. And as for Canada, I am my father's daughter. The further I can get from my family, the better."

She held her breath. It was one thing to think so little of her relatives, quite another to say it. Not to mention implicating her father in the same loathing. However, the worry was wasted. Jasper was still staring past her. Amelia refused to turn and stare, fearing Miss Allen was dancing in the clearing, naked as a sprite at the full moon.

"So long as you're happy." He patted her hand the same as their grandfather did when he was on his way to the study for cigars with his grandsons. "If you'll excuse me."

He stood with an enviable grace and strolled off, his legs making short work of the climb and his boots leaving divots in the moss. The group he joined, the friends her parents believed she'd cultivated in London, wore his same bored expression as they waved their fans and checked their watches.

Amelia could stay still no longer. Getting to her feet, she walked away from the party and toward the river, using trees for balance as her boots slid against the mud and wet greenery. Tears filled her eyes. A hand closed over her arm, and she shook it off. "Leave me be. The grooms will lead you back." The last word broke on a sob.

She ran nose first into a satin and wool covered brick wall. "Amelia? What's happened?"

Richard's warm voice, his strong arms around her, stopped her flight and dissolved her into a weeping mess. "It isn't fair, Richard. He's going to inherit three other houses and more money than he can spend," she cried into his jacket. "He's going to put some awful mistress at Oakdale, who doesn't care about the hollyhocks my mother planted below the bedroom window so she could see them first thing in the morning. His brats are going to trample the kitchen garden and the mint we use for tea. Some oldest child will become a baron without even knowing my father and how much he loved this land. And I won't be able to do anything about it, because I'll be in Quebec."

"No, you won't." He pulled away enough that she could see his smile once her vision had cleared. "Fake, remember?"

Dear God, he'll think I'm a ninny, forgetting my own plan after only a day. She ignored her hot cheeks and grinned. "I suppose it's a consequence of everyone assuming it's genuine. I've been defending myself all morning."

"I'm sure that's not all you've been defending." He brushed his lips across her forehead. "Thank you."

Amelia would have argued if she'd been able to speak. Her entire body tingled from his touch, his breath on her hair. At the last moment, she resisted curling her fingers against his jacket to keep him close. It would never do to have him think one touch, and a brief one at that, had affected her.

"You'll be their dotty cousin in a cottage over the hill, living with a drunk tabby cat and causing a scandal by wearing split skirts and meeting regularly with a dour man in a dark top coat," Richard said. His hands still rested on her waist, too light to restrain her but heavy enough to tease her imagination.

"But I still won't be able to do anything about it," she sighed. She wasn't sure which was worse, never seeing what became of her home, or seeing changes progress every day.

"Then tell them the truth." Richard stepped back. The breeze that had been pleasant only moments ago now chilled Amelia's nose. He offered his arm, and she took it, tucking her fingers against his elbow as she moved close enough to smell the cinnamon and horse on his coat. "You had no problems negotiating with me. You can do it with them."

Of course she could. She could go back to the house, march into her father's library, and tell him she'd been haring about the countryside at all hours of the day and night without a chaperone and regularly meeting with a former smuggler. That she was running a business that employed tenants' children whose families needed support. That she'd been making whiskey for years and had almost set herself on fire at least twice. That she didn't want to marry. She could ask Jasper to sell her the house, or at least make her his steward.

She could shock everyone.

But if the whiskey came out of those barrels as bitter turpentine, she'd be a laughingstock. She'd lose her family's support. She'd default on her loan and lose her inheritance. She'd have to marry anyway, and her options would be dismal.

"I'll find a way," she murmured as they approached the party. "This will work." It had to.

And, if not, there was always the nunnery.

HE'D KISSED HER.

Richard raked his hand through his hair as he walked the length of the stable. Again. He stopped in front of the pig pen. Pinky snuffled through his new bedding, rearranging it into a pattern only his piggy brain understood.

"It wasn't a real kiss," Richard muttered. It wasn't a lie. His lips hadn't touched hers; he didn't know what her tongue tasted of, or how her breath felt across his cheek.

But he knew how she felt in his arms.

"She needed comforting," he told the pig's curly tail.

Her tears had gutted him. It was different than seeing his sister cry, because he had usually been the cause of it—though Oliver had played a hand here and there. Simon's tears had been easy to solve with food, a nappy, or his favorite toy. Oliver's had been horrible because there hadn't been a damn thing he could do about them, not when he felt the grief as keenly.

Though Richard would debate the loss. He'd had Julia for years longer than her husband. Seven years on from her death, and he still found himself thinking of her—of jokes they could share, places she'd enjoy seeing, how she'd scold him for misbehaving.

Julia would have loved the glade where they'd picnicked today. The wind whispering through the leaves splashed with bright fall colors that glowed in the sunshine in random patterns, much the way the ripples in the water glinted gold and silver as they sluiced past. The contrast of white blankets and dark riding habits against the last of the green grass.

Richard rubbed his thumb across his fingertips, feeling deep blue velvet instead of calluses.

"You're well-dressed to feed a hog."

Richard flexed his fingers and turned from the luxury pigsty. Oliver strode down the stable path leading his team, Mars and Mercury, to their stalls. Despite tight reins, the horses held their heads high and tossed their manes in rebellion.

"What have you been up to?" Richard asked. For years, he and Oliver had shared almost every experience. Whenever they'd worked separately, they'd returned with detailed explanations of their accomplishments or Simon's latest milestone. It had been one of the first things Richard had missed once Oliver had sailed.

"Trip to Brandon, on the other side of the forest." Oliver slipped the bridles from one horse, then the other, giving no further explanation. "Where are you off to?"

"Heading back to Oakdale for dinner." Richard walked toward the door, careful to give the horses and their master a wide berth.

"Rich?" Oliver put a hand on his shoulder, halting his retreat. "What's going on?"

"Amelia's expecting me." He wasn't looking forward to the evening, but he wasn't going to leave her to face her guests alone.

"Fighting the bit already?"

It was an old joke, begun by Julia when he'd refused to be bound by the harness of marital bliss. She liked to say he preferred a sulky to a gig. "No. I'd just rather not attend a party."

"Since when?" Oliver gave a wry chuckle.

It was a fair question. In the four years between Julia's death and Oliver's departure, Richard had familiarized himself with the insides of every pub, club, and brothel in Quebec. He'd always been careful, but he'd rarely been lonely. "People change, Oliver."

His brother-in-law gave him a long look, his head tilted slightly. Richard had seen that look for years, every time Oliver had assessed a business deal or a stand of timber, looking for the flaw.

"Is it so difficult to believe I love her?" Richard met Oliver's stare. After years together, they each knew the other's tells. "Or is it more of a wonder that she loves me?"

His best friend blinked, then again. "It's just very fast."

"Some people don't take years to admit they're in love, Ol." Richard backed away. This close, it was impossible to hide for long.

"What of the distillery?"

There's water, grain, and fermentable ingredients in Canada. Not to mention space and freedom. None of which she wants. "That's between us, I believe." Richard increased the distance between Oliver and himself. "And it may be a moot point if this weekend doesn't sway her parents." It was going to be a moot point anyway. He went to his waiting horse and swung into the saddle. "I'll see you at breakfast."

Once away from the stable, Richard put his heels in the horse's ribs. He'd foregone a hat this evening, which gave them a chance to fly down the lane and onto the road before veering onto the shortcut Amelia had taken after their first meeting.

Beneath him, the giant gelding tensed and surged, leaping over even the smallest shadowy obstacle in the failing light. Richard bent low and tucked his knees close, his smile widening as he turned toward a low fence. "Go on then, boy."

Speed and power gathered as they neared the jump. At the last moment, the horse gave a grunt as his hooves beat the ground. Then they were aloft, beast and man holding their breaths as they sailed for a briefest moment. They landed with a solid thud, and Richard glanced over his shoulder, whooping at the distance they'd cleared. He slapped the horse's neck. "Good man."

They stayed at a gallop until the Manor came into view, the light from the windows creating square stars. Richard slowed to a trot as they reached the fountain. The door opened, and Simms's shadow stretched toward him. A groom took the reins.

Richard gave him an extra few shillings. "He's earned a good rubdown and a helping of grain, if you wouldn't mind."

"No, sir. Looks like he's given you a good ride." The lad grinned. "I might have a carrot or two put back."

Richard nodded his thanks before climbing the stairs, straightening his clothes as he went. "Thank you, Simms."

"You're welcome, sir." He put his hands out. "Your coat needs a good tug. May I?"

Richard nodded. Under Simms's care, the coat snapped to his shoulders like a piece in a puzzle. Sleeves were forced to his wrists.

"Horseback does poor service to a suit." Simms's eyes sparkled as he pulled the front of the coat into place. "I served as the old baron's valet in a pinch. He enjoyed a good ride."

"How's my hair?" Richard whispered.

"Fine, sir. Pomade works so well they ought to put it on the hems of ladies' skirts." The older man flushed. "Oh. Forgive the—"

Richard was laughing so hard he didn't hear the rest of the apology. "I'll have to remember that one."

"Just don't credit it to me." Simms led him toward the gathering room as though it was his first visit. Augustus Chitester's jovial voice grew louder with every step. "They've only just come down."

"Tell me." Richard got shoulder to shoulder with Simms. "The household gossip. Is everyone...happy?" It shouldn't make a difference. It wasn't supposed to matter. Still, he hoped Amelia had allies in her own home.

"We have long known Lady Amelia wouldn't settle for average," Simms said. "And if adventure is involved, all the better." The butler faced him and put a hand on the door. "If she is happy, we are happy, Mr. Ferrand. Titles be hanged."

A traitorous peace came over Richard's soul as the door swung open and Simms announced his arrival.

"Richard." Augustus greeted him with a hearty handshake. Though pale, he was steady on his feet. "Whiskey?" He pointed toward a lurking footman bearing a tray.

"Thank you." Richard took a sip before bowing to Amelia's

mother. "Lady Chites—"

"Marian, remember." She squeezed his fingers. "It is lovely to see you, Richard. How are things at Felton House?"

"It is amazing how much noise such a small family can make," Richard said. Two years ago, he'd teased Oliver about the joy of having the house to himself. However, after just a few weeks, the quiet had grated. He had run from it until he'd worn himself out.

"I can sympathize." She tilted her head toward his. "I wasn't quite prepared for having this group traipse through the house at all hours. Thank goodness it's only for a few days."

Richard's eyes swept the room, thanking his lucky stars Fiona's attention was focused on Jasper Warren. One of the men from the picnic raised his glass in salute. Richard returned it. Charles Grayson had asked so many questions about Canada that Richard had felt like a zoological exhibit, but he'd been well-intentioned.

It was too easy to imagine Amelia and he entertaining in his home, the faded wallpaper replaced, the house full of noise and life. Her using the tea set to test mash flavors. Making their own life.

She was near the window in conversation with Ethan Raymond. Her pink skirts ruffled so that she resembled the peonies in the garden at home. Her white silk glove went past her elbow and contrasted with Raymond's hand on her arm. Amelia's elbow moved; his fingers tightened. The color on her cheeks matched her dress.

"Excuse me," Richard said to Marian as he moved past her. Avoiding everyone else, he reached Amelia's side. Over her head, he shot Raymond a warning glance.

The man's gaze narrowed, his mouth flattened to a straight line. "Ferrand. We weren't certain you'd arrive in time for dinner."

"*You* weren't certain, Mr. Raymond," Amelia said as she drew closer to Richard. "I never doubted."

Maybe it was Richard's imagination that her skirts were cool against his trousers. Perhaps it was wishful thinking. Regardless, he took her hand and pressed a kiss to her silk-covered knuckles. "Thank you for your faith, *chéri*." He tucked her hand into his elbow and met the other man's stare as he guided Amelia away. "I'm not really the *early to bed* sort, Raymond."

"I can vouch for that," Fiona Allen all but purred as she stopped beside him on the arm of Jasper Warren. "As can you Amelia, I'm sure."

"I haven't had the opportunity to be aboard ship with him." Amelia's fingers tightened on his coat. "Yet."

"Well, surely the kisses he's stolen keep you up all night in anticipation. I know I—"

"That's quite enough, Miss Allen." Richard covered Amelia's hand with his. "You read far too much into our acquaintance."

Fiona's dark eyes flashed. "I don't recall you being an unwelcome recipient of—"

"He's correct, Fiona. You've taunted my cousin quite enough." Despite his words, Warren's smile was as relaxed as the hand holding his whiskey tumbler. "Are you joining us for shooting tomorrow afternoon, Ferrand?" He looked past them, toward the windows. "I'd imagine you'll put some of us to shame."

"Wouldn't miss it," Richard said. "Though I'll have to fight the temptation to change targets."

Warren tilted his head back for the loud laugh that was apparently a family trait. "Perhaps we could convince my cousin to add boxing to her list of entertainments for the weekend."

"You two aren't funny at all," Amelia said, though she wasn't as stern as she should have been. "There's Simms at the door. Dinner's ready."

Richard slowed their march toward the dining room and pried Amelia's fingers from his arm. They left a mass of woolly wrinkles in their wake.

"What's wrong?" he asked in a whisper. "Did Raymond say

something to you?"

"Ethan, Fiona, Jasper…and all I can do is be vague and smile as though—" She stopped in mid-sentence and glanced toward the footman who stood within earshot. "I'm not upset, Richard. I'm angry."

She really was like the peonies Julia had planted their first year in the Quebec house. Even without someone to tend them, the flowers had stayed strong and hearty. Julia would have liked her.

"As you wish," he murmured.

He led her to her place setting, almost the full length of the table from his. He was destined to sit nearer her mother. Amelia would be close to her father and her cousin. Raymond would be nearby as well. She'd be on her own unless Richard chose to feign ignorance and sit wherever he damn well pleased.

"Don't let them goad you," Amelia said as she stopped him from claiming the neighboring chair. "You have more manners than they do, and I'll be fine." She kept hold of his hand, and her ocean-deep eyes met his. "Your wine has arrived at the distillery. After the party, wait for me in the stable with the horses. I'll be down in ten minutes."

It was a romantic notion—a young lady sneaking out of her room for a tryst with her betrothed. Two lovers alone in the dark. But they weren't lovers, and this wasn't a tryst. No matter what Fiona Allen might tease. No matter what his imagination might spin.

What this happened to be was a complicated mess. The best thing would be to cry off before he got in too deep for his own good. Amelia could handle Raymond on her own. She'd proved it several times already.

Just like she'd proved that she'd go into the dark with or without him.

"Ten minutes. No more."

CHAPTER TEN

TWENTY MINUTES AFTER everyone had gone to bed, Amelia descended the back stairs, fighting the impulse to rush. If she thumped her work boots against the steps, she'd wake the household. She also refused to run to Richard's side.

He didn't need to know how relieved she'd been when he'd swept her from Ethan's odious lecture. The man actually believed she should have informed him of her engagement before announcing it to the entire party, since he *had been there first*. As though she was India and had to accept him simply because he wanted her. And if she heard "he's fine, for a tradesman" one more time, she'd scream.

Which she couldn't do, because polite young ladies didn't screech at their guests, especially a cousin who prowled the house as though he already lived there. Amelia was smart enough to realize that if her plan worked, if she got to stay on the shelf, she'd need Jasper's good will. If the distillery failed, or even had a bad year, he would hold the family purse strings. If the distillery was a moderate success and she got to live in her own little corner of Norfolk, Jasper would be her neighbor.

Amelia clicked the kitchen door closed and stood in the courtyard, her gaze trailing up the worn brick walls her grandfather had helped patch as a childhood punishment. Stars pricked the sky, and the moon was nothing but a sliver.

He wouldn't be her neighbor. He'd put Fiona Allen out here as his mistress and give her a large enough allowance to bribe her to stay. She wasn't fit to marry, and she was too indiscreet for a house in London. *I'll have to spend the rest of my life listening to her stories of kissing the man who threw me over.*

Amelia had gotten a taste of it this afternoon, when the women had taken tea while the men had played billiards. All but Richard, who had left to spend time with his nephew and change for dinner.

Belinda Martin had shot a sly glance toward her a moment before she'd asked Fiona about her time in Paris and her crossing of the Channel. Once she got to the point of meeting Richard, the recollections had been peppered with *I'm sure I don't need to tell Amelia.*

But she *did* need to tell Amelia some things, which made her feel naive. That was irritating by itself. But knowing Fiona knew them because she'd actually kissed Richard, perhaps more given her veiled hints, was infuriating. All Amelia could do was sip her tea, smile, and make vague agreements about her betrothed and how they'd fallen in love.

The stable door was ajar, and a thin rectangle of yellow light spilled across the paddock. A gray shadow lurked just inside. Amelia slowed further. She never feared being out at night, but this was later than she usually traveled.

"Don't be a goose," she scolded herself. "If Richard has already left, then that's Henry. You told him to have Molly ready."

She walked through the door, chin high. She'd never been afraid here, and there was no need to begin now.

Richard was waiting at the opposite door, flanked by their horses. Relief flooded through her, along with a shiver she now equated with him. She'd experienced it when he'd surprised her with their betrothal, and again at the picnic when he'd kissed her.

She took a bit of feminine pride in his waiting well past the ten minutes he'd allotted. *Take that, Fiona.*

"You're late." Richard handed her Molly's reins. "I sent the groom to bed. I thought it best he not see us out this late."

Amelia grasped the saddle, put her foot in the stirrup, and swung herself onto Molly's back. "You needn't have bothered." She arranged the cloak around her, made sure its hood covered her hair. "I pay him to keep my rides a secret."

Richard stood at her knee, one eyebrow cocked high. "You're out with a lot of men in the dark of night, are you?"

Only him. Amelia drew a deep breath, pressing her breasts against her shift and making her aware of those parts of her anatomy that had been a mystery. Richard made this ride different, more thrilling and adventurous. He made her the same.

At least for now.

She nudged his chest with her toe and scoffed. "Get on your horse. Drake won't wait forever."

Once they'd exited the rear paddock, Amelia nudged Molly into a trot. They crested the ridge, and she tilted her head to the sky. Out here in the open, stars gathered in drifts, some so dense they changed the color of the sky. "Are the stars like this in Canada?"

"Out in the forest, it seems like they'll tumble through the trees."

Though she was sad to learn this wasn't hers alone, she thrilled to see him staring upward as their horses found their own way. "Do you spend a lot of time in the forest at night?"

"Not as much as we used to," Richard said. "In the early days, when we were doing most everything ourselves, we spent most of our nights in tents, sleeping in shifts to guard against bears and wolves."

There was wistfulness to his words. Drake teased that she spoke the same way about whiskey. "You miss it."

"I hated sleeping in tents. It's cold and damp, and Oliver snores." Richard cast a sideways glance. "But I loved making something from nothing. Watching it come to life around us."

"Do you feel that way about wine?" She'd toured wineries with her father when they'd visited France and Italy. The greenness had struck her, as had the crowd of people involved in harvesting the grapes. With whiskey, it was her and the still.

"I don't know how I feel about wine yet," Richard said. "It's property I never knew existed, in a country I never wanted to visit. I have employees I didn't hire, and we don't yet know what to expect from one another. I don't know if they're lying to me, and all they know of me is that I share the name of a man who let them down."

He was in profile in the darkness, but it was easy to imagine his muscles bunched near his ear, as they'd been earlier when he'd dealt with Ethan. A tingle began low on Amelia's back, where Richard's hand had rested, and spread outward until it reached her fingers, which he'd covered when they'd faced Fiona.

The feeling took on a new meaning in the dark with him, alone. It made her aware of how he handled the large gelding, where his boots stopped near his knees, how his breeches fit his thighs, his straight back and broad shoulders, his large hands and long fingers holding the reins.

It was easy to imagine how Fiona must've been affected by time alone with him. After all, according to her, Richard had done more than kiss her on the forehead.

"You're quiet all of a sudden. Not asleep over there, are you?" he asked.

"I had no idea house parties were this exhausting," she said. "Perhaps I should have scheduled fewer activities, but it's really no more than what we might do in a day if we added a dinner party."

"You play croquet when no one else is around?"

"Well, one must practice." His chuckle made the darkness richer. "Mother and I play often. Father grouses about the holes in the garden." She muffled a yawn.

"Perhaps it's a good thing your guests have less time on their hands. Some of them seem bent on mischief."

She couldn't be blamed for Fiona, but he wasn't wrong about the others. She should have paid more attention to Mother's guest list. "Some aren't." But it was clear they were put off by those like her cousin.

"I can't figure out Miss Gerard," Richard said. "She seems every bit a society miss, but everyone keeps her at arm's length. Even you."

"Margaret's mother has pushed her to be part of the *ton* all her life, which is difficult for a country baron's daughter." Realizing how that sounded, Amelia rushed to continue. "Not that I'm any better, but I don't want it, which only seems to make me more appealing."

"I don't think it's just that," Richard said. "She's much different than you."

"Margaret was engaged to Garrett before his death."

"Oliver's brother?" Richard asked. "It's difficult to imagine her in Thea's place."

It was. Margaret had been chosen by Oliver's mother, who saw a kindred spirit and a girl smart enough to count her blessings and stupid enough to attach to a spendthrift, womanizing, drunkard.

"Her loss of that title has both soured her disposition and made her more desperate to escape. The *ton* is like any pack; they smell weakness and turn on the culprit. The harder she tries, the more they run. And the harder she tries."

They'd arrived at the distillery. Amelia dismounted and led Molly to the manger. Richard followed suit. His horse chuffed against the hay and shook his head, rattling the buckles in his bridle. Amelia stroked his head from coarse forelock to velvety muzzle.

"What's his name?" She met Richard's gaze, ignoring the shadows cast by the lantern.

"Rabbit." Richard said as he combed through the dark mane.

She'd expected something darker, more pagan and dangerous. "Not Bacchus or Faustus or…"

"He leaps like a rabbit, and he's as quick as one." Richard turned away. "Shall we go?"

They crossed the dirt plot that served as a delivery dock, now dominated by a hulking wagon loaded with barrels stacked two high. A team of six draft horses, their backs too wide for Amelia to straddle, waited patiently, their heads drooped. Perhaps they were simply exhausted from the load.

She swept through the barrel room and into the bottling room. Drake waited there, one hip resting against the table, one elbow resting high on the middle of a barrel. He was all in black, even his gloves, and he'd forgone his usual waistcoat in favor of a coal black one. A pistol dangled at his side. "If it isn't the happy couple."

Richard's hand curved to her waist, pulling her so he could stand in front. Amelia nudged him aside. "Don't be silly. He dresses like this when he's out at night." She smiled at her man of business. "Those horses look like they need a good rest and some care."

"Which they'll get after you leave," he said, his lips quirking in a wry smile. "I've sent the driver to The Goat for a meal so he won't be around to see you come and go." He offered them each a glass. "Ready?"

"You've tapped it already?" Richard asked.

"It's a skill I picked up along the way."

"Wine or whiskey?" Amelia eyed the barrel, trying to determine for herself. After two years, her barrels had mellowed to a yellow-gray. This barrel was more silver. It also smelled sweeter. "Wine."

"It could be whiskey." Drake's smile widened, transforming him to a younger, more dangerous version of himself. "It wouldn't take but a moment."

Amelia's tongue curled, imagining the taste of wheat, honey, berries, cloves, and ginger. In a week, it would be two years. What difference would seven days make? She dug her nails into her palm. If she gave in and it was turpentine, she'd never know if it mattered. She shook her head and placed her glass beneath the tap. "Let's try this wine."

Burgundy liquid rushed into the glass, sloshing against the sides as though it had been waiting years for freedom. Amelia lifted the drink to her nose, closed her eyes, and drew a deep breath, searching for flavor in scents. Past the bite of fermentation, there was a grape not unlike her favorite jam, but beneath that was warm earth after a good rain, carnations, a hint of salt.

She could imagine herself there, in the sunshine, surrounded by green vines and flowers, the surf crashing in the distance. "Lovely."

"You haven't tried it yet," Richard murmured as he clinked his glass to hers. "Partner."

The taste was much like the smell. "It's good."

Drake nodded his agreement, but Richard looked to her, both eyebrows raised.

"It doesn't compare—"

"It doesn't have to." Amelia put her hand on his arm to reassure him. "This business has taught me there's a place for each spirit. Just as whiskey doesn't go on a dinner table, this wine has its own place." An idea struck her. This wine needed a party, and she just happened to have one. "Drake, can you get a case of this to the manor tomorrow?"

"The young people will be here before school, so it shouldn't be a problem."

Richard still had his eyebrows arched, and she itched to smooth them back into place. "Are you certain?" he asked.

"We have several of the party set as a captive market." Amelia schemed as she talked. If they liked it as she predicted they would, they could be persuaded to order more for London. Their recommendations would drive more orders. No one in London wanted to be without the goods their neighbors enjoyed. "They might as well be good for something."

"Well thought out," Drake said. "What shall we label it?"

As they worked out the details, Amelia went to the still room. The copper monsters she loved hulked in the darkness, waiting for her to return. She tapped the edge of a mash tub, and the hollow thump echoed through the quiet room. It was a blessing, the quiet, after all the useless commotion of the past few days.

The scent of drying wheat, of home, drifted down from the loft and enveloped her like a blanket.

"There you are." Richard's quiet words doubled the warmth. "Drake is anxious for us to be away before the driver returns."

Now that she was here, she didn't want to leave. "He'd never let someone else in."

"Our horses will be difficult to hide, especially yours. Everyone in the village will recognize her."

This driver wouldn't be from the village. Drake would have hired him in Ipswich or Cornwall, wherever the ship had docked. "Without me on her, Molly is just another gray horse."

"With an expensive saddle," Richard countered as he took her hand. "As much as I like watching you work, we must go."

His hand was gentle, as were his words, but his profile was stern. "I don't agree with much Miss Allen says, but I have to confess she and I share an opinion about the pomade in your hair."

"You two have discussed my hair?" She didn't need to see his face to know he was smiling.

"Not discussed, exactly. She mentioned how dashing you'd appeared with your wild hair tossed by the winds in the Channel." The comment had made Amelia recall her first encounter with Richard. "And I have to agree. You look much more yourself when your hair is curly."

"I see." His thumb stroked the top of her knuckles, sending sparks up through her wrist with every bump. "What else has she spoken of?"

"She never fails to goad me about having kissed you, which is as inappropriate as it is irritating."

"Irritating?" His rumbly voice was as warm as his fingers curving around hers.

On one vacation, in Calais, she and her parents had been forced to stop at a posting inn to avoid the rain. As it had been a downpour, they'd chosen staying dry over being fashionable. The fire was warm and the food was tasty, even if the crowd was more working class. Amelia had enjoyed watching everyone, until two women had begun squabbling over the same man. Harsh words had quickly escalated to slaps and hair-pulling. Father had whisked her out before anything else had happened, and he'd refused to explain what had happened. All he'd said was that one day she'd understand.

Amelia desperately wanted to pull Fiona Allen's hair.

"It is very boring to sit, smile, and drink tea. All I can do is nod and say '*Yes, he is quite dashing. Of course I was totally swept away. Certainly he takes my breath every time—*'"

"I see your point," Richard said. "Why not try using that magnificent imagination of yours? Take a kiss you've had and plop me in the proper spot."

"Oh, I don't think that would work at all." She could almost hear his eyebrows rise. "It wasn't an encounter where you'd want to be plopped."

"*An* encounter?" He faced her. "You said you were familiar with kissing."

"Well, I *am* familiar with it, and since he almost chipped my tooth, it *was* memorable."

Richard's dry laugh teased her ears even as his boot slid along hers, as though he was searching for firm footing on a dark path. "I agree. I don't want to be plopped into that scenario."

His features were visible now. His lashes low over his eyes, his lips curved in a half smile. His fingers slid up her neck and under her hair. His nose brushed her brow as his breath coaxed her eyes closed, leaving her to feel his slow trek to her mouth. His nose brushing hers, his lips sweeping from her ear down her cheek. By the time he reached her lips, she was trembling.

It was a sweet pressure, encouraging her to shape her mouth to his, to cling to it until he pulled away. His fingers stroked the curve of her neck.

"Breathe, *chéri.*"

When Amelia obeyed, he returned to her mouth and swept his tongue over her lips in a wet plea that she answered.

Richard's groan rumbled over her teeth as his tongue slid against hers. He tasted of wine and whiskey and of something darker that urged her to do the same as he. She tangled her tongue with his, tested the firmness of his lips, felt him smile.

"Ahem." The deep cough came from neither of them.

Richard stopped kissing her but kept her shielded from the lantern light in the room. His eyes stayed on hers as he spoke. "Fletcher?"

"Yes. You two are out of time." He left the lantern as he closed the door.

Richard dragged his hands from her and backed away, kissing her knuckles as he lifted each hand from his coat.

Amelia wanted nothing more than to put out the lantern and return to the dark, to the circle of his arms. "No wonder Fiona—"

He stopped her words with a quick, hard kiss. "No. *That* belongs to us alone." He kept one hand, twined their fingers together. "I need to get you home."

CHAPTER ELEVEN

H E EXPECTED TO be alone as he slipped through the kitchen door. Some of it was the hour, most of it that he was accustomed to an empty house. But when Richard entered Felton House through the kitchen door, a baby's whimpers greeted him. A low fire in the hearth gilded the red hair of an otherwise shadowy figure.

Thea turned, half-shielding Carys, the fire poker in her other hand. "Good lord." She nudged the logs, sending sparks flying before returning the poker to its perch. "Are you late or early?"

Richard spread his hands wide. "I thought the hens might appreciate a tailcoat."

She snorted a laugh. "Whatever makes them lay better."

Carys's whimpers grew to cries, which wavered in time to her bounces against her mother's hip. Richard recalled a similar evening, years ago, but with an exhausted father and a terrified uncle.

"She's teething?"

"God yes, and she has her father's temper."

The kettle grumbled on the stove, a precursor to its screech as sure as Carys's cries were to wails. Richard reached for the baby.

"Give her over. I make lousy tea."

Thea surrendered her daughter on the way to the stove.

"Thank you. Oliver has ears like a bat, and I've just gotten him back to bed." She removed the kettle from the heat and filled two cups. "He's had a long day."

Richard dipped his index finger into his scalding tea and then stroked it over Carys's irritated gums. She gave up fighting after a moment, gnawing his finger until a hard, sharp tooth pricked his skin. Richard switched fingers, heating it before soothing the child.

"You're good with her," Thea said. Her curls were escaping from her loose braid and crawling up her robe—an odd, faded patchwork thing. She blinked slowly, her eyelids going only halfway up.

Richard switched fingers again. "It looks as though you both have had a rough time of it. What happened in Brandon?"

Her gaze widened as she straightened. "We go every Saturday." She sipped her tea. "Our son, Jamie, is buried there."

Richard stared at Carys's chubby face, calculating in his head. It was possible that there could have been another child, before her or after. Before might have explained Oliver's hasty remarriage. Though why would their infant son be buried a village away?

Thea placed her cup on the table without making a sound. "He was…from before. He and I lived in Brandon while Oliver was in Canada."

That made no sense. The man Richard had known, the man who'd married his sister and carted their son into forests and business meetings, wouldn't have left family behind. *Would he?* "Do you mean to tell me he—"

Thea stopped him with a shake of her head. "He had no idea until he returned." Her smile was sad. "He didn't tell you."

"Rich, I've remarried. Against all odds, I've found Thea again and, unbelievably, she still has use for me. I cannot wait for you to meet her. She has found her way through so much and has emerged as a great lady, equal to only one other. I hope you can share my joy. I believe Julia does."

"He doesn't like to talk of death." Richard shifted so that he could cradle Carys, who had fallen asleep. "Does Simon go as well?"

She nodded. "We make a day of it, the four of us alone on a picnic. We play and pick flowers and tell stories, but Oliver..." Her eyes shone in the firelight, bright as glass. "It's difficult for him to reconcile a life only possible because of loss." She covered Richard's hand while still staring into the fire. "We both are keenly aware of it."

The woman had a heart and courage he hadn't seen in many. His sister sprang to mind. Julia had always had an iron will she'd cloaked in silks and curls.

Amelia shared those traits as well, though he preferred her in her linen and wool work clothes, her hair caught back simply. She was fighting a life that would be changed by loss. Her father. Her home. Her freedom. Richard wanted to tell her that the battle she'd chosen was going to be difficult, but she'd likely scold him for stating the obvious.

Besides that, she'd already achieved modest success—at least enough to risk a larger investment. In a few years, he had no doubt she'd make a name for herself and he'd be...

Back in Canada.

Thea refilled his tea. "Perhaps you can drink this one instead of feeding it to Carys. Do you want me to take her?"

Richard flexed his fingers against the blanket and shook his head. "She's no trouble."

"Enough sadness," she said. "How was your day?"

"I'm glad this party is almost over." The incongruity of *him* dreading a party wasn't lost. "Between croquet and fending off insults, I'm exhausted."

Not to mention kissing Amelia. Even after a ride, in this kitchen, by the fire, he could close his eyes and catch her scent on his coat. He didn't want his tea because he could still taste her.

Richard snatched his teacup and downed the drink in one lukewarm gulp.

"Insults?" Thea asked. "About you having a profession?"

"Some of them, yes. I swear but I've never seen a group of people so opinionated about their own laziness." He looked to her. "How do you manage it?"

"It helps that Oliver hates town, so we only go for lords and bolt for home whenever possible." She relaxed in her chair, stroked a frayed and faded ribbon on her cuff. "I suppose, too, that I've never tried to live down my past. I won't apologize for having made a living, or a life, before Oliver returned. Just as he had a life in trade before he had a title. Those experiences made us suited for the future now in front of us." She sipped her tea. "But be wary of branding them all lazy, Richard."

"What?" Surely she, of all people, wasn't going to perpetuate the myth that men with no calluses on their hands were somehow better simply due to the luck of birth.

"There is good and bad in every class," Thea said. "You've seen it. Some people *are* lazy, but others work in different ways, the ways they are allowed, to ensure the lives of the people dependent upon them. And, like Oliver, some choose that."

Amelia was doing the same thing, in her own way. She'd been passionate this afternoon at the picnic, explaining how her whiskey had been sourced from local ingredients. Even now, her still was full of the apples she'd stealthily advised Fletcher to buy from a farmer Richard now suspected was a tenant of the Chitesters.

"He didn't know what he was getting into," Richard argued. Oliver had left Canada as a black-sheep second son and had landed in Britain as the heir to a title. Amelia knew what she was choosing.

Just like you know it's a waste.

"But he didn't have to come at all," Thea said. "He could have remained in Canada. He could have returned and run his estate by proxy. I could have refused his proposal and stayed an innkeeper. In some ways, those lives would have been simpler. But the fact that we chose this life, that we work together, makes it easier to withstand any gossip."

What if the gossip was true? "It's not just about my profession," Richard confessed. "Fiona Allen—" How on earth did he explain that he'd spent so much time avoiding society ladies that he hadn't recognized one when she'd caught him? At best, it made him sound naïve; at worst, it conveyed how much time he spent in bad company. "She's quite forward."

Fiona had approached him aboard ship, on her own. She'd introduced herself by her Christian name and struck up a conversation. But it said something about him that he'd equated those behaviors to a doxy. Didn't it?

"I dislike that word," Thea said. "It just means she's bold. You and Oliver were bold, and no one criticized you. The *ton* considers you odd, but, if pressed, those men would have to admit they admire your accomplishments. Fiona is considered bold, but Mr. Raymond is considered determined. Maybe stubborn. I'm bold." She shot him a sideways glance. "So is your betrothed."

His coat sleeve had smoothed out quickly, but it was easy to recall Amelia's grip on it. *It's very boring to sit, smile, and drink tea.* "Perhaps indiscreet is more accurate. Fiona seems to delight in making Amelia uncomfortable."

Richard couldn't totally fault her, though. Fiona's persistence had led to that unexpected kiss in the dark. On the face of it, Amelia's behavior wasn't that much different than Fiona's. His reaction, however, was.

He couldn't wait to kiss Amelia again, and that eagerness told him he'd be safer kissing Fiona.

Life was complicated.

"I have not told you, but I am thrilled you and Amelia are marrying," Thea said. "Though all of Norfolk will miss her—and her whiskey. Whether they know it or not."

And all of Quebec would miss getting acquainted. Even if they didn't know it, he did.

As he'd said—complicated.

AMELIA DISLIKED SHOOTING. She saw no point in getting up early only to stand around and do nothing but wait for an animal to wander by. She dreaded the noise and the cold, for it was always dismal during hunting season. Most of all, she hated the animal's panic if the shot was missed or they sensed their killer, when they knew they were being hunted.

This morning, she added an extra reason. She was going to be trapped in a blind with Ethan Raymond.

It wasn't on purpose, though he was acting as if she'd chosen him deliberately. It was really more of a consequence. He'd chosen Anthony Ashton, heir to the Viscount Burwell, as his partner. Amelia believed Tony, a good-looking rather serious fellow, would make a good match for Annabel Pearce. To do the matching, she needed to be in the blind with them.

Across the carriage, Annabel hid a yawn behind her hand. "Do forgive me."

"It's far too early," Amelia said. "I should have devised an indoor activity for the ladies, but it seemed fair play to watch the men shoot if they are going to join us for archery."

"And they will only join out of fair play," Annabel teased. "If we want them at archery, we must hike through the countryside at the crack of dawn."

"Because if they don't appear for archery, none of the ladies will go." Amelia did her best imitation of a *ton* matron. "Everyone will be left to their own devices."

Annabel put her hand to her chest in mock horror. "Which should never happen at a house party."

They fell into a fit of giggles, which ended only when the cart struck a rut and sent them scrambling for a handhold. It would be grand to have Annabel close enough for visits.

She always reminded Amelia of a swan, tall, graceful and serene. She even had quiet hobbies. Today she carried her sketchbook in her lap. Amelia looked to the hills and fields that were home, seeing them with an artist's eye as the morning sun burnished the crest of each before sweeping into the valleys below.

"I haven't had the opportunity to congratulate you on your betrothal," Annabel said. "He is an intriguing choice."

"But?" Amelia asked. When Annabel stayed quiet, Amelia refocused. "I'm sorry. Most well wishes have come with a qualifier."

"I think most are surprised because they knew Ethan had settled on you, and they expected you to swoon at his feet." Annabel shifted her grip on her sketchbook. "For myself, I'm glad you didn't. Your Richard is a far better match, and a much better man."

Your Richard. Amelia enjoyed the sound of that and, as her heart swelled, she liked the feel of it far too much. Just his name conjured the memory of his kiss, which was never far from her anyway.

"We were placed together at dinner, and while he only had eyes for you, he listened and participated in the conversation around him, something I've never known Ethan to do. Trade or not, Richard is astute and clearly well-educated. I am glad he turned your head, though I wish you weren't leaving for Quebec so soon after we've become acquainted."

"I'm looking forward to the adventure," Amelia said. Her conscience twitched at the lie, but not as much as her heart.

It was utterly foolish. Her home was here, her business was here. She was doing all of this so she could stay *here.* And Richard was only helping her because he wasn't staying. He'd said as much.

It was only one kiss.

She could visit Quebec on her own. Perhaps they could have dinner and laugh over the time they fooled an entire village into believing in a whirlwind courtship.

The cart drew to a stop, and Belinda Martin was the first out.

"Do you really believe she can shoot?" Amelia asked. "Or do you think she's playing it up to catch Lord Trentham?"

Amelia had been shocked when Alexander Hyde, the newest Earl of Trentham, had accepted the family's invitation. He was the only attendee with a title. Even Jasper didn't have one yet.

"She may shoot, but she'll be lucky if someone doesn't mistake that feather in her hat for a grouse," Annabel bent to whisper. The sunlight caught her hair and transformed it from soft brown to dark blonde. "Perhaps you should mention it to her cousin."

Amelia didn't wish to speak to Fiona Allen so early in the morning, not about her cousin's hat at any rate. She was saved when Lord Trentham himself flicked a finger across the feather and sent it flying. Belinda looked equal parts outraged and pleased.

Hoof beats announced a rider coming up behind them at a gallop. Amelia turned, heart in her throat, hoping nothing had happened to her father.

Richard slowed his mount as he reached them, the horse dancing below him as he stopped. His dismount was as graceful as a dancer, and he stopped to speak to the groom who took the reins. In the past few days, Amelia had learned he was always late, as though he put off leaving his family until the last minute.

"I do like what he's done with his hair," Annabel said.

So did Amelia. He'd left it dry this morning, and the mass of loose, dark curls were wilder from the wind and his ride. Cut short, they framed his brow and stopped near the tops of his ears. More than that, he'd done something she'd asked of him. He looked to her and smiled, wide and bright.

Her ears buzzed as she swayed on her feet. She was *not* swooning over a man, no matter how handsome and charming he was. No matter that her tongue dipped across her lower lip, recalling his taste. She'd simply forgotten to breathe.

Dragging in a deep inhale brought another thrill as the tips of her breasts brushed her chemise. It worsened as he joined them, staring at her with a wicked glint in his clear blue eyes.

"Oh my," Annabel murmured. "Adventure indeed."

Given the day's scheduled activities, he was dressed more casually. It was easy to imagine him coming home after a day in the forest.

Not home, Amelia. He will not come home to you. That's against the terms of your contract.

"Good morning, *chéri*," Richard said before he lifted Amelia's knuckles to his lips. His breath teased her skin even as his finger stroked her palm, reminiscent of the way he'd caressed her nape during their kiss. "I apologize for being late."

It was a good thing he had hold of her hand. All she wanted to do was tangle it in his hair and see if it was as soft as it looked, if it would wind round her fingers.

The twinkle in his eyes sparked to something darker, deeper as his hold tightened. "I was awake far too late last night."

"Kiss me and you're forgiven." The words were out before Amelia could consider them, but as Richard kept her close, she was glad she'd said them.

He kissed her on the nose and pulled away to wink. "I'll not scandalize you in front of your guests no matter how sweetly you ask," he whispered as he kept her close. "I'm sorry to give you a fright. I stopped at the house so Simms could direct me. He says your father is having breakfast in his library. That's a good thing, yes?"

It was a return to normal, which was an excellent thing. Tears clogged her throat as she nodded. It would be so easy to lean against him and weep at the cruelty of hope.

"Amelia, we don't have to—"

"I'm fine." She cleared her throat, squared her shoulders, and left his embrace. However, she put her hand in his elbow as he followed their—her—guests. She couldn't stop touching him and, when he covered her hand with his, she considered whether he felt the same. However, maybe it was just to convince everyone else of his affection.

"I'm afraid we're separated this morning," she said in her most businesslike tone. "Jasper asked to partner with you, and I had already decided to match make."

Richard nodded. "Everything seems to be going to plan."

It was not Amelia's plan to deliver him into Fiona Allen's clutches and then walk away, but she did it. She also took a lower position behind the blind so that she didn't have to watch them across the field, or the carnage that would certainly ensue.

"I suspect we'll have to keep on our toes to best Warren and Ferrand," Tony Ashton said as he checked his rifle.

"I suspect that's why Miss Chitester chose it," Ethan replied. "Is that so, miss?"

"We chose it because Oakdale has fine game and plenty of room for an activity young men enjoy." Amelia glanced toward their gamekeeper's son, and apprentice, who was serving as Ethan's loader.

The pride on his face, and the respect in his nod, made her wistful. She remembered when the family had arrived on the estate, and how hard they had worked to restore Oakdale's herds and flocks. She hoped Jasper kept them on.

"And not because your betrothed has likely had to scour the woods like a wild man for his meals?"

Heat bubbled in Amelia's chest. Not only was he insulting Richard, he was also demeaning the young man next to her. A skilled huntsman, he kept several families in meat during harsh times. "I'd value any man who could care for himself and his family, rather than simply hunting for sport."

Ethan balanced his rifle on the wall of the blind, his back to her and his stance wide. "Trust me, Miss Chitester, I know the value of the hunt and overcoming my prey."

Tony Ashton caught her gaze, his eyes wide. "I say, Raymond, all this talking is scaring the game."

"Not just the game," Annabel whispered as she plucked up a charcoal stick. "Your Richard may find himself mistaken for a stag."

"Or Ethan may be recognized for the boar he is." If Amelia could find a long enough stick, she'd be tempted to poke it up the man's arse. "Though Mr. Ashton seems more pleasant."

"Tony has always been kinder than Ethan deserves. They're cousins, you know?" Annabel swept her tool in a wide arc, making the creation of hills seem effortless. Amelia couldn't draw without leaving finger marks on the paper. She invariably ended up with charcoal on her nose.

"Would their relation be a drawback to forming an attachment with Tony?" Amelia whispered. "I've heard he's a fine catch."

More precisely, she'd heard that he didn't gamble to excess, didn't drink himself into oblivion, and that he treated his servants well. His father didn't keep a mistress, so it was assumed Tony wouldn't either. He certainly wasn't rushing to the altar as though he needed financing. But Annabel had likely heard the same gossip.

"I appreciate your efforts," the young woman said without raising her eyes from her sketch. "But it is wasted on me."

"You are too harsh on—"

"Amelia, my father invested heavily in a foolish scheme that has depleted his living. He's using my dowry to stay one step ahead of collectors and debtors' prison. You must have noticed my dresses are from last year."

She did recall that the green dress Annabel wore today had been worn by her sister in a prior Season. Though her sister was shorter and wider, and the dress had been altered with an expert hand.

"I am sorry, Annabel. Is there anything I can do?" Amelia's mind was already spinning with how she could connect her newest friend with the ladies in the lending circle. Perhaps they could fund an art gallery or a dress shop—assuming Annabel had done her own alterations, of course.

"Your friendship means everything to me, and I hope you will agree to keep it." Annabel rested her charcoal near the page, keeping it in place without leaving an errant mark.

"Of course." Surely she didn't expect Amelia to turn her back simply because her father was foolish. "And perhaps there is a chance to make a match with—"

"No titled man will take a wife without a dowry." Annabel said it like they were discussing the weather. "You and I both know that. My father knows that."

"Then why…" There was no proper way to ask why her father had tormented her with a Season where women like Belinda Martin would look down their noses, where men like Tony Ashton might call only to turn away once the books were opened.

"My choices are governess or mistress." Annabel's mouth flattened into a thin line. "My father is too embarrassed to let me go into service or to ask my sister's new husband for help. He's sent me here to catch a…benefactor."

Amelia's mouth fell open. "What?"

"You have a viscount, a soon-to-be marquess, and several earls on your guest list. He's hoping I'll be appealing enough to have one of them take me off his hands, at least temporarily." Annabel's eyes blazed with hatred, matching the color splotching her cheeks.

"Graves—my chaperone—was my governess once upon a time." Amelia patted her friend's hand and kept her smile bright. "She'll know exactly what to do."

CHAPTER TWELVE

"SIMMS TELLS ME you've gifted us with a case of your wine," Augustus Chitester said. "You certainly know how to bribe a father."

"I'll take whatever advantage I can get," Richard said, laughing. He didn't have to force the humor. The man's good nature was contagious. However, it left a bitter aftertaste. He didn't believe in dishonest negotiations, and leading Amelia's father to believe they'd soon be family was the largest lie he'd ever told.

Augustus' chuckle ended in a deep cough that shook over his shoulders, through his barrel chest, and down into the gig seat so that it trembled beneath them. It reminded Richard why he'd agreed to Amelia's madcap plot in the first place.

"You certainly earned Marian's favor by agreeing to be my driver this afternoon," Augustus said once he caught his breath. "I'm sure you'd rather be down there in the fray."

As he spoke, one of Amelia's arrows went far wide of the target. It wasn't the first that had done so.

"I believe I'm safer up here," Richard said. "She is remarkably bad at this."

"Archery has never been her sport, but she knows many young ladies like to use it to show off their figures," Augustus replied.

It was something Richard would have expected. Just as he'd

been known to bid too high on a contract when he and Oliver didn't enjoy working with their counterparts, Amelia's determination to remain unmarried would lead her to choose activities where others outshone her.

"She's deadly at croquet, though." Augustus nudged him with an elbow. "Goes after it like a general wading into battle."

It wasn't the first time the sport, if it could be called that, had been mentioned. "Why croquet?"

"She liked the mallets." Augustus's wide smile belied his flat statement. "I still remember the first time Marian put one in her hand. It was taller than she was by almost half, but she'd carried it around like a sword, whacking everything in sight." He chuckled. "Be forewarned, young man."

It sounded very much like they were going to get Augustus's permission to marry. Before Richard could stop it, tingles shot through his blood to every extremity.

All of them.

He shifted in the seat, hoping to stop his body's happy reaction to something that wasn't supposed to happen. Wasn't going to happen. His silent fidgeting drew Augustus's attention.

"It's not a foregone conclusion, mind you," he said. "We have a few remaining concerns."

Of course they did. Having been in almost the exact position almost ten years ago, he could guess what they were. "Miss Allen?"

For almost a year after Oliver's arrival in Quebec, he'd talked of little else but Thea, the girl waiting on him at home. For a year after that, he'd mourned her betrayal. When he had finally awakened from his heartbroken stupor and begun to pay attention to Julia, she'd been overjoyed.

Richard had been less so. No man wanted a woman in his family to serve as a consolation prize.

"She has been quite vocal about your previous connection," Augustus said. He had lowered his voice and pulled a cigar from his pocket. Rather than lighting it, he tapped it on his knee as though he was considering its purpose.

"I didn't compromise her, nor did I raise her expectations." Richard inhaled a breath so deep it reached his toes. He hadn't been a monk, but he wasn't going to discuss it in detail. "The moment I met Amelia, all other women vanished from existence."

That wasn't a lie. Every time they were together, Richard forgot there were others nearby. It didn't matter if they were at dinner or surrounded by trees. He'd arrived for hunting and seen only her. He'd missed several open shots because he'd been looking for her across the valley, her hair a halo in the sunlight.

It would be silly if it wasn't so alarming.

Augustus harrumphed an agreement. "That's a fine answer. But if it changes, remember—"

"She has a mallet," Richard joked.

"And I have a shotgun." Her father was deadly serious. "Though it would be difficult to reach you in Quebec, which leads me to our other concern."

Trade. It had to be. A baron might be the lowest rung on the social ladder, but he was still *on* the ladder. Most wanted their daughters to move up a rung or three, not step off entirely.

Oddly, Richard's concerns over Oliver had been the reverse. Quebec had its share of titled, and entitled, Englishmen—and Frenchmen for that matter. Richard had seen them escort their wives to church on Sunday and their mistresses upstairs on any other night of the week. He'd monitored Oliver and Julia's eventual courtship carefully.

He'd never been so glad to be wrong. And he'd make sure Augustus—

You'll make sure of nothing.

Augustus waved away his concern. "It's reassuring that you don't need her dowry. But…" He faced Richard with watery eyes. "I'm ill, and Quebec is a long distance."

*Damn. Damn, damn, damn, damn, **damn**.*

Richard's tongue itched to tell the man the truth. "Augustus—"

"I want her to be taken care of, to have—"

"Amelia has a good sense about her, sir. You know, the wine was her idea." He tiptoed into the discussion. "I'd mentioned the arrival of my first shipment, and she introduced me to her tenant—"

"Eamon? She argued with me for days to let him build on the property. He's your distributor?"

And your daughter. "He is. But Amelia suggested that if I brought you the case, perhaps the party would help carry the word back to London. She has a good business sense, Augustus."

"She's a lot like your nephew. Before Marian and I married, Amelia spent a great deal of time with me. She picked up more than I thought. But she's not a man, Richard. You know that—"

An arrow thwacked into the carriage box, just below their feet.

"What the hell?" Richard snapped his attention to the clearing below. Jasper Warren dropped his bow to the left, pointing toward Amelia squaring off opposite Ethan Raymond.

Richard leapt from the gig. "Excuse me, Augustus," he said without looking back.

He jogged down the hill, as much to keep his balance as to reach Amelia's side, treading mint and thyme underfoot and dragging the scents with him. Once on level ground, he straightened his coat and cuffs, nodding his thanks as he passed by Jasper. "You're handy with that thing."

"I don't want to inherit that badly," the other man said in his typical bored drawl. It was as though he couldn't be bothered to open his mouth properly. "Raymond's been poking at her all morning, but it only just got heated."

"Let me pass, Mr. Raymond." Amelia's command cut through the air. "I have had quite enough of this."

Richard strode across the makeshift archery range, his stare fixed on her tormentor.

"*You've* had?" Raymond sneered, his arms crossed like any

schoolyard bully. "You flirt with me endlessly in London, vanish into the countryside so I had to chase you, and then spend the weekend playing hard to get. Only to turn around and invite me to house party where you announce your betrothal to a *tradesman* who is only after your dowry." He pointed behind them. "He is likely up the hill now, scheming how to separate you from your funds and your home."

Amelia raised a fist, and Richard hesitated, hoping he'd see her lay into the man.

Instead, she raised her index finger. "I danced with you, and we rode in the park. Just like half a dozen other girls." Another finger. "We returned to the country because the Season was over." Another. "You arrived without invitation and without notice." Another. "I'll give you that point. Though I dare say none of the other young men considered it an invitation to a proposal."

Her thumb. "Richard could buy and sell you if he so chose, but he has better breeding. You will cease these tasteless remarks or you are welcome to pack your bags."

She stopped just short of stamping her foot, but her skirt twitched. Her glove was taut over her knuckles as she gripped her bow.

Richard went to her side and tugged the weapon free before she bashed Raymond over the head. "And sixth, I don't need another home. I have two fine ones, along with two businesses, on two separate continents." He curved his hand to Amelia's waist, coaxing her to look up at him. Her blue eyes were full of sparks. "As a matter of fact, I've been talking to your father about us staying in France for a few months after the wedding. What do you think, darling?"

He could imagine her at Rosnay, surrounded by sunshine and flowers, the sea breeze catching her hair. She'd be pestering the winemaker about his process, no doubt.

The image was still in his brain when she grasped his shoulder and stood on her tiptoes to kiss his cheek. Her fine cotton dress did little to mask her body heat as she lingered, her hair tickling his nose and her breath warming his ear. "I think that would be lovely. Thank you for asking."

Even if this was just for the other man's benefit, Richard wasn't going to complain. Instead, he flexed his fingers against the ridges of her stays and turned enough to inhale her sweet scent. After a few days away from the distillery, she smelled of flowers and sunshine instead of fruit and sugar.

He didn't know which he preferred.

A shadow loomed in the corner of his eye. Keeping Amelia close, he shielded her from Raymond's hard eyes. "We'll be along in a moment."

Richard didn't know if Raymond slunk or stalked. He didn't know if he grumbled or growled. He only knew the odious bastard was gone and the day was the better for it.

Richard tipped Amelia's chin and brought her lips to his. The sweetness made him hungry, and he happily surrendered to it, sweeping his tongue against hers. Her gasp made his lungs swell, and her fingers in his hair made his knees wobble.

He came up for air, but the world kept spinning, and when he focused on her, he realized he was in danger of more than falling over.

"I forgot..." He was doing that a lot lately. He cleared his throat. "We should go before anyone thinks I've compromised you."

Just saying it made him think of little else. He backed away and took her hand, tugging her behind him when she didn't move quickly enough.

"Isn't that the point?" she half-giggled. "To make sure I'm on the shelf?"

She wasn't helping matters. "Amelia—"

"Fine." She anchored her feet and tightened her arm. "But you aren't going to ruin my enjoyment of finally telling that man what I thought of him." She yanked her hand free. "And you aren't going to drag me back to the house like I'm an errant child."

Standing there, one eyebrow arched, one hand on her hip, telling him off, she was…adorable. And though Richard's brain told him to run the other direction as fast as he could, his body fell into place beside her. His elbow waited for her hand. His feet fell into step.

"And you aren't going to dampen the thrill of kissing you," Amelia sighed. "I can't wait for Fiona Allen to tease me again. She's going to get an earful."

Chuckling, Richard looked skyward and silently prayed for mercy. "What am I going to do with you?"

AMELIA LET HERSELF into the distillery and stood in the doorway, shaking the rain from her hat and cloak. The barrel room was dark and cool even on the brightest days, but tonight, the weather and the lack of moonlight gave it a gloomy, cold air. The barrels hulked in the shadows like great beasts waiting to drag passers-by—

Enough of this imagination. It's gotten you into plenty of trouble already.

Dry fingers brushed her ankles, startling a shriek and inspiring her to fumble for the matches and candle that always waited by the door. As the flame sputtered to life, the hand reached for her again, and she shrank into a corner until Caspar's purr rumbled against her feet.

"Silly girl," Amelia chided herself as she bent to stroke the cat's short orange fur. He was fatter than last month, which hopefully meant he was doing his job rather than begging for the children's breakfasts. "Incorrigible creature."

She straightened and lifted the candle high, showing the path between stacked wine casks. Sweet oak and dust tickled her nose until she sneezed. The sound echoed back to her.

"Bless you." The dark rumble paired with an even blacker

shadow in the doorway, tall and ominous.

"Who's there?" Amelia hated the shake in her voice, but her heart was in her throat. She raised the candle higher, and relaxed only when it glinted off the pattern of Drake's waistcoat. "Oh, it's you."

He reached for her hand and led her through the path and toward the still room. "What's frightened you?"

How could Amelia explain that having Ethan tower over her and carp about his expectations had been unnerving? His harsh face and hard eyes had made him almost unrecognizable. She'd fought back out of self-defense as much as anger, though she'd found it liberating to be honest in her opinions. "It has been a long day, and the ride was far darker than normal."

It had been a relief when Richard had arrived and played co-conspirator.

For that's what he was, though it was difficult to remember at times. Especially when he befriended her father and spoke of France as though he was focused on keeping her near her family, even when he knew she'd never be leaving.

All afternoon, the thought had chafed much like a pebble in her boot. She'd always thought in terms of fighting to stay in Norfolk, in Thetford, near to Oakdale. She'd wanted control of her own life and her own future. Today, listening to Annabel's story of her father's losses, Amelia saw that control meant risking failure and poverty.

If she failed, she wouldn't *get* to stay here. She'd be *stuck* here. On the outskirts of everyone else's life.

"Richard should be with you," Drake said as he lit a lantern.

The soft glow burnished the copper giants, which were waiting for a task. Tonight, rather than creativity, they inspired exhaustion. But if this is what control looked like, she'd seize it. No matter the work involved.

She would not be a spectator in her own life.

"You do realize our betrothal is a ruse?" she asked as she climbed the stairs to the loft, her boots heavy against the treads.

"You don't say." Drake infused a cartload of sarcasm into those three syllables. "That doesn't relieve him of escorting you."

It did if she'd told him she was staying in. "I'm fine." Amelia knelt at the edge of grain bed and gathered a handful of wheat. It was fuzzy against her fingers and smelled of fields after a summer rain. In the lantern light, the kernel was a soft green. "This is ready to kiln."

"Oh good." Drake trudged up the final stairs.

Amelia understood his grumpiness. Sweeping grain was dusty, heavy work even in the sunshine. Doing it at night, after a long day, was almost enough to make her cry. "I'll be glad when this party is over."

"You'll get no argument from me." Next to her, Drake's face was in half shadow, the lamplight mapping the thin line of lips and the tenseness in his jaw. She thought there were shadows under his eyes. She wasn't the only one who'd been working all day.

Not to mention, he'd stuck himself in Thetford to keep her business on track for the duration of the party. "I can do this so you can go rest."

Drake lifted a broom in one hand, a lantern in the other, and walked down the narrow scaffolding like it was level ground. "How was dinner?"

Richard had cried off early because Simon had requested his uncle's presence for bedtime stories. It was easy to imagine the seven-year-old saying it just that way. But it had left her to deal with Ethan Raymond's growing churlishness, and Fiona Allen's annoying gaiety. Even her cousin Belinda seemed weary of her.

Who would have guessed that the savior of the evening would be Margaret Gerard at the piano forte? She played with exquisite skill, but she sang even better. Even Jasper had been impressed as he sipped his ever-present drink. Charles Grayson had sat spellbound for most of the evening. He might still be in the drawing room, alone in the dark.

Drat. She had nearly forgotten. "Jasper would like a case of

Richard's wine to take back with him, as would Charles Grayson." Amelia used her boot to flip open the lid to a chute built into the loft's railing.

"I had the children label extra bottles. We can deliver the cases tomorrow." Drake pushed the grain toward her in powerful swipes.

"Thank you." Amelia shoveled the wheat kernels down the chute, where it whispered its way into the kiln pot waiting below. "They aren't missing school?"

"Of course not." Drake stripped from his coat and rolled up his sleeves. "How long do you and Richard expect to get away with this cock-eyed scheme?"

"Long enough." Her shirt stuck to her back. It just needed to long enough for Ethan not to offer and Father to change his mind, which she hoped would be before her feelings were more twisted. The point of her plan was that she'd pretend to be broken-hearted, not that she actually was. "And it's not cock-eyed. We are in business, and me staying unmarried is related to that business. My parents need to stop their matchmaking."

"They worry over you," Drake said. "It's what parents do."

"It's what daughters do as well." Amelia's back twinged. Perhaps she should have stopped her day at archery. Though malting was one of her favorite things in the distilling process. Wet grain slipped through her fingers like heavy silk, and dry grain like sand. Up here in the loft, the routine push and pull was calming when her thoughts were a muddle.

Which was all the time lately, because trying to be two people was exhausting. It's what had led her to the lending circle in the first place. She'd thought that having money for salaries and supplies would ease her workload and her mind. It had been naive. Once she wasn't burdened with the tedium of bottling and bookkeeping, her imagination had sprung to life. There were few things she could smell, or taste, without thinking of it in whiskey. But that taste, ultimately, came down to the grain.

Which is why she was shoveling wheat into a kiln in the

middle of the night.

Drake's muttered curse drifted on the too-warm, nut-scented air, and Amelia's conscience spasmed as much as her back. It wasn't just herself she was putting through this. "Thank you for being here. I'm sure you've given up something in London."

"Helping you isn't a chore." His smile flashed. "Well, *this* is. But the rest of it isn't. I enjoy being in the village, and most of the day I'm at loose ends. In London, I'd be doing little but keeping the boys out of trouble."

Boys? It was the first time he'd ever mentioned a detail about his life. "What boys?" *Had he been married? Was he married?* "Do you have children?"

His silence added weight to the air. It grew heavier with every swish of the broom. "Brothers," he finally murmured.

As an only child in a large house, Amelia had spent most of her childhood wishing for siblings. If she'd had them, if one had been a brother, if he had doted on her, perhaps she wouldn't be in such a quandary. "How many of them? How old are they? What of—"

Drake heaved a sigh. "There are too many of them and they aren't old enough to see sense most days. And don't change the subject." He leaned on his broom. "How do you see this scheme of yours ending? What do you want from it?"

That had been one of his first questions to her when they'd formed the straw relationship that fed her unladylike ambition. *That* had sprung to life when she'd seen her father's smile after tasting Eamon Brewer's first good batch of white whiskey.

The question had also led to Drake's primary lesson. *Always begin with the end in mind.*

"He'll cry off and go back to Quebec, and I'll stay here as a broken-hearted spinster."

"That will never work," he said. "No matter how much your parents may like Richard and understand your grief, they will want to see you matched. And the *ton* will never leave you be. You're too pretty and your dowry is too tempting."

"Perhaps he can do it after he sails then. He wouldn't be the first man to sail for a new country and change his mind. Oliver—"

"That wasn't what happened with Oliver. And I wouldn't put it past him to sail for Quebec and drag Richard back by his hair."

Amelia slid her fingers along the shovel handle, feeling instead the way Richard's silky hair twined through them. "Then I'll cry off and send him packing."

"Over what? Because anything bad enough to break an engagement will leave Oliver and Thea with a scandal. I'd like to think Richard wouldn't do that, I don't believe you'd do it, and you *know* I won't allow it."

Amelia was glad she hadn't discussed this plan with him earlier. "Then maybe he can just ruin—"

"Stop." Drake's command rang across the rafters, and his steps made the floorboards bounce under her feet. He stopped far enough away to be proper but close enough she could see his glare. "If you are going to barter your virtue for whiskey, I'll take an axe to every barrel right now."

"How dare you threaten me with that." Amelia closed the distance between them. "And how dare you talk to me like I'm a child. I have worked my arse off for my freedom, and you will not take it from me. There are plenty of women in the *ton* who have traded their virtue for less."

"Which is just as wrong," Drake said. "But if Richard has agreed to that particular term, I'll drag him back from Quebec by his bollocks. Though I'd probably have to fight your father and Oliver for a turn."

Unless Father was no longer here and Mother was grieving. Which was much too unreliable. Because if Richard kept kissing her and Father lingered, it would be difficult to keep avoiding—

Tears sprang to her eyes. She was a selfish and self-centered daughter. And apparently, too stupid to figure a way out of this mess.

CHAPTER THIRTEEN

"WHAT ARE YOU saying?" Margaret Gerard asked, her eyes narrow. "That I'm foolish?"

Oh dear. "No," Amelia said as she dropped her cup into the saucer, the clatter adding to her jangled thoughts. This is what came of trying to help, which she'd decided to do early this morning when she'd collapsed on her mattress in an exhausted stupor. "That's not what I meant at all."

"Meringue is only flattering with desserts, Amelia."

"I didn't say you looked like a meringue; I said all the frothy lace at the neck of your dress made me think of a meringue."

It was a fine line, and Margaret's unabated glare told Amelia she was too close to it. Regardless, there was no graceful way to stop. "I didn't intend to hurt your feelings or be unkind. I was just meant that…sometimes a pie is prettier when it is simple."

This conversation had sounded so much better in her head as Rose had styled her hair. But, then again, Amelia had only gotten a few hours fitful sleep filled with nightmares of Drake keelhauling Richard as they returned from Quebec on a rough sea.

Annabel came into the room. "Good morning." Her spirits were much higher than yesterday, and Amelia made a note to hug Graves's neck the next time she saw her.

"Good morning, Miss Pearce," Margaret said, her nose in the air and her mouth in an ugly line. "You're just in time to hear

Amelia's logical comparison of pie and dresses."

Annabel slid a sideways glance toward Amelia and smirked. Amelia hid her dread behind a sip of chocolate. Young ladies wearing that expression were unpredictable. Had she misjudged Annabel's intentions?

Likely so, because nothing was going to plan during this dreadful weekend. Even the weather today was frightful. Rather than burning off ill feelings by smashing balls with mallets, they were going to be stuck inside listening to the rain pelt the windows.

"Are you discussing all the lace at your neck, because it does remind me of a confection," Annabel said. "Which is a shame because it distracts from your other qualities."

"Mother says the lace enhances my…" Margaret looked toward the door before waving her fingers toward her breasts.

Or where her breasts would be if she had any.

"The frills only serve to draw attention to them, not make them larger. There are other ways to flatter your figure." Annabel cast a discerning eye over Margaret's dress, an appealing butter yellow silk that contrasted nicely with her dark hair, but was festooned with enough lace to make a coverlet. "A simpler bodice would also call attention to your neck."

And away from her nose.

"You have lovely posture, Margaret," Amelia said. It would never do to let Annabel dig her out of a hole alone. "I noticed it while you were singing last evening. You have a fine voice, and it's clear you enjoy music. Charles Grayson seemed particularly impressed."

"Mother says that the feathers in my hair make me appear taller."

They reminded Amelia of the parrot her grandmother had owned years ago, especially when Margaret preened as she was doing now. They also made Charles Grayson sneeze.

Annabel shot her another conspiratorial look while she sipped her chocolate. "I've known Charles for years, and he's always been fond of music. He's quite talented himself. He plays the violin."

"Does he truly?" Amelia said. "I wish he could play for us."

"He's not as well situated as the marquess," Margaret murmured as she pushed her fork across her plate. "Mr. Warren cuts a fine figure, too."

Not for the first time, Amelia cursed the social requirement that her father's heir be invited to every occasion. His good looks and nonchalance made him appear the ultimate catch. "Mr. Grayson is shorter, true, but he has a much better disposition than my cousin."

It wasn't betraying her family if it was fact. Her father had been the only one to escape his ancestors' taciturn moodiness that led to boredom, which led to meddling just for the fun of it. He'd credited Norfolk weather for the difference.

"And he's heir to Viscount Ledbury," Annabel added. "My mother is a cousin, so we've visited the estate. It's lovely, and the income is generous. The family has always run it well, and Charles will be no exception. He loves it there. Whoever he chooses to marry will be well-respected in the *ton*."

Margaret was quiet for several moments. "My maid would never go against Mother's decree about my dress."

"Come early for dinner." Amelia put her hand over Margaret's and squeezed her delicate fingers. "We'll help sort it. My maid, Rose, can help with your hair."

"I can work on the dress," Annabel said. "As a matter of fact, we can do something about this one as well if you'll meet me upstairs." Her lips quirked. "My room is to the right of the landing, second door on the left."

"On the right," Amelia said. "I believe I put you nearer the garden."

"So you did. I'm forever getting turned around in new houses," Annabel said. "Why don't you go up now, Miss Gerard? I'll be along as soon as I talk to Charles about his violin. He usually travels with it."

Once they were alone, Amelia turned to Annabel. "Thank you for your help with that. The more I spoke, the worse it sounded."

The other woman brushed off her concern. "I wouldn't have stepped in, but I've caught Charles staring at Margaret when he thinks no one is looking. I believe he'd approach her if it weren't for those feathers—they make him sneeze. Plus, Belinda and Fiona poke fun at her, which I can't abide."

Amelia had considered Margaret Gerard many things, but laughable had never been one. Not until this weekend. "A word of warning, she can be a bit of a social climber."

"Charles can sand off her edges. He has that way with people. Though she might help him as well. He never knows who anyone is." Annabel placed her utensils on her plate without making a sound. "And most women are social climbers. We've no other way of controlling our future."

They rose from the table and left the dining room, the taller Annabel shortening her steps to match Amelia's so they could continue their conversation.

"Miss Graves has been very helpful, and I believe I have a path to some sort of independence," Annabel said. "But this will likely be the last party I attend."

"I will miss you." Amelia grasped her hand. "Please write."

"Most certainly. You'll need my address for the wedding list. Assuming you still want—"

The front door opened, letting the fall air chill the house and teasing Amelia's nose with the scents of mud and moss. Richard stood there, shaking the water from his coat before he handed it to their footman. He was laughing with Simms.

"Of course I still want you at the wedding," she murmured to Annabel, lost in her thoughts.

She wanted *everything*.

⌢

THE ONLY THING worse than a house party was a house party on a rainy day. After breakfast, the men had played billiards and cards while the women had indulged in backgammon and chess.

After playing so many rounds of *vingt et un* that he'd stopped paying attention to his wagers, Richard had planned to leave after luncheon. But here he was, on the sofa near enough to Amelia to allow conversation, but far enough to avoid scandal. Fires blazed in every hearth, beating back the damp chill, and gaslights and candles were a poor substitute for the sun. On the other side of the windows, the world was a misty green and gray.

"You've been quiet this morning," he said.

"We've hardly been in the same room until now." Amelia's smile was limited to a lift at the corners of her mouth, and there were shadows smudged below her eyes. "But I didn't have a restful night."

For a moment, he wondered if she'd lain in bed staring at the ceiling. Had she missed his breath and his warmth? Perhaps she'd touched herself, wishing it was his hands—

"I had to talk to Drake about extra cases of wine," she whispered. "And the grain had to go into the kiln."

It had just been him lost in fantasies then.

"You went to the distillery in the rain? Alone?" They were silly questions. He could almost hear her roll her eyes. "Why didn't you tell me?"

"I've done it long before you arrived, and I'll—"

Be doing it after you're gone. He didn't need to hear her say it. Didn't want to.

"Besides, you were needed at home." Her lack of sleep gave her a languid softness that was as lovely as it was dangerous. "How did Simon enjoy his story?"

"The boy has a mind like a steel trap. It took twice as long because he kept stopping me to point out contradictory details from the nights before."

"You invent them?" she asked.

He nodded. "Simon grew bored easily when Oliver and I

were working, but we couldn't carry a book with us. So we all spun the stories together." Her furrowed brow encouraged him to explain. "A two-year-old has a *why* for everything. At first, we answered everything as honestly and reasonably as we could, but it didn't take long for it to become maddening." Richard smiled, remembering. "Imagine trying to explain why you can't see air, or why vegetables are good for you. But Oliver forbade *because I said so*. Apparently, his mother said it a lot."

"I can see that," Amelia said, chuckling. "She didn't like to explain herself."

Not for the first time, Richard was glad he'd never met the dowager duchess who'd bullied her son to Canada and his lover into poverty. "One day, rather than snapping at Simon that I didn't know why trees weren't as tall as mountains, I kept quiet and he answered his own question—that they grew that way somewhere else. We trudged through the forest all day, imagining a land of giants while I surveyed a stand of timber."

Amelia's smile was shy. "I used to imagine—"

"Should we play a parlor game?" Margaret Gerard asked the group. "Perhaps Jacob and Ruth?"

Richard resented the interruption of his quiet conversation. Besides, the last thing this crowd needed was a blindfold and a chance to grab one another. Coffee had given way to cider, which had progressed to wine and sherry. Billiards had encouraged whiskey, in part to ward of the chill of the games room.

"That is a poor idea," he whispered to Amelia. "Think of something—"

"Let's test our brains first," Amelia said. "I have it on good authority that Richard writes fine limericks." She went to the writing desk, returning to distribute paper, ink pots, and quills. "Why don't we all try?" She rejoined him on the sofa, quill in hand. "Can you give us one as an example?"

Oh, dear God. His reputation for rhyming was based on risqué poems and a little boy's naiveté. Oliver would find this hysterical. Given Jasper's muffled laughter, he did as well.

"Let's see." Richard searched his memory for a limerick that didn't mention scandalous topics, but nothing came of it. Closing his eyes, he pieced the simplest of words together.

"Men scour the *ton* for a girl,
A lass that is all silk and pearls.
You may call me a fool,
But linen and wool
Do more to set my head awhirl."

"Well done." Jasper lifted his glass, a smirk on his face. "I wondered how you'd accomplish that."

"How clever," Amelia said as she squeezed his hand. "You really are quite talented." Her blue eyes widened, drawing him to the brink of the sea, but then shifted before he could fall in. "Everyone, let's take fifteen minutes and see who can craft the best rhymes."

The guests spread across the room in search of writing surfaces. For the next quarter of an hour, everyone else's quills scratched over paper while Richard hoped good natures and good manners would prevail.

"Time," Amelia called. She returned to the sofa, fluttering the page to dry the ink. "Who wants to be first?"

"May I?" Margaret asked.

"Certainly." Amelia's curls bounced as she nodded, her smile bright. Her joy made him hope that much harder for success.

Margaret cleared her throat.

"Their once was a lady in feathers,
Who thought that they made her much better.
Until her friends did harangue
To shed her meringue;
She's glad that they all came together."

She finished to mild applause, her smile lighting her face. Richard recalled how she'd arrived, just two days earlier, with her nose in the air and trying too hard to fit in. What a difference this party had made.

"That was lovely, Margaret, and so kind of you," Amelia said.

"Who's next?"

Charles Grayson cleared his throat. "Me, I think." He drew a deep breath and began.

"There once was a lass who could sing.
As well as a bird on the wing,
And a man with a fiddle
Who wrote a poor riddle,
And couldn't find a proper ending."

The applause were heartier, and the ladies' gasps of disappointment brought good-natured teasing from the gentlemen. No one needed to suggest the correct rhyme. It only took one look at the blushing couple to realize the *ring* was implied.

"I'll claim hostess's right and go next," Amelia said. Rather than staying seated, she went to the liquor shelf across the way and lifted a familiar bottle. The pride on her face was a secret she shared only with Richard.

"There once was a bottle from Brewer.
Who said 'I have heard the best rumor.'
That I sit on a shelf,
Which I've built for myself,
In the hopes it will make me much smoother."

"Well done, well done," Jasper rumbled as he applauded. "Your tenant has a fine champion."

"I learned that lesson from Father," Amelia said as she reclaimed her seat.

Richard took her hand and squeezed her trembling fingers. "I am very proud of you," he whispered. It was the truth. That rhyme was as close as she'd come to admitting who she really was, what she did when they weren't around, and how good she was at it. The men had been commenting on those spirits throughout the party.

He also couldn't help comparing. His limerick had been of her, but hers had been of whiskey. Across from them sat a couple truly and honestly in love, separated only by custom and permission. He and Amelia were bound by business, by contract.

Soon they'd be separated by an ocean.

"Annabel next," Amelia cheered, clapping.

The other woman stood and curtsied to her hostess, a wicked glint in her eye. Richard braced himself. It was always the quiet ones who caused the most trouble.

"There once was a man with a daughter,
Whom he led like a lamb to the slaughter.
And though she did bleat,
He swore she was sweet,
But pity the young lad who caught her."

After a moment of stunned silence, the ladies leapt to their feet in wild applause. "Huzzah, huzzah. Well done. Well done."

"Indeed," Richard said as he tipped his head in a bow. "Rhyming *and* clever. Well done, Miss Pearce. You've captured the spirit exactly."

"There was a young lady who teased," Raymond shouted over the din. The group looked to him, their smiles fading, their eyes wary. Like animals sensing a storm or a forest fire.

"And she did it with beautiful ease." He swayed on his feet and gripped the mantel for balance.

"But I'll give some advice,
She'll discover the price.
Of doing whatever she pleased."

"Damn him," Richard muttered. He pushed up from the sofa, but Amelia pulled him back to his seat.

"Leave it," she whispered. "No one has any idea of yesterday, and he didn't mention me by name. Let it pass and they will as well."

Jasper shot him a glance and nodded. Richard responded in kind, making a silent agreement that this one trespass would be allowed. Raymond had reached the end of his lead.

"Mine seems appropriate here," Fiona said, avoiding her cousin's restraining hand.

"The was a young man on a horse,
Who was handsome and dashing, of course.

And though he did try,

His plans went awry,

Because love is not something you force."

Amelia sputtered into a cough, poorly concealing her laugh. The others took her cue, smirking behind their hands. Except for Fiona, who looked Raymond square in the eye. Richard had the wild urge to throw himself in front of her.

"There was a young woman named Allen." Raymond's eyes narrowed.

"Who had a particular talent.

She lifted her skirt."

Jasper lunged for Raymond, pushing Fiona behind him.

"Her knees in the dirt," Raymond continued.

Richard reached him, grasped his other arm, and joined Jasper in pushing him toward the door.

Raymond twisted against their hold, and shouted over his shoulder. "And all of the men with her time spent."

They forced him into the hall and Richard shut the door, but not before a sea of gasps rushed after them. A lone sob echoed.

"She can serve it up, but she certainly can't take it," Raymond slurred. "But, come to think of it—"

Jasper jabbed his elbow backward, much like a piston in an engine, and Raymond became dead weight. Richard had never been so happy to drag a drunk to a chair, and the happiness mounted when he saw Raymond's bloody face and swelling nose.

"He won't remember how that happened," he said. "I should have stopped Amelia when she suggested that game."

"There is no easy way to tell your betrothed anything in public," Jasper sighed. "Which is what makes that state so bothersome. At least it was better than being blindfolded." He pulled the bell by the stairs. "And he will damn well remember it because I'll be writing to his grandfather. If Fiona's rooms in London aren't filled with flowers within the week, there will be hell to pay."

Simms practically skidded to a stop at the base of the stairs.

"Do we need a doctor, Your Lordship?"

Jasper looked to him and then to Richard. "Simms, please take Mr. Ferrand to see his lordship. Then fetch Mr. Raymond's valet and driver. He's leaving."

"You'd best alert everyone below stairs, Simms," Richard said as he followed the butler up the stairs and around the balustrade. "I believe the party will be ending."

"Thank God for small favors," the butler muttered before he knocked on the door and announced Richard's arrival.

Richard entered a dainty sitting room, dominated by a large chaise lounge under the window. Amelia's mother stood beside the lounge, smoothing her skirts while Augustus wrestled with a pillow stuffed behind his back.

Richard fixed his gaze on a safe, empty corner. "I'm sorry to disturb—"

"Don't look so embarrassed." Augustus chuckled. "After luncheon naps are the best way to waste a rainy day. Is something amiss downstairs?"

Richard gave them the main points of the afternoon, and rushed to help Marian out the door so she could see to the young ladies.

"She'll tear a strip off Raymond's hide before he leaves," Augustus said. "Jasper's with him now?"

Richard nodded. "And his valet's been directed to pack. He may be gone from the house before she can reach him."

"I hope so for his sake. He was her favorite in the suitor race, and she doesn't take well to being disappointed." He swept back the coverlet and stood, using the back of the chaise for balance. "Pull the bell, would you? I'll want to send everyone else on their way personally."

Richard did as he asked and then kept on a path toward the door. It stung that Amelia's mother preferred Raymond to him. "I'll see what else I can do."

He emerged from the sitting room into a completely different house. The halls were full of maids and valets rushing from room to room. Chaperones were flying up and down the stairs like great ravens. The downstairs door was open, and Jasper was half-dragging Ethan Raymond from the house.

Richard brushed past the younger man's valet, who was babbling a string of apologies to anyone who would listen, and helped shove the unconscious scoundrel into his coach. A heedless Raymond lay sprawled, halfway on the floor.

Together, he and Jasper watched as the coach leapt to a start and sped away.

"Well, I'm certainly glad he's not marrying Amelia," Jasper drawled in his lazy way. And then he broke into an Augustus-like laugh.

Richard joined him.

They were still laughing when they returned to the drawing room, and every lady there turned to give them a horrified stare. All except Miss Gerard, who was locked in a quiet conversation with Charles Grayson. Jasper went to comfort a stricken Fiona.

Amelia left her guest's side and folded herself into Richard's arms. "This is all my fault," she whispered against his chest.

"It is not," Richard murmured as he kissed her forehead. "He should have had more sense. Even Fiona knew to behave—"

"He was drunk, Richard. He didn't know what he was doing because he'd been drinking whiskey. *My* whiskey. If this is what comes from it, then maybe I should let Drake take an axe to it after all."

He led her to a quiet corner and backed away enough to see her clearly. She'd been crying. Over some spoiled bastard who retreated to the bottle when he hadn't gotten his way.

"Amelia, you know alcohol in excess gets people drunk."

"Of course I do, but I didn't know it makes people hateful." She looked past him, her lips trembling. "I wanted to stop Fiona teasing me, but I never wanted her to be hurt like that."

She was an amazing young woman, facing her tormentors one moment and then worrying she'd wronged them the next. If he let himself, he could fall in love with her.

Richard's heart stuttered in his chest. She'd made it clear, more than once, that theirs was a business arrangement. She enjoyed kissing him, but she didn't want to marry. She didn't want to live anywhere but here, where she could have success on her own terms. His job was to keep anyone from endangering that. Including him.

"I want you to hear what I'm saying." He waited until she focused on him. "Being drunk does not make people anything other than what they really are. If they're happy, they grow exuberant. Sad people become morose. And angry people…"

"Grow hateful?" she whispered. "Are you certain?"

If she only knew how hateful Oliver had been before Julia had set him straight, or how morose he and Oliver got every year on the date of her death. They'd banned alcohol from the house for so many years that he still went out when he wanted a drink. "I am. Raymond was angry before he ever picked up a bottle. You saw that yesterday." The memory made him wish he'd gotten a lick in before Jasper had delivered punishment. "And if you give up your goals because of him, he wins, Amelia."

She nodded once, then again, stronger. "Thank you, Richard. I am so glad you were here to deal with the awful parts." She frowned, and he stopped himself from running his finger between her brows to smooth the lines. "Though I don't quite understand all of it," she continued. "The lifting the skirts thing is fairly obvious, but the dirty knees—what on earth does that have to do with anything?"

Laughter gurgled in his throat, only to be dammed by her earnest stare. No woman who made whiskey for a living, dressed down earls-to-be like a fish wife, and kissed a man until he was dizzy could be that innocent. Except that she was. She was supposed to be. He'd spent too much time in clubs and brothels, where the women knew every trick. Some had even taught him a few.

Richard banished the images from his mind, because it wasn't a prostitute he wanted on her knees in front of him. It wasn't a courtesan he wanted in his bed.

"Richard?" she asked, her frown deepening.

"I'll explain it to you later." It was an automatic answer, one he often gave Simon when he couldn't stop what he was doing. Most of the time, the boy forgot his question. Richard hoped to bloody hell Amelia forgot this one, because he couldn't explain it to her.

And he didn't want another man doing it.

Ever.

CHAPTER FOURTEEN

THE MANOR WAS quiet again. Amelia paused at the top of the stairs, soaking in the morning light made that much warmer and brighter after yesterday. No more croquet or shooting, no more wondering what to wear. She didn't have to worry about entering a room and coming face-to-face with someone she wished would disappear.

Fiona Allen sprung to mind, and Amelia's cheeks heated. After the way Ethan had treated Fiona, perhaps she deserved some mercy.

The sun shifted just enough to gild the oak rails and spark off the highly polished baluster. As a child, she'd pretended the wood was gold and pillars of diamonds, and that she was leading her comrades in storming the castle to claim its treasure.

Her friends then had been as imaginary as the treasure. Now she knew the pleasure of having had real friends here. She wouldn't miss the fuss of hosting a house party, but she'd miss chatting with Annabel over breakfast or helping Margaret with her hair. She'd even miss Jasper and his odd sense of humor.

And Richard.

"Good morning, miss." Simms was at the bottom of the stairs, bearing a tray with Mother's favorite tea service. Father had found it in Austria for their anniversary. "Your parents are breakfasting in the conservatory. Miss Graves is with them."

"Thank you, Simms." She finished her descent and joined him on his walk through the house. "And thank you for taking fine care of our guests over the last few days. They were a handful."

"Thank you, miss. I'll pass that to the others as well." The old butler tilted his head toward her. "We're glad to have things return to normal, though the younger staff were looking forward to the farewell ball."

Amelia had to admit she'd been looking forward to it as well. She enjoyed everything about a ball—the colors, the music, the refreshments. Mostly she enjoyed dancing. She'd been looking forward to doing it with Richard.

The conservatory was Mother's space in the house, just as it had been her first mother's. Amelia always wondered if it was Marian's love of flowers that had first attracted her father, who hadn't been able to walk in the garden for months after his first wife's death. Now he sat surrounded by plants collected over years of travel, some of them too delicate for English weather and others recently brought inside for the winter. Those still smelled of wet earth. There were likely some very confused worms in the soil.

The row of windows looked out over a terrace of chrysanthemums and lilies, ringed by roses and lilacs with rain-heavy heads. The space had been her mother's last addition to the garden before her death. Amelia had helped plant everything except the roses because her mother was worried over the thorns, but they'd sung nursery rhymes while the prickly shrubs had gone into the ground.

Her stepmother had won Amelia's undying affection for her care of a garden she hadn't planted. That affection had influenced almost every choice Amelia had made since she'd come of age, and it now sparked her guilt over the ruined house party. "Mother—"

"Amelia, I really must apologize," Mother said. "Had I known what Mr. Raymond was capable of, I never would have encouraged you."

"I don't believe any of us suspected," Amelia said. "He certainly displayed none of those traits in London."

"Nor when he visited," agreed Mother. "Perhaps he was simply disappointed."

"That may be," Father said as he buttered a scone, "but life is full of disappointments. Earl or not, I'd prefer not to saddle Amelia with a childish husband, nor settle her funds on a drunkard."

Mother nodded as she sipped her tea. "I must say, I was quite impressed with how well Jasper and Richard managed the situation."

Amelia had been as well. They and Simms had worked efficiently to have all the guests in their carriages with hampers of food for the drive back to London. Except for Charles Grayson, who had escorted Margaret to her father's estate.

"Is your heart still set on Richard, my girl?" Father asked, smiling.

A thrill went through her, a delicious sensation reminiscent of their kisses. The memory of Richard's fresh, clean scent overpowered the transplanted bougainvillea hulking in the corner, and his sweet, sinful taste replaced the bite from her tea. She didn't need to close her eyes to recall his face. His dazed, hungry gaze wasn't her favorite, though. It was his determined stare from yesterday as he lectured her to keep to her mission.

And if you give up your goals because of him…

The taste of tea returned a moment before the smell of mud. Amelia set her cup in her saucer before sliding her fork under a bite of eggs. "I am." She curved her lips in a smile. "Even more so."

He was the perfect partner for her. Not husband. Partner.

Just as she was for him. Even Ethan had taken a case of wine back to London, though he might have been influenced more by keeping up with Jasper, and he just might drink it all himself. Perhaps Richard could take her whiskey to Quebec. That would be a good consolation prize. It would be lovely to think of him drinking it when he was at home, and maybe he would write and ask for more, or come visit and restock. He would have to return to France at some point, wouldn't he?

And perhaps, Amelia, he'll find a nice French girl and bring his wife and their dozen children to play with their cousins. You'll be the old maid dinner guest. And she would not feel bad about that. At all.

"I'll go over today and talk with him," Father said. "And your mother and I were discussing a party to celebrate."

Not another one. And not one to celebrate something that wasn't intended to be real in the first place. It was already difficult to stay unattached. "Are you certain that's wise after yesterday?"

"Just a dinner with his family and a few of our neighbors," Mother said. "We aren't embarrassed by him, and we want our neighbors to know that. We especially want the duke and duchess to know that we are happy to be connecting our families."

They weren't, though, and there was no way to escape in any direction. Amelia's tears had as much to do with that as with her parents' ability to accept Richard simply because of who he was, not how he was born. "Thank you," she said as she dabbed her eyes.

"If I may?" Graves said. "This seems to be the best time for me to begin searching for a new position."

"No," Amelia blurted. It was a knee-jerk reaction. Graves had been in the household, in her life, since before she'd gone off to school. For a girl who had been used to entertaining herself, Graves had been a Godsend. Though the chaperone's presence had chafed at times, Amelia had seen the other side of the coin in Fiona Allen. "I can't do this without you."

"You most certainly can." Graves's warm smile matched the hand she put over Amelia's. "You are an almost married woman now, and you and your betrothed don't need shadow. It's time for me to find another girl."

Which set Amelia to weeping again. "Well, you'll get an excellent reference from us." A horrible thought hit her, and she spun to face her father. "She will, won't she? The house party shouldn't affect her. She raised me to be better. This was all my fault."

Father patted her other hand. "I believe it was Mr. Raymond's fault, dear." He focused across the table. "You will have a glowing reference, Lillian. What's more, we will all be looking for a family nearby who needs you as much as Amelia and I did when you arrived. You will be missed."

Amelia squeezed his hand. Not long ago, his fingers had been thick and strong. Now, though the strength was still here, she could feel the knobs of his knuckles. Despite the sun through the windows, he was pale and there was a knitted throw across his lap.

"And you must come back for the wedding," Mother said to Graves. "If you are gone, that is."

"Of course she'll have another situation by then," Father decreed, much like his former self. "Cream always rises to the top."

The freedom Amelia had schemed for was within reach. No more shadow. No more secretive rides in the dark of night. Even when her engagement ended, Graves would already have a new situation. She wouldn't return. Mother would be busy with Father, which would limit trips to London. That, in turn, would lessen the need for another chaperone. Though, really, who would want to chaperone a supposedly broken-hearted, shelf-sitting, young lady?

Amelia's world was about to change. And it made her want to hide under her bed.

RICHARD SWIPED THE back of his gloved hand across his brow, dashing sweat away before it dripped into his eyes. Sawdust drifted from his forearm and his work shirt peeled from his shoulders. It had been years since he'd worked like this.

And he loved it.

"If you've finished preening," Oliver said. His brown hair was darker at the ends where it stuck to his forehead and temples, and a wide smile spread over his damp face.

Richard hefted his end of the freshly hewn log into the wagon and walked it backward until his heels bumped against the stack already waiting. "Careful, I'd *hate* to drop this on your foot." He balanced the log on its companions and kept a steady hand on its rough head.

"Thea wouldn't know whether to punch you for damaging me or hug you for making me stay home." The last words came through a grunt as he shoved from the bottom. "Did you save this bloody great beast for me on purpose?"

Bark splintered and flew, and Richard leaned away to avoid being stuck in the eye. "It's smaller than the ones we began with. Perhaps your age is showing."

The log slotted into the crease on the pile, completing the second to last row in the pyramid. Richard gave the structure a shove and a hearty kick to ensure it was stable and then leapt to the ground. The landing jarred even his teeth. Perhaps age… "But then maybe it's just been a difficult few days." He slapped Oliver's sweaty shoulder. "You're up next."

With Oliver serving as guide in the wagon, Richard pushed against the next log's weight, his boots sliding on the gravel and his shoulders aching with the strain. He relaxed only when it dropped into place with a deceptively soft thud and didn't send the ones below it into a slide.

Oliver leapt from the wagon, bouncing on his feet as he landed. He'd done the same almost ten years ago when they'd cut their first load of timber. "How difficult could a party have been?"

Richard had a headache, which was either from the hangover or from the sudden release of tension. "You know what *ton* people are like." He'd never been so glad to see the backs of carriages as they'd crossed under Oakdale's gates.

"I do," Oliver said. "But I also remember what you said when

I harassed you about your nights in clubs. *You have to meet people where they are.* I actually repeat that every time I enter the chamber at lords or a ballroom during the Season. It's my job." He shrugged and gave a lopsided grin. "One of them anyway. We'd best get back or the lads will have nothing to saw."

Given that two heavily loaded wagons had already rocked and rumbled out of the forest, the saws could likely run for days. Oliver hated to be idle. It was a trait Richard shared, which was one thing that had been so trying about helping Amelia over the past few days.

"How did she cope with the abrupt end to the house party?" Oliver asked as they lurched toward the turnaround, the harnesses straining over the draft team's broad backs.

"She's been burning the wick at both ends, so I believe she's glad it's over," Richard said.

"I'm guessing she wasn't happy with the interruption they brought in the first place, given that she's building up her stock." Oliver maneuvered the team into the turn while Richard kept a wary eye on their cargo. He didn't know if he had the energy to reload the wagon.

It was a relief to talk about Amelia's business rather than their supposed romantic connection. "It will do her good to return to regular hours." He wouldn't have to worry over her haring about in the dark or, more dangerous, accompanying her. Nights alone in the shadows were far too tempting.

"And Fletcher can go back to London," Richard continued. He liked the man, but Amelia's comment about him taking an axe to her barrels rankled.

"They do spend a great deal of time together," Oliver said. "But I never expected you to be jealous."

"I'm not jealous." At least he hadn't been until now.

And that was the largest part of Richard's headache. He kept forgetting that he was helping her, just like Drake. Though Drake was getting paid while Richard was getting insomnia. All he could do last night was stare at the ceiling and remember how she'd felt in his arms, how she'd run to him for comfort. "I just think it would be good for her to get back to normal."

Never mind that her normal would not include him for long.

"Until you two leave for Quebec."

Oliver's flat statement reminded Richard of his purpose. "Of course. Assuming that her parents agree." After yesterday's debacle, that was no longer certain.

"I believe that's why Augustus is here." Oliver pointed ahead and to their right, where a barouche sat waiting.

Richard's heart clogged his throat, pounding so that it echoed. It heightened everything, the salty taste of his lips and the sweat drying on his clothes, stiffening the coarse linen. His boots were too heavy, and the sun was too hot on his bare head. The nagging itch crawling across his skin warned that he had sawdust *everywhere*.

If they were going to discuss Amelia, they should do it in a library over a drink, when he could look like a gentleman. They shouldn't be on the side of the road.

The wagon drew even with the barouche, and Augustus lifted his hat—the tam he'd worn when watching archery—and the wind lifted his thin hair. "The duchess told me I'd find you two out here." He was in his shooting jacket, and his cravat had been done in a simple loop. "It's a fine day for it."

Being outside and around working men, it was easy to see how pale the older man was, how his jacket hung slack on his shoulders. In contrast to Richard and Oliver's sweat-soaked state, Augustus had a lap quilt draped across his knees. He was fading in increments, and Amelia had to watch from the sidelines.

It would be a slow process—until it wasn't. But the lead-up to death would have allowed Augustus time to settle his daughter's marriage to Ethan Raymond. He might have even lived to see her married and made miserable by a spoiled *ton* layabout who had no idea of the gift he'd been granted.

Better the man have no son-in-law than one like that.

Richard removed his splinter and dirt encrusted work glove

and extended his hand. "Good afternoon, sir. Is everything well?" An arrow of worry struck a nerve. "Is Amelia—"

"She's fine, lad," Augustus said. "Out for a ride. Though it does my soul good to know she's your first worry. Speaks well of a husband."

His quirked brows called attention to the word as much as his sly smile. Richard was dumbstruck. A baron had given him, a half-debauched tradesman covered in sweat and grime, permission to marry his beloved daughter.

Oliver's elbow in his ribs reminded him to speak up. "Thank you, Augustus. It's an honor."

"For us as well." He looked to him and then Oliver. "We plan to celebrate with a dinner at the house. Tomorrow evening, I think. Just us and a few neighbors."

They'd all be celebrating a lie. "Are you certain? With everything from yesterday?" Richard asked. "We will be no less engaged."

"We won't hear of anything less," Augustus said. "It seems we still have a great deal of food laid in on account of the ball-that-wasn't, and it can't go to waste." With that, he thumped his cane on the carriage floor. The barouche rolled forward. "Come early, both of you. We'll review the marriage contracts."

Richard sat, staring at his grubby boots. He couldn't help but wonder if Amelia had inherited her negotiation skills from her father, or what Augustus would say if they wrote an addendum focused on the distillery. He could imagine her pacing outside the library, itching to impose her own terms, just like when she'd bowled him over the first time they'd discussed a partnership.

Then, he'd been too stunned to answer. Now? Now, he didn't care. Whatever Augustus gave him would be hers. It could go to their...

Damn it all to bloody hell. He'd done it again.

"Congratulations," Oliver said. "She's the perfect match for you."

"Mm-hmm." Richard stared at his boots. She was perfect if

for no other reason than she didn't want to marry any more than he did. Or had. Or would have.

This was getting far too confusing.

The wagon lurched forward, rocking him forward and back, leaving him dizzy. The field grass muffled the creaky wheels. Richard didn't need to look behind them to know they'd left a steady path from where he had been toward where he was going.

"Did you hear anything I said?" Oliver asked, laughing.

"No." He'd been busy thinking about contracts he couldn't sign without lying and about children he and Amelia wouldn't have.

"Didn't think so," Oliver sighed. "Have you thought about how to handle everything here?" He stared over the backs of the team. "With Augustus's health, he might go while you're sailing."

"Die, Oliver." It was annoying, at times, that Oliver refused to acknowledge death. It was also embarrassing that Richard's throat closed over the word. He liked his fake father-in-law-to-be. More than that, though, he knew it would gut Amelia, and that she would have to face it alone. She damn sure wouldn't be sailing to Quebec with him.

"We've discussed taking our wedding trip to France." Well, he and Augustus had discussed it. Amelia had seemed excited when he'd mentioned it later—until she'd remembered they were pretending.

"You could stay here," Oliver said.

They crested a hill, and the mill lay below them, spread like one of Simon's toys across the carpet in their offices back home. It resembled the mills they owned across the province, but the lack of rugged mountains was a constant reminder they were no longer in Canada. He needed to be in Canada. "I think not."

"Why? Your families are here. Her business. You're my partner in this." He swiped his hand across the valley. "And it's closer to the winery." He kept his eyes on the team and on the road as they navigated the switchbacks that let them descend at a safe angle. "Potter can keep the provincial mills going without us. You said so yourself when you wrote about this trip." They reached the lumberyard, and Oliver slowed the team to a stop. "Stay, Rich. We miss you."

The simple words warmed him through. Being here made him realize how much he'd missed—how much he'd miss in the future. But only part of his family was here, and Amelia's plan didn't work if he didn't leave.

CHAPTER FIFTEEN

AMELIA PUT HER palm flat against her stomach. Past the satin and stays, a giant flock of geese thundered against her ribcage as though she were thwarting their migration.

"You are lovely," Mother said as she stared over Amelia's shoulder and into the mirror. "I am glad you have made your own match, Amelia."

One day soon, Amelia wouldn't feel guilty every time she spoke with her parents. She would be able to ride to her distillery in the daylight without sneaking down the back stairs. She'd be able to work in the same space, and at the same time, as her employees. Today wasn't that day. "I'm proud that you and Father have accepted him."

"Whether the *ton* admits it or not, we all benefit from someone's hard work," Mother said. "And some families are only a few generations from trade themselves." She put a gentle hand on Amelia's shoulder, encouraging her to turn. "But I owe you an explanation. I wanted to improve your standing because I thought it was what your true mother would have done if she were able." Her eyes teared. "I wanted to prove that I had been…"

Oh, hang it all. Amelia had accepted her parents' eventual disappointment when she ended up on the shelf, but she'd never expected it to come if she was actually engaged. It was one of the reasons she'd devised this plan. Besides that, who could be disappointed with Richard? But here Mother was, dabbing her eyes with a handkerchief that was more lace than useful fabric. "You can't still have your heart set on Ethan?"

Mother shook her head, sending her curls bouncing and making her appear younger, though she was closer to Amelia's age than Father's. "Heavens, no. That young man fooled me well, but he will only do it once." She took Amelia's hand in a tight grip. "When I married your father, my mother's only question was to my happiness. And I can see how happy you are with Richard in your life."

"I am." It wasn't a lie. She'd enjoyed her horrible house party because he'd been there to laugh with, and his words of encouragement stuck with her. More than that, he knew her secret and had proved he could be trusted with it. He didn't treat her like she was foolish, and their sales of his wine had added much needed capital to her coffers. But it was all bittersweet.

"I will miss you, dear girl. And I don't know what I'll do without you when…"

The rest of her sentence was lost in her handkerchief, but Amelia knew enough to fill it in. She pulled a chair close and eased Mother into it. Rather than confessing her plan, she knelt without care of her skirts or her aching back. "I will be close by." She cut off her mother's protest. "Richard has mentioned a wedding trip to his winery in France."

"What a kind thing to do." Mother turned to the mirror and blotted her tears. "And you will enjoy that. You've always loved learning about how things are made. Wine will interest you more than lumber, I think."

But not more than whiskey. *Besides that, she's never heard Richard speak about forests and trees.* "Perhaps, but I won't know that if we don't get downstairs."

"Your father should be up in a moment." Mother stood and leaned close to the mirror. "I don't look like I've been crying, do I? It bothers him if I'm weepy. And I would hate for Lady Gerard to gossip that I'm not happy about Richard joining the family."

Amelia suspected any red-rimmed eyes would be counted toward happiness. She put her chin on her mother's shoulder and grinned into the mirror. "Lady Gerard will be far too busy turning every conversation to Margaret and Charles Grayson."

A knock at the door had them both straightening. "Come in."

Father closed the door behind him and stopped, his eyes wide. "Two of the most beautiful ladies in England, under my roof at the same time."

It was the first time he hadn't addressed her as a *young* lady. Amelia's eyes stung. "And the most dashing man."

His laugh boomed against the ceiling as he strode to them, his arms outstretched. She walked into his embrace. This was her father of old, strong and commanding attention, but she knew he'd rested most of the afternoon in preparation for tonight.

"You wouldn't say that if you saw the man waiting for you downstairs." His voice rumbled through her ear and warmed her heart as much as his arms warmed her suddenly cold body. He backed away much too quickly. "And I'll get an awful scolding if I muss your dress."

He cleared his throat and offered a long, wide jewelry box, its velvet cover as black as a moonless night. It had been in his safe for as long as Amelia could remember, and she'd heard the history of its contents all her life. Her tears slipped free.

"None of that," Father blustered. "Your mother would have wanted you to have them tonight." He opened the case, revealing an oval sapphire set in the middle of a double strand of lustrous pearls. The companion earrings were sapphire bobs with pearl drops. He'd bought them as a wedding gift for her mother because the gems matched her eyes.

Father motioned for her to turn so she could watch him slip the pearls around her neck. The sapphire rested just below the base of her throat and was cool against her fingers.

"It's lovely, Father." Amelia searched for a memory of her mother wearing these, but the only image she could grasp was the portrait that hung in her hallway. Her true mother had been painted in her garden, in a simple day dress, so there hadn't been a need for jewels.

The earrings were heavier than she'd expected, but they were too pretty to leave behind. The sapphires caught the light when she moved her head. The pearls, cool at first, warmed against her skin. The lady in the mirror had little in common with the child who'd grown up in this room or the distiller who shoved her work clothes under the bed.

"Enough, ladies." Father offered Amelia his arm. "Let's go celebrate an engagement."

Amelia stopped at the door long enough to kiss Mother's cheek. "You have nothing to prove. Who I am is a reflection of both the women who raised me."

Father patted her hand as they waited a moment for composure. "She's going to be weepy all evening, I'm afraid."

Mother finally joined them and took Father's other arm. Then the three of them walked down the hall, past the portrait of the angel in the garden who'd watched over Amelia since she was ten years old, and to the top of the stairs.

Below them, the hall was full of friends and neighbors. Richard stood close to Oliver and Thea, nearest the stairs. He was in the same tailcoat he'd worn the night they'd announced their fake engagement and started down this road. Every man in London wore a tailcoat, but Richard's wavy mop of hair gave him an irreverent air, and his white waistcoat and shirt called attention to his broad chest and his height. His cravat, simply looped and pinned, contrasted with his complexion. Though he was clean-shaven, it wasn't difficult to recall the stubble on his jaw or how it felt against her fingers.

It didn't take a trade to set him miles apart from any other man she knew.

He was looking up at her like she was the cake Cook had hidden for dessert. Torn between flying down the stairs into his arms and running back to her room and hiding in the closet until everyone went home, Amelia hesitated. She was safe here, on her father's arm. If time could stop here, she'd be happy.

"We should have hired an orchestra," Father whispered. "Or come down sooner. This is like a Quaker wedding."

"We're a bit too colorful for Quakers," Mother giggled. "And the orchestra will be here for the wedding party."

Amelia's feet twitched on the stairs, pushing her to take one step forward, then another. Her father let her go.

Richard stepped up to reach her. "You are stunning," he whispered. His lips brushed her knuckles, his warm breath soaking through her gloves, but his eyes stayed on hers. And then he winked.

Her laugh bubbled up like fermented mash. She clasped his hand and finished her descent so they could greet their guests. Mingling amongst them were the family's staff in their best livery. The women's aprons were so starched Amelia imagined they'd shatter at the briefest collision. Simms hovered on the edge of the room like a commanding general surveying the battlefield, flanked by footmen he could send into the fray.

Richard tucked her hand into his elbow. His arm was thick and solid. "Shall we?"

Smiling up at him was easy to do. "Let's."

"How do you do this?" Richard asked Oliver.

"Propose?" His brother-in-law grinned. "Didn't you watch me do it once?

"Not that." Richard swept his half-full glass across the drawing room. "This."

Going from the forest to a formal dinner had made for a long, disorienting day. By rights, he should be exhausted. Instead, Richard was the odd sort of alert that only came from being on his feet too long and being fed rich food and alcohol. He kept imagining there was sawdust on his shoes or leaves in his hair.

"It's jarring, sometimes a little boring, but you get used to it."

Time was, Oliver had dreaded events like this to the point of being surly. Julia had rationalized that he was restless, driven to prove himself to the people he'd left behind. She'd be insufferable if she could see how right she'd been.

"It's just like home, Rich. We've done this before." Oliver put a hand on his shoulder. "The clothes are just stiffer, and no one discusses business outright." With that, he turned so he and Thea could speak to a neighbor whose name Richard couldn't recall.

Which was the issue. Everyone's faces and names had blended together. Charles Grayson was across the room with the Gerard family, nodding as he listened to Mr. Gerard who, by all accounts, was to be his father-in-law. But he glanced Richard's way and rolled his eyes before lifting his glass in a silent salute.

Richard returned the toast, priding himself on his choice of family.

His eyes found Amelia, as they'd done all evening. Her dress matched her eyes in some alchemy that only dressmakers knew, and her jewelry caught the light every time she turned, echoing her smile. The pearls were just a shade lighter than her skin, except for her flushed cheeks. She looked every inch the happy bride-to-be.

The ring in his pocket, bumping against his thigh with every step, made him feel very much like an eager groom.

"She's beautiful, isn't she?" Drake asked from behind, his voice as quiet as his approach had been.

No matter how glad Richard was to see a friendly face, the other man's stealth unnerved him. So did his appraisal. "The world is full of lovely faces, Fletcher. That's not what makes Amelia special."

It wasn't lip service. In a room where everyone was celebrating and not discussing business, Amelia offered his wine to guests with a smile and a nod. Almost all the gentlemen carried a tumbler of her whiskey. Though she moved through the room on her father's arm, speaking with people who had known her all her life, Richard recognized the stiff posture from a hard day. "She was at the distillery today?"

"The wheat was ready to mash," Drake said. "And before you say anything, I've told her to have the boys do it for her, but she insists. It's like trying to remove a cook from a kitchen."

Richard had watched her sample his wine, seen her tongue trace flavors across her lips. Where he only found alcoholic fruit, she'd found something that had drawn out a secret smile. Instead of asking her, he'd gone in search of it when kissing her. Now he couldn't drink it without tasting her instead. "What flavors did she select?"

"Apples, of course, since she pressed me to buy a cartload. And sharon fruit. Florence, our newest clerk, brought a few to work for sharing and, before I knew it, I was negotiating for bushels of them."

Amelia took great pride in knowing the source of each ingredient, of supporting her father's tenants, of having her product strongly identified with her home. She'd gone to great lengths to ensure it.

"She says you threatened to take an axe to her barrels." Richard looked Fletcher square in the eyes. "That best never happen again."

The other man's mouth flattened to a straight line. "If she bargains her virtue as part of her scheme for freedom, barrels won't be the only thing I take an axe to."

The heat in his words gave Richard pause. He'd had a similar conversation with Oliver years ago, warning him not to break his sister's heart. But it was different. Julia had loved Oliver long before either man had realized it. Amelia had made her intentions and plans clear. "I would not take advantage of this situation."

Fletcher nodded once, short and sharp. "That young lady put her future in my care. Keeping her from making it harder than necessary is a task I take seriously."

Because you are not in her future. Drake didn't have to say the words for Richard to hear them.

"You two are far too serious," Amelia said as she joined them.

The moment she threaded her hand through his elbow and onto his arm, Richard relaxed. The room wasn't so close, and his cravat wasn't so tight. He glanced over his shoulder to where Oliver stood with Thea, recalling him in rooms with Julia in a similar posture.

Damn.

"We were just discussing the finer points of axes," Drake said. His smile widened. Richard imagined it was how he'd looked at Julia. At least he hoped it was, because Fletcher's pride and affection were evident, but it wasn't the same way Oliver had looked at Julia, or the way he looked at Thea, which was different still.

"No talk of axes at a party," Amelia scolded gently.

"Certainly," Drake replied before lowering his head and his voice. "Something has arisen, and I have to return to London."

She nodded. "I'll see you there then."

Richard looked between them. "You're going to London?"

"My investors have a quarterly meeting in a few weeks." Amelia squeezed his arm. "Our guests are leaving. Please come help me say goodbye."

Not for the first time this evening, Richard was grateful that the Chitesters had kept the celebration small. Though his face ached from smiling and his mind spun with names, the hall contained only family in short order.

"Shall we do another toast?" Augustus asked. "We seem to have wine remaining."

"Could Amelia and I have a few minutes alone first?" Richard's face heated, and he blamed it on not spending enough time in polite society. It never bothered him to enter a brothel and ask for his favorite hostess, but to stand here surrounded by family was something altogether different.

"How silly of us not to consider that," Marian Chitester said. "The library should be fine."

Avoiding Oliver's and Drake's stares, Richard led Amelia to the library and closed the door.

"Thank goodness that's over," Amelia sighed. "It was good of everyone to come, but this has been a long day."

She twisted her head and neck in a move Richard had done often himself to relieve overtaxed muscles. It wouldn't work unless she'd been hunched over ledgers, which Fletcher had said she wasn't.

"Sit," he said as he urged her toward the chaise lounge. He waited as she did so, admiring how the light gilded her hair. "Which hurts worse, your feet or your back?" As he sat behind her, straddling the lounge, he knew he should pray for feet, but he didn't.

"Back."

Richard chafed his hands together to warm them before lightly touching her shoulders. "Stop me if you get uncomfortable."

She nodded but didn't speak. Her muscles shuddered under his hands.

"Relax, *chéri.*" He laid his fingers along the warm, smooth pearls circling her neck before pressing his thumbs against her spine.

The knobby bones were delicate under her soft skin, but the muscles around them were knotted.

"You should have told me you needed help today." He worked his thumbs out and then down, splaying his fingers wider across her collarbones while trying not to think about how much of her skin was bare.

"I've done this for as long as I have—" Her sentence ended in a groan that tightened every inch of Richard's skin.

He cleared his throat and kept going, easing his touch in the hopes of minimizing her reaction. "I know you have, and I know you like to do it, but you shouldn't be working so hard."

"I'm perfectly capable." She moaned again. "That feels marvelous."

"Shh. If you keep that up, I'll have a room full of angry men." Not to mention how difficult it was going to be for him to walk out of here.

"Why?" She turned her head, pushing another knot against his thumbs, and the pleasure on her face made his mouth water.

This had been a horrible idea, but Richard couldn't make himself stop. "I'll explain it later," he mumbled as he shifted away from the heat of the fire and changed the direction of the massage, hoping her neck would make him stop thinking about how easy it would be to skim her dress from her shoulders.

He should have known better. A woman's nape was one of his favorite spots. The skin there was a cross between satin and velvet, always warm.

"I know you're capable, Amelia, but let me do the shoveling and heavy lifting, please."

"Are you doing this to get me to agree?" She dropped her head with another sigh, this one quieter. She'd bitten her lip to keep it contained.

It didn't matter to his body, which had hardened to the point of pain. "No. It's not to get my own way." He simply couldn't resist touching her. His thumb found the hollow at the base of her skull and his fingers slid into her hair. He gentled his touch to keep from mussing it. "But I want to help you."

"But when you go—"

He didn't want to think about that. He leaned forward to reach into his pocket, bringing his nose near her ear. She smelled of flowers and fruit, and he filled his lungs with it. "Let me do it while I'm here," he whispered.

She turned to him wide-eyed and nodded mutely. Richard pressed a soft kiss to her lips and slid one hand to her shoulder while the other pressed the box into her hands. "Thank you."

She eyed the box before giving him a cheeky grin. "Will you give me presents every time I agree with you?"

"This time is special," Richard said. He nudged her with his torso, meaning to encourage her. Instead, it sent a domino reaction down his body. "Open it."

The box fell open, and her gasp made him swell with pride.

Richard had intended on a simple ring, but the only jeweler in Thetford happened to have a small client list and a good supply of gems, thanks to a cousin who had recently gone out of business. The ring consisted of a small sapphire circled by blue topaz rounds and then surrounded by narrow slivers of yellow topaz and garnets.

"It's lovely."

He took it from the box and slid it over her finger. It was slightly too big, but they could have it resized. Otherwise, it was perfect.

"You didn't need to do this," she whispered.

He shifted so that his thumb could stroke her jaw, encouraging her to look at him. "I wanted to."

Her mouth met his and opened easily to give him access to her sweet, hot tongue. He tempted it to follow his, taught her how to kiss him, growled when her fingers tangled in his hair. Her silk covered breast filled his hand, the peak pebbled against his palm. He slid his thumb across it, and reveled at the way she arched, silently begging for more. He gave it, rolling the nub between his index finger and thumb and claiming her mouth to muffle her sigh.

He kissed her until she needed air and then kept going, shifting to her jaw, then her neck, and finally her shoulder. The soft swell of her breast against his fingertips brought him crashing back to earth.

Richard straightened as much as he dared and waited for her eyes to refocus. "That shouldn't have happened, Amelia. I'm so—"

She stayed pliant in his arms for an extra moment before sitting, her spine curved in a languorous arc that tempted his fingers and mouth. Her lashes hung low over her eyes, and her lips were swollen. "Don't you dare say you're sorry unless you really are."

He wasn't. "I lost myself in the moment," he whispered.

"So did I." She rested her forehead against his temple before kissing his cheek. "We'll do better tomorrow."

I publish the banns of marriage between Richard Pierre Ferrand of this parish, via Quebec, Canada and Rosnay, France and Amelia Christine Chitester, daughter of Baron Kilverstone, of this parish. If any know cause or just impediment why these two persons should not be joined together in Holy matrimony, ye are to declare it. This is the first time of asking.

CHAPTER SIXTEEN

AMELIA WAS AWAKE to see the sunrise, which would have been ideal if she'd slept at all.

Instead, she'd tossed on a bed made from rocks until the sheets were tangled around her legs, which left her cold. When she straightened them and covered, she was warm, but when she closed her eyes, she was back in the library with Richard's arms around her, his lips on her skin. Just thinking of it had made her nipples harden, which had restarted the cycle.

The sun made the fog go from white to silver. "Time to get started," Amelia whispered, her words making mist on the window. She turned toward the bed and banged her ring on the edge of her dressing table.

"Drat." She lifted it to the sunlight and smiled at the prisms it cast over the curtains and the wall. It hadn't been damaged, which was a relief, but it reminded her to leave it behind. It was loose, and she didn't want to lose it on her ride or in the mash. Her finger already felt odd without it.

She shrugged into a topcoat and slipped down the back stairs, ignored by the staff getting started with their day. Outside, the chickens huddled in a feathery pack, clucking unhappily about the temperature. The newest litter of kittens stared shyly from behind a miserly stack of hay.

The stable was warmer, but wisps of steam rose from Molly's

back as she waited, and her breath came out in giant puffs. It was easy to imagine that she had created the fog with her impatience to be off for the day.

The chill prodded Amelia to hurry to the distillery, but hurrying made the air bite harder. By the time she arrived, her fingers were stiff.

She lifted Molly's saddle, wincing as her back twinged. Just like that, she was in the library again with Richard's fingers on her bare skin. Heat poured through her, pooling in mysterious places so that Amelia was surprised steam wasn't rising from her coat.

After seeing to her horse, Amelia hurried into the distillery, ignoring the temptation of the barrel room in favor of the bottling room stacked with crates of wine. A movement to her left pulled her up short. "Hello?"

The young girl spun on her stool, her dark braids flying behind her and her eyes large in her freckled face. Her palm was flat against her plain white blouse. "Oh!" Ledgers lay open behind her.

"Florence?" Amelia hoped she was right. Otherwise, she was facing a burglar—or a spy—with nothing but her straw hat for defense.

"Yes, Miss Chitester." She hopped to the floor and dropped a quick curtsey. "May I help you? Mr. Fletcher said you might stop by seeing as you're Mr. Brewer's landlord."

"Yes, er, do you mind if I walk through? I've not been here since Mr. Brewer began operations in earnest."

"Certainly. I'll go with you." The young lady held open the door to the still room. Her clothes were tidy and well-tailored, but there were spots where the pattern had worn almost white. If she thought anything of Amelia's more casual clothes, she didn't show it.

"Is Mr. Brewer a good employer?" Amelia asked as they walked through a room which she could navigate blindfolded. "Does he require you to be at work this early?"

This damned ruse was trying.

"Yes, miss. Though he keeps odd hours. We come in to work, and it's obvious someone's been here in the night," Florence whispered as though she was in church. "But he pays us well and the building is always warm when it's supposed to be." She leaned in. "Mr. Fletcher is dreadful scary until you get used to him."

"He is rather like a giant raven." Amelia chuckled. "But why are you here so early? Alone?" The irony of the question was not lost on her.

"I wanted to review my figures," Florence said. "A great deal of the wine has been sold very quickly, and Mr. Fletcher says the percentages are important to Mr. Brewer. Plus, I worry after Caspar up here all alone."

The marmalade tabby looked up from his breakfast of roast beef and potatoes. Amelia would swear he smirked.

"Will you have enough for lunch yourself, Florence? Because I'm sure Caspar could find some mice." *If he could waddle away from his dish.*

"He catches plenty, but I'd get tired of eating the same thing every day, wouldn't you?" Florence shrugged. "And Mother sends me extra since I go to work before school." She led them back to the door. "I need to go. Mr. Fletcher says we aren't to leave anyone in here."

Amelia would have to discuss that rule with him. "Of course. Thank you for your help, Florence."

She went back to the stable and Molly, making a show of saddling the mare while the girl locked the door. She waved goodbye before taking off over the hill toward the road.

"What are we waiting on?"

The hoarse, deep whisper sent Amelia's heart to her throat and her hand to her chest. The laughter under the words, however, had her spinning on her tormentor.

Richard's wide smile stole her words for a moment, but only just. She pushed him backward and kicked his shin. "You are awful."

He dissolved into laughter. "Fine thing to say to your be-trothed. Especially since I brought you firewood." He motioned to the cart behind him. "Where would you like me to put it?"

A few unladylike suggestions sprung to the tip of her tongue.

His eyes twinkled as he leaned closer. The kiss was so quick and light she didn't have time to respond. "Why don't you get to work? I'll put it where you and the children can get to it easily."

She did as he suggested, but only because she was headed that way of her own accord. Once inside, she went to Florence's desk and reviewed the ledgers the girl had been so nervously review-ing. Her figures were neat, her work visible, and the percentages were accurate. She also had a kind heart and a sensible nature. Drake had been right—she was a good employee.

Satisfied, Amelia hung her coat on the rack in her office and retrieved her favorite stool. An empty bucket and a crate of bottles sat waiting next to the white whiskey still.

Before settling in for the long job of decanting, she lifted a paddle from the wall and pushed it into the mash tub until it struck the bottom. The wheat eventually yielded as Amelia put her shoulder into the paddle and walked around the tub. The water created a current that swirled the ingredients together. The scent of autumn floated upward, and the stirring became easier.

After five good turns around the tub, she returned the paddle to its resting place. Hands on her hips, she rolled her shoulders and stretched her back. The quiet of working alone usually appealed to her, but right now, her attention was outside in the cold. On a whim, she set coffee to brewing on the cast-iron stove in the corner.

With no other alternative, she took her place on the stool, put the bucket under the still, and turned her head to avoid the fumes as the top of the whiskey poured from the tap. It didn't take long for the smell to turn sweeter, until all of it smelled of figs and oranges.

The glass bottle was cool against her fingers, making it easy to mark how fast it filled with warm whiskey. One bottle. Two.

Three.

"Amelia?" Richard called.

"Behind the still."

He carried a load of firewood to the stove and poured a cup of coffee. "Thank you for this."

She thought he might leave and battled disappointment. It was foolish to expect him to stay when he had work to do as well.

"You need a taller stool." Richard placed a chair beside her and sat, his knees level with her ear.

"I tried that. I have to bend too far to fill the bottles." She kept her focus on the tap. She couldn't afford to waste any of her product. "Besides, this is my lucky stool."

"How so?" He nudged her hand with an empty bottle.

Amelia set the full bottle to her left and took the empty one. "I was sitting on it the day I brewed my first drinkable whiskey." It sounded foolish out loud.

"Oliver and I have our first axes mounted in our primary office. They remind us of where we started. Why we did it."

She tried to imagine him in his office. "Are you the bookkeeper?"

"I'm the surveyor and the buyer. Oliver does the numbers." He toyed with the bottle while he waited for her to finish the one in her hands. "Or he did. Now I do it all, at least most of the time."

The words were missing his smile, and she understood why. "It's a big job to do alone," she said. "Solitude is good for thinking, but too much of it…"

"Exactly," he said. "I've missed having family nearby."

"Which is why you're sitting with me, watching me fill bottles." *Drat. That sounded wrong.* "Not that I'm family, of course."

While that held to the terms of their agreement, it left an ache.

"Of course." He tugged one of her curls. "Even though I'm spending the day with your father."

"He most likely wants a walk away from the house. We do it

all the time." The scent of the whiskey turned again, less fermentation and more fruit. She switched off the tap and began stopping the bottles. "He'll bring home enough game to fool Mother, but mostly he just loves being outdoors."

Richard shifted his place and joined her in her work, his large hands surprisingly agile. "Will you join us?"

She shook her head. "I can't stand shooting small animals. I know they end up in the pot, but I prefer to see them in the forest when I ride."

Richard lifted the full crate and balanced it on his hip before offering his hand to help her stand. "Are you finished here then?"

There was no way to start another batch and have it bottled before she had to go London. "I am."

She had no idea what she'd do all day. After weeks of having to be in two places at the same time, having a day to herself was a luxury.

Richard went to the bottling room while Amelia fetched her coat. They stopped in the barrel room while she fished in her pocket for her keys.

"You could uncork one of those barrels and have a tasting session." He waggled his eyebrows.

"Tomorrow." A day might not make any difference, but she wasn't going to be impatient. Not now. She followed him out and locked the door.

He was already in the stable, saddling Molly.

"Are you rushing me off so you can break in and uncork that barrel?" she teased.

"I'm sending you home to put your feet up and read a book." He brushed his fingers along her jaw.

Amelia was kissing him before she knew what was happening. Richard's sharp inhale stole her breath a moment before he tunneled his fingers in her hair, cradling her to him. The sinful heat made her toes curl.

"I wanted to do that the moment I saw you out here," he murmured, resting his forehead against hers.

Amelia closed her eyes and imagined what could happen if they got lost in the moment again, out here alone. It was a dangerous path to travel. "I don't think we should arrive at the house together."

"Probably not." His laugh dusted her cheeks. "I'll pick up the road and come that way. You go through the fields. We'll look surprised at the door." He pressed a kiss to her forehead. "And I'll try to miss as many rabbits as I can."

"Is your eyesight failing?" Oliver asked as he broke his shotgun open to empty the barrels.

Richard followed suit, even though his shotgun was already empty. "What gives you that impression?"

"I've never seen you miss so many times." His friend clapped him on the back, laughing. "Marriage is ruining your focus."

"It isn't that." Richard followed him the front door into Felton House's grand front hall. "And If Augustus thought I'd be scrambling about the woods all day to feed my family, he'd have never agreed to—"

Simon was sliding down the banister with an ease that was both impressive and terrifying.

He reached the bottom and looked up at them with a wide smile and frantic wave. "Did you see, Papa?"

Oliver's breath came out in a *whoosh*. "I did, *hijo*. Well done."

"I did just want you told me." Simon leapt to the floor and came running at them. "How was hunting?"

Richard knelt for a hug and lifted the boy in one arm as he stood, though his knees buckled with the extra weight. He considered surrendering until Simon slung an arm across his back. Oliver's snicker doubled his resolve.

Lionel took their weapons and carried them past the stairs to the back of the house.

"I did well," Oliver said. "But Richard missed three out of four shots all day."

"Are you sick, *Oncle?*"

Given that *sick* had always been the best explanation for a hangover, Oliver's laughter rang through the hall. A baby's wail followed a moment later.

"No, I'm not." Richard lengthened his stride to keep up with Oliver as he headed for the drawing room. Simon's boots thudded against his thighs with every step. "I was trying not to embarrass your papa in front of his friends."

"So now your father-in-law thinks his daughter will starve." Oliver rounded the doorway and met Thea's glare as she comforted Carys. "I'm sorry, *pepinilla.* Simon—"

"Do not blame our son for your humor, good or otherwise." Despite her scolding, she laughed. "And come take your daughter. She's tired of me."

Richard knelt and put *his sister's* son on his own feet, ruffling his hair before he stood.

The boy made a beeline for the sofa, where he wedged himself between Oliver and Thea and patted his sister on her apricot-colored hair. "I went down the staircase faster than ever."

"You did, did you?" Thea asked, drawing his attention from brotherly ministrations. "Was anyone else in the hall?"

"Papa and *Oncle* were there at the end." Simon grinned at her. "Don't be cross. I only went down the lowest one, and I did it just the way Papa showed me."

Richard suspected the butler had stayed close by but out of sight.

"At least the carpet will stay nice," he said. They'd slid down the banister in Quebec so often that Julia teased they were afraid to ruin the carpet.

Oliver met his gaze. "I was thinking the same."

The sadness in his eyes made Richard feel better, which pricked his conscience. "At least he didn't do it with the baby."

Simon had begun riding down with Oliver when he wasn't much older than Carys. Richard had waited until after his first birthday.

"Which you will not ever do," Thea said to Simon in her sternest mother voice. "It's enough that the maids won't have to dust the stairs until you leave for university." She shifted her gaze between Richard and Oliver, signaling a change in topic. "You didn't bring anything for the pot, did you?"

Oliver shook his head. "We left most of it with Mrs. Bell, but I dropped a brace at the dower cottage for your mother."

It was almost impossible to believe that the black-clad, unsmiling woman was Thea's mother.

"I'm sorry for the reception you likely received," Thea said. "The post arrived today."

Oliver stopped bouncing Carys and put a hand on his wife's shoulder. The baby didn't appreciate the change.

Richard took Carys in hand, sat in a chair, and resumed the jostling to calm her. Oliver had always hated the post, and it seemed Thea shared the sentiment. "Bad news?"

"A letter from my sister." Thea covered Oliver's hand with hers, chafed it over his knuckles. "Same song, different verse. Nothing from Italy, though."

"Small graces." Oliver glanced at Richard. "My mother is in Milan. Painting."

He'd written that he'd exiled his mother for her treatment of Thea, but he'd never mentioned Thea's sister. Richard wanted to ask, but he understood they might not wish to share the story outside their family.

"Simon?" Thea asked. "Would you please go fetch Carys's favorite blanket? I think she's cold."

The rosy-cheeked child in Richard's arms was putting off enough heat for two people, but he stayed quiet as his nephew bolted from the room.

"And come down the stairs on your feet, not your bottom," Thea shouted.

Oliver leaned forward, his elbows on his knees. "Thea's sister, Milly, is in prison for blackmail, kidnapping, and attempted murder," Oliver whispered. "She blames us because we put her there."

If they were responsible for her arrest, there was only one possibility of a kidnap victim. Richard's blood ran cold. "Who did she blackmail?"

"My mother. And when we rescued Simon, she almost drowned him. Would have, if not for Thea."

And Oliver, who hated bad news and talk of death, hadn't said a word. "You should have told me." Richard cleared his throat to banish the tremble in his voice.

"I tried, but on paper it read like a penny dreadful." Oliver leaned back and pulled Thea close, kissed her hair. "It's still difficult to imagine."

In this sunny room with a crackling fire, with Carys gurgling in his arms and Simon thumping down the stairs, it was too easy to imagine Oliver without the woman in his arms. Richard had seen it before.

"Ben Latimer stopped by today." Though Thea was speaking to Oliver, she stared into the fire. "He's back from Scotland and looking for work. I don't have anything for him at the inn. Do you need anyone?"

"I wish I did. Ben's a good hand, and I'd like to help a soldier." He focused on Richard. "Ben came home after the war in Spain only to be faced with parents who were in ill health. Once he was on his own, he deeded the property back to me and went for a walk."

"How long ago?"

"He said he's been to Skye," Thea said. "He looks fit and ready to work, and his appetite hasn't lessened. He ate until Hazel stopped filling his plate."

"Why don't I hire him for the distillery?" Richard said. "I'd like to have someone there to help Amelia."

The couple exchanged a look. "You want to hire Ben for Amelia?" Thea finally asked.

"Is he a drunkard or unreliable?" When she shook her head, Richard pressed his points, ticking them off on his fingers. "Amelia can't keep being in two places at once, especially right now, and neither can I. Drake can't be expected to put his other ventures on hold simply to make it more convenient for us. She needs help with the heavier work, whether she'll admit it or not."

Carys began to whimper, prompting Thea to cross the room for her daughter. "You sound as though she's going to continue production."

"She is, at least until she's exhausted her supplies." Richard spun his tale as he spoke. "We're not in a hurry to leave, especially with Augustus's health."

Simon came into the room as Richard was finishing his semi-lie. "You're leaving?" The little boy's bottom lip trembled.

"Not right away, *hijo*," Oliver said. "But he and Amelia are getting married and—"

"And then you're getting a new house, like we did." Simon's mood shifted like fog fleeing the sunshine as he dropped the blanket in a pile over his sister's head. "And carriages, and a cook, and a garden." His devilish grin looked just like Julia's. "And a *baby*."

Richard joined the laughter, but there was a spot deep under his ribs that warmed at the thought, much like having Carys and her blanket in his lap. It was easy to put himself in Oliver's place—surrounded by family and love.

No. He had to be honest with himself. Not *a family*. His and Amelia's family. Them, their children, Marian as a doting grandmother. Amelia's drunk cat. Oliver and Simon nearby. It was even easy to see Thea there. He could help Amelia at the distillery before going to the mill every day.

But that wasn't his deal with Amelia. It didn't matter how much he liked her parents, or how much he admired her. The vicar could read the banns from now 'til doomsday; it wouldn't matter. She wasn't marrying him.

He was going home, to a business that practically ran itself, an empty house, and a row of graves. There was a neat rectangular spot at the end, waiting for him.

"Let's start with an employee before we graduate to babies." He stood. "Where can I find Mr. Latimer?"

CHAPTER SEVENTEEN

"Good morning, Amelia." Mother entered the dining room and went directly to the sideboard. "Are you ready for today?"

Amelia froze with her teacup halfway to her lips. "I've been looking forward to it for a while."

Her oldest barrels were ripe today. In a few hours, she'd know if she'd been wasting her time putting gallons of whiskey aside to age only to see them ruined.

Today, she was a businesswoman or a fool.

How did Mother know? How had she been discovered? Had someone said something? Had Richard told Father yesterday while they'd been hunting?

"Always a good sign." Mother kept her back to the table as she filled a plate. "Wedding dress fittings shouldn't be dreaded."

"Quite so." Amelia exhaled in relief. "I thought I might take Molly out for exercise this—"

Her mother's pale face and shadow-smudged eyes stopped the plot mid-formation. Amelia scrambled to her feet and rushed to help her sit. "What's happened?" she asked as she clasped Mother's hand. "Is he worse?"

"No, dear." Mother clasped her hand. "He had a bad night is all." She sank bank in her chair, as though making a breakfast plate had exhausted her. "It's the result of his schedule over the past few days, no doubt. I've convinced him to stay in bed this morning."

"Which is where you should be." Amelia rose from the table and pulled the bell cord.

"I have too much to do." Mother fought to keep her plate from Amelia's grasp, but it was far too easy to take from her. "I need to review menus with Cook, and we need to begin preparing the house for wedding guests, and—"

This is all of a waste of time. There isn't going to be a wedding. Not now. Not ever. Amelia bit her lip to keep the words from spilling out.

"All of which I can manage," she said instead as she handed the plate to a footman and looked to Simms. "Please help the baroness upstairs and tell Hayes she's to rest until time to prepare for the modiste." Mother's maid would guard her health like a hawk. "Send a maid upstairs with a breakfast tray."

The old butler dipped his head. "I'll send Mrs. Carter in."

Amelia went back to her place at the table, placing her utensils over the plate as she'd been taught. After tucking her chair under the table, she smoothed her skirt and squared her shoulders. The old housekeeper had always been the personification of every evil queen she'd stormed the staircase to battle as a child.

After a moment, she sought a distraction that wasn't nibbling on the half-eaten scone on her plate. The garden caught her attention. Pale sunlight swept over the asters and Queen Anne's lace that her true mother had planted to help fill the garden as the lilacs and roses faded, awaiting their spring rebirth.

If only people were flowers.

"Lady Amelia?"

She spun from the window with a squeak. If it were up to her, they'd have put a bell on Mrs. Carter long ago.

"Simms said the baroness has gone up ill, but you haven't sent for the doctor. I believe—"

"Doctor Anderson will be visiting Father later this morning." Amelia reestablished her posture. "If Mother worsens, he can see her then as well."

"But surely—"

"Calling him out early will worry Father, which will in turn concern Mother." Amelia resisted rubbing her temple. "She claims to simply be tired." She raised her palm to stop an argument. "Let her rest before we panic, Mrs. Carter."

The ring of authority in her voice shocked Amelia as much as it did the housekeeper.

"As you wish. If there's nothing else—"

"There is. Mother is concerned about the rooms for wedding guests, but I assume you already have the staff working on those and you will let me know if you need anything."

"Yes."

"The wedding is two weeks away. Does Cook have the menu in hand?" They would be sending baskets to all the tenants for months after the wedding was canceled. Or they could use it for—

She would not think of a funeral and she would not cry, no matter how badly her eyes stung.

"We know your favorite foods, but what of Mr. Ferrand's?"

He could like liver and onions for all Amelia knew, though he didn't taste like it. Based on that, she'd guess he preferred berries and cream. "I'll ask."

Mrs. Carter's dubious expressions said it all. *Lady Amelia is marrying a stranger on a whim. She always was an impulsive girl.*

The *ton* would be saying that about her for years to come. Would that be what her friends said of her whiskey?

"Cook would welcome you in the kitchen to discuss the cake, and the gardener would like to discuss flowers that will be available." She frowned again. "They will be less show stopping than in summer."

No *flowers will be even less show stopping.*

Amelia's glanced to the window, watching her chance to escape leave without her. It couldn't be helped. She was needed here to plan an imaginary event, waste her parents' money and her servants' time.

Worse, the wedding became more real each time it was mentioned. She had counted on her parents' insistence on formality to allow time to formulate an excuse to cry off. She hadn't expected reading the banns to weave a romantic spell. Sleep evaded her as she created a wedding guest list of her own, shorter than her mother's, but more meaningful. Her dreams were full of lemon chiffon cake and bouquets of fall flowers. And her dress? In her head, it was the gold one waiting in her closet.

Crying off was going to be painful. The best she could do was minimize the disaster.

"I'm sure whatever they decide will be fine." Amelia brushed past Mrs. Carter on her way to the door. "I'd planned for a ride this morning."

"And your parents?" The arch question matched her arched brow. This was the woman who had ruled with an iron fist in the era between one mother's death and another's arrival.

"I will be back well before Dr. Anderson arrives. The modiste is scheduled soon after. Mother says Father is simply tired. I have told you *she* is as well. That should be enough."

"Young lady."

"That is *My Lady*, Mrs. Carter. Whether or not you agree with my decisions." Amelia met the housekeeper's hard gaze and locked her knees to keep them from knocking. "Now...I am going to enjoy my home for the precious little time I have left to do so."

"The job requires discretion," Richard said. "Secrecy."

"But the distillery isn't illegal?" Ben Latimer was a tall, lean man. The latter likely a consequence of his recent walk through Scotland and back. His hair, the color of Carys's, was clubbed back in a neat tail that wasn't fashionable, but he was clean shaven and his clothes were soldier-neat. He could have been mustering for drill.

"Not illegal at all." *With the exception of the charade over its origin.* "Just…unusual, which you will come to understand."

"And you want me to be a watchman and do any heavy lifting?"

"Mr. Brewer has hired local children who work before and after school, and his landlord stops by on occasion. Baron Kilverstone's daughter."

"Lady Amelia?"

It was good that he could recognize her if she showed up in the middle of the night. "Yes."

"You two are marrying, correct?" Latimer dropped to his haunches to scratch Caspar behind the ears. "I was in church on Sunday."

Richard had known the announcement was coming, but hearing his name connected to Amelia's in such a public way, then receiving congratulations from the Chitesters' tenants and other villagers, had done something unexpected to him. He had walked away feeling connected to the community in a different way.

Hiring a guard wouldn't just ease Richard's mind about Amelia. He'd be helping a respected member of the village with a job and a home, and Latimer would be well-suited to watch over the children when they were here. Even Amelia's drunkard cat liked him.

"We are." The conviction landed soundly in his chest, giving Richard a moment's pause. "Lady Amelia and Mr. Brewer have a close relationship. She's taken a special interest in the distillery."

An interest? She's willing to give up everything to make a go of this.

"Will that concern you?" he asked Latimer.

"For a pound a week and a roof over my head?" The other man looked up at him, squinting in the late morning sunshine. A smile creased his face. "Lady Amelia can come and go as she pleases."

He stood and stretched out his hand. Richard took it. "You can move in whenever you'd like."

A horse approached, and Richard turned to greet Amelia with a smile. The one she returned was thin, at best. "Good morning, gentlemen."

Latimer took Molly's reins. "It's a pleasure to see you, Lady Amelia." If he was surprised to see her in a split skirt, it didn't show.

"It's good to see you home, Mr. Latimer. I didn't have a chance to speak to you at church on Sunday."

"You were busy, my lady. Congratulations on your betrothal."

"Thank you." Her gaze flicked between them, but she ended staring at Richard. "What brings both of you here without Mr. Brewer or Mr. Fletcher?"

Though her voice was light and cheerful, Richard recognized the challenge in her eyes. "I've hired Mr. Latimer on Mr. Brewer's behalf. As security and manual labor since Mr. Fletcher has been called to London." She'd see reason, he was certain of it.

"*You* have." Her face was frozen in the pleasant mask she'd worn during the house party. She focused on Latimer, and Richard was immediately warmer. "I'm certain you'll be good at your job, Mr. Latimer."

"Thank you. If you'd like, I can see to your mare before I go into town for my things."

"For your things? Are you going to live here?"

"Security isn't useful if it isn't available, Amelia." Richard had dealt with it for years as he and Oliver had begun mill operations in other parts of the province. She was new to the idea. It would get easier to accept. "I've offered him the room behind the stable."

"I see." She stayed focused on the other man. "Thank you for your kind offer, Mr. Latimer, but I wouldn't want to delay your errand. I can see to Molly."

Latimer shot a quick glance to Richard before he nodded. His friendly expression had faded into a frown and then into military coldness as their exchange with Amelia had evolved. "Certainly, my lady."

His cart rattled across the path and disappeared around the corner of the distillery. As the sound faded, Amelia walked her horse to the stable.

"You were rude, Amelia." Richard walked beside her. Despite being almost twice her height, he had to quicken his pace to keep up.

"*I* was rude?" She stepped in front of him to loop Molly's bridle over the post nearest the trough. "You two were in my place of business uninvited."

"I wasn't aware I needed an invitation." He reached for the feed bucket and winced when her elbow struck his ribs. "Ow."

"My apologies." Her flat tone belied her words. "I'm used to doing this myself."

Which was his point. She didn't need to struggle alone. "But I am right here."

"Mm-hmm." Amelia gave Molly a solid pat before she walked away toward the distillery.

"You're angry with me." Richard waited at the door while she unlocked it.

"I am."

Inside, the barrel room was cool and dark, and the musty air tickled his nose. Furtive scurrying in the deep shadows told him they weren't alone. Amelia inhaled sharply and didn't release the breath until she'd lit a lantern. "Those children have to stop feeding Caspar."

"Amelia. I'm right on this. You'll see—"

"I won't." She positioned a sluice-like ramp near a barrel and a wheeled platform at the end of it. "You'll tell him you've overstepped and that he doesn't have a position here."

With a grunt, Amelia pushed the barrel on the ramp and eased it down until it reached the platform. Another unladylike noise and equally scandalous squat lift, and she positioned the barrel so she could roll it into the bottling room. She lost her hat in the process.

She faced the table and the barrel, tilting her head the way he did when he was deciding how a tree would fall. With a sigh, Richard stepped forward, lifted the barrel, and carefully set it on the table next to her hat.

Amelia wheeled on him. "Do not come in here acting like you know everything about my business and what I need, or how—"

"You couldn't get the barrel onto the bloody table," Richard shouted back.

"You didn't let me try. You just decided I needed help and did it without asking. What if I came to Quebec and hired a house-keeper for you?"

What if she came to Quebec? "Amelia—"

"This is not your business, Richard. It is *mine*." She put a hand over her chest, calling his attention to the tiny buttons on her thin linen shirt. "I have worked hard to learn this craft and taken a huge risk to expand it. And I've done it on my own."

No, she hadn't. "Your *child labor* force works here unsuper-vised most days."

"I hire tenants' *older children* because their families need the money." She didn't back down. "It keeps them close to home and allows them to stay in school."

Richard glared down at her. "You hire them because they don't ask questions about an employer they never see and work that's done in the middle of the night."

"Drake—"

"Put everything on hold to come babysit your distillery and workforce while you couldn't get away. Now he's in London." He pointed a finger at her nose. "Which is where you're going for a few days. Your business will be unguarded."

She opened her mouth, as though waiting for an argument to fly in, only to snap it closed again. Richard's satisfaction doubled when her stare began to simmer.

"With him here, I can't come and go as I please."

Which wouldn't be a bad thing. "Maybe it will keep you from haring about in the dark while you live a double life."

"It is my life." Amelia slapped her hand on the table, a small sound in the big, empty room.

"So that makes it all right that you could be dead in a ditch for hours before anyone missed you? What would happen if you surprised a thief here?"

"It won't be necessary for much longer. Father will be dead—" Her eyes went wide and glassy as she slammed her hand over her mouth a moment before she folded in on herself. "Oh God—"

Richard pulled her to him, her head crashing into his chest as he cradled her quaking shoulders. The sobs rattled down her back, and he let his hands follow them over the curve of her spine. "It's okay."

Her blonde hair was stuck in his waistcoat, and it clung tighter as she shook her head. "It isn't. It won't ever be again. All I could think of—"

"Shhh." He wished he could change things for her, but more than anything, he wanted to take the pain he knew was coming, the ache that would stay with her the rest of her life. All he could do was let her cry.

It took a few minutes for the storm to subside to sniffles. Richard pulled his handkerchief from his pocket and held it where she could see it. Her damp fingers brushed his.

"Thank you," she whispered. "But I'm still angry with you."

He tugged one of her curls. "I know." He wasn't sending Latimer packing, though. He was right on this. He knew it. "Why are you here this morning?"

Amelia backed away from him, dabbing her eyes before cleaning her nose. "I wanted to tap the barrel. Today is its second birthday."

"We could still do it."

"Because the morning has gone *so* well," she muttered before retrieving a mallet, awl, and tap that were waiting nearby.

Richard held out his hand for them, only to be met with a disappointed sigh. She was looking at him like he was daft.

"You're too short." She wasn't much taller than the barrel they were about to sacrifice.

Amelia dragged a stool across the stone floor slowly, prolonging every screech and bump. Then she stood on it with an exaggerated flourish. "The world is too tall."

She set the awl against the barrel and swung the mallet, her mouth set in grim determination. Richard stood to the side, ready to help if the barrel slipped or the stool shifted.

"There are two glasses in the office." She picked up the tap.

God save him from stubborn women. Richard strode through the door and the still room, his long legs making quick work of the distance. The glasses sat on the shelf, sparkling in the sunlight as though they knew their roles for the day.

By the time he returned, Amelia was easing the tapped barrel into a cradle. The stool screeched on the stones as she adjusted her posture.

Richard thumped the glasses on the table and reached for the barrel.

"Stop it." Her voice was as sharp as the awl. "I have to get used to the weight and how it moves or I won't be able to do it on my own."

She wouldn't be able to do it at all if she broke her neck, but he clenched his fists and waited for her to get into trouble. He didn't breathe until she stepped down from the stool.

Amelia filled two glasses and set one in front of him. "Let me try it first, please."

The amber liquid glinted in the light, reminding him of the topaz in the ring he'd given her. The moment he'd seen the stones, he'd known they were perfect.

She hesitated for a moment, closing her eyes as though she were praying. Her first sip was tentative, and the way she ran her tongue over her lips made him weak in the knees. Her smile shaped to the rim of the glass with her second sip.

Richard lifted his glass and took a drink. It was smooth and warm on his tongue, and the fragrance lingered in his nose after he'd swallowed.

"It's good, isn't it?" Amelia whispered. "I'm not imagining it?"

He took another sip, longer this time. God help him, it was like kissing her. "It's delicious, Amelia."

"I did it," she whispered as she stared at the liquor swirling in her glass. Her smile broke wide. "I really did it."

Richard recognized the look. He and Oliver had shared it the first time they'd filled a skid with hewn lumber. They still shared it whenever they pushed felled trees into a wagon on their own. Just like he'd found a home in the middle of wild trees, Amelia had claimed her space here.

He touched the rim of his glass to hers. "Congratulations."

I publish the banns of marriage between Richard Pierre Ferrand of this parish, via Quebec, Canada and Rosnay, France and Amelia Christine Chitester, daughter of Baron Kilverstone, of this parish. If any know cause or just impediment why these two persons should not be joined together in Holy matrimony, ye are to declare it. This is the first time of asking.

CHAPTER EIGHTEEN

THE RUSHFORD COACH rocked past Oakdale's gate and onto the road, sloshing Amelia in her seat. She kept a tight hold on the handle mounted to the wall to avoid falling against Richard. He was too busy admiring the scenery to notice.

"I apologize for the ruts," she said. Father had always sent stewards out to smooth the road after a rain. She should have thought of it, but her attention had been divided between a very real worry over her product and her panic over an imaginary wedding that was ten days away.

Plus, she'd had an extra employee to train.

"I'd be happy to send someone over to help your stewards," Oliver said.

"Thank you, but I'm sure the household will get back to normal while I'm not underfoot to distract them." Father wouldn't want his neighbors, no matter how friendly, to think him incapable of managing.

"There is no need to pretend, Amelia." Richard's shoulders heaved like a swell over the open ocean.

She'd ridden over them aboard ship when they'd traveled. There was thrill in standing on the bow as they'd gathered speed and height; the spray in her face promised wild adventure. But as they'd neared the crest, panic had always fluttered in her stomach. There was no turning back. It was either crash or race down the other side. Either way, the world was different.

"That's a bit harsh, Rich."

"I'm only saying there is no shame in accepting help when friends offer it." Every time he spoke, her stomach fluttered. Even when she was angry with him. Even when he looked at her like he'd rather be anywhere else.

Well, she didn't want him on this trip either. "Accepting help is different than having it forced on you."

The wheel struck another hole, and Amelia was tossed against Richard's solid arm before she could grab an anchor. He touched her just long enough to make her crave his warmth, and then she retreated like a turtle into its shell.

She brightened her smile and faced her hosts. "At least that one wasn't my fault."

Oliver had an arm around Thea's shoulder, securing her to him as though he was worried she'd shatter. "I won't complain," he chuckled. "But we might end up covered in spirits before we ever reach London."

Amelia looked to the ceiling. Her first case of aged whiskey was up there, meant for the lending circle—to prove their faith in her hadn't been misplaced. There were also two more cases of wine for Jasper. He'd written with the request and an invitation to a private ball. He claimed it was to celebrate her engagement, but she didn't believe he needed an excuse for a party.

Regardless, it gave her reason to travel to London with a duchess as her willing chaperone. The only issue was her fiancé. "They should be safe. Mr. Latimer wrapped the shipment for safe travel."

"You're welcome," Richard muttered.

Amelia chose to ignore him rather than start another fight. She retreated to her corner of the coach and tightened her grip on her anchor.

"It's wonderful that you had a position for Ben, even if it's only until the wedding," Thea said. "You'll need the extra time he can buy you over the next few days."

That appreciation would likely vanish when she didn't marry, didn't leave Thetford, and still let Mr. Latimer go. "I didn't count on having another employee so soon, especially not a resident. It's difficult to come and go without raising suspicions."

"If you were honest with him, it might make things easier," Richard said.

It wasn't that Amelia didn't grasp his reasoning. She even appreciated it. The last few weeks had left her exhausted, but this morning had been deeper than that. Father's illness, and Mother's necessary focus on his needs, left the household looking to Amelia for direction. From the moment she woke, someone was asking her questions or telling her what they thought she should know. There wasn't a quiet space in her day. "Easier is a matter of opinion."

It wasn't an accusation, but Richard focused on her like a large owl. "What does—"

"It's like going into the woods alone, Rich." Oliver's gaze met hers. His smile told Amelia he understood her dilemma. "Sometimes, work isn't about work."

Thea's rich laugh rippled through the coach, coaxing smiles before she even spoke. "Hazel caught me mopping the hall a few days ago. She was halfway through scolding me before I could explain that I simply needed to busy my hands and quiet my thoughts."

"She's not used to a duchess who thinks, much less one with busy hands." Oliver kissed her hair.

"Don't be so hard on your mother," Thea chided. "Being a duchess is a job all unto itself." Her steady gaze met Amelia's. "Any society lady really."

Richard snorted. "I think there are people who would trade places with you in a moment."

Oliver stripped from his coat, folded it, and put it behind his back as a pillow. "Thea knows more about the businesses in Thetford than I will ever."

"But they are your responsibility," Richard argued. "Not

everyone has those same demands."

Oliver barked a laugh as Amelia turned to stare at Richard, her eyes wide.

"What's your favorite flavor of cake?" she asked, only to interrupt him. "And your favorite fall flower if we want to have them on the table for the wedding breakfast? The modiste is coming. Do you want peach silk or blue velvet for your traveling dress? This is the household budget for the kitchen this week. Would you prefer beef or pork roast from the butcher? The upstairs maid has taken ill, but one of the houseboys can step up to help with the fires so a younger girl can step up to help with linens; will that be acceptable? The coach needs new paint and upholstery. Which styles would you prefer? Margaret Gerard's wedding should be held soon. Will you stay for it or return from France? The bills are on your desk for review when you have a moment. Mr. Gray is ill, so we'll be sending a basket. Do you want to take it when you go by? Poor family, they're going to lose their harvest unless they get help. The Wood family lost their father to a farm accident. Without a means of support, the younger children will have to be sent out to family in Suffolk. The Jones's home needs a new roof before winter, especially since she's been ill. They could afford it if they could sell the rest of their pears. Doctor Anderson will be visiting at teatime. You'll need to be here to entertain. And—"

Richard raised his hands in surrender, but his eyes held a challenge. "Then why make the choices you have?"

If he was inclined to consider her responsibilities a chore, he would never understand that her inspiration for whiskey was born, in part, out of her involvement with her family's tenants. She knew what they were harvesting, what they needed, how they worried for their children.

"You're marrying a baron's daughter with a substantial dowry," she said, arching an eyebrow. "Why don't you count your looks as currency and try for a better purse? Why don't you sell your business interests and trade in gossip?"

Richard stared at her for a long moment before nodding his understanding, but he didn't say anything further. Which was fine. Amelia was talked out.

On the other side of the coach, Oliver stretched his legs across the seat, bracketing Thea in his lap and offering his chest as a pillow. She took it, pulling a blanket over them both as she snuggled against him.

They had a love match that was also a partnership. As a child, she'd seen them in the village. They'd been inseparable, two halves of a whole. They were the same now, each filling the other's empty spaces. If Amelia were ever to marry, she'd want a marriage like theirs.

The road had smoothed out, so Amelia released her grip on the hand hold and rubbed her tense knuckles. If she and Richard had discussed hiring Ben Latimer, she likely would have handled it better. But he'd ambushed her with it, leaving her adrift as he'd pointed out her shortcomings—like her height, which she couldn't control anyway.

She rested her head against the wall and watched the road unspool behind them. She'd been grateful for Mr. Latimer's help this morning, but seeing him had made her wish for Richard. Wishing for him reminded her he wouldn't be here much longer.

Her eyelids grew heavy as the coach rocked steadily toward London, and she crossed her arms over her middle to stay warm. Her fake fiancé never failed to surprise her.

When one led a life of secrets, surprises were rarely good.

As unbelievable as it had been for Richard to grasp that Oliver had a title and a country home, it was even more difficult to fathom that he had a London townhome and his servants traveled ahead to open the house. The street was apparently fashionable given the amount of carriage traffic that was traveling past despite the late hour. The gas lamps spat shadows over his ceilings, and a hackney with a squeaky wheel rumbled past for the fifth time since they'd retired.

Granted, it had been early when they'd all gone to bed. Eight hours in a coach was exhausting whether you napped or not. Oliver could sleep anywhere, a trait his wife seemed to share. Though perhaps they were simply exhausted from their responsibilities. Because Amelia fell asleep pressed against the opposite wall like she'd been caught in a spell while trying to escape. Her neck must be killing her.

Richard had tried to help, but she'd pushed him away without waking. It had left him nothing to do but sit facing her, watching to make sure she didn't hurt herself. His back ached from the middle of his shoulder blades to his tail bone.

That wasn't what kept him awake as he flipped on the mattress and punched his pillow to redistribute the feathers he'd punished less than hour ago. Amelia's diatribe kept repeating in his head. The words were a blur, but the disappointment in her eyes was clear. He'd hurt her feelings. Worse, he'd damaged her pride.

He'd never imagined she'd take Latimer's hiring as an insult and, frankly, her reaction had insulted him. He'd apologize for his reaction, but he didn't regret the impulse. Ben was a good man and a good fit, and it would be easier to leave knowing she was protected.

Because he was leaving. Today's discussion sealed it. Amelia's commitment to her tenants and her craft were admirable, but she had to be in Thetford to tend to her responsibilities. He had to resume his in Quebec.

But one day, she'd be able to look at Latimer and realize someone had loved her enough to keep her safe even though he'd let her go.

He'd tell her that if his brother-in-law had any pity. Instead, Oliver and Thea slept next door with Amelia on the other side of them. There was no way to approach her alone, and he couldn't sleep until he told her.

Surrendering to the torment, Richard sat on the edge of the bed and lit a candle so he could find his slippers and dressing gown. He'd bought these especially for the trip, given that he hadn't worn his others since Julia's death. He and Oliver had given up on them as they'd raced to comfort a wailing baby, each braving their panic because they swore the little monster fed on it.

He'd worn a lot of brave faces over the years. He could do it again.

Out in the hallway, Richard kept the candle high and focused on the stairs instead of the bedroom doors to his right. Though after watching her sleep all afternoon, it wasn't difficult to imagine Amelia in bed, her face buried in the pillow. Of course, in his imagination, she was naked and her breath teased his skin.

It was a miracle Richard reached the bottom of the stairs without breaking his neck. It was also no small feat that he found the library on the first try. All the doors here looked the same.

He entered the room, relieved to see a fire. Gas lights poured through the cracks in the drapes, making bright stripes against the carpets and halfway up the shelves. Oliver had told him he had purchased a copy of *The Count of Monte Cristo*. Richard found it in the corner opposite the door, alphabetized with its binding in a perfect row with its shelf companions. It was the same way their library was organized in Quebec.

A flash of white in the corner of his eye stopped him cold. If it was an intruder, he was literally cornered with no weapon but a floppy shoe.

"Hello," Amelia whispered.

She was curled in a chair, her loose blonde hair bright in the candlelight. Her dressing gown was a thin cotton wrap that matched her night dress, which hung loose enough to expose her collar bones.

"I thought you'd be asleep." He kept a tight grip on the book. She'd lost weight since she'd purchased that gown, either from worry or hard work. Perhaps a combination of the two.

"Thea offered her copy of the Currer Bell novel everyone is reading." She tucked her hair behind her ear. "I was hoping it would help me sleep, but I can't put it down."

"Mm-hmm." There were things he wanted to say, he remembered them clearly, but he couldn't stop staring at her hair. Her braids had left it wavy, reminding him of a frayed rope.

Amelia unfolded from the chair. "I can go up and leave you to it—"

"Stay." He hadn't meant to bark like that. "Please don't go on my account. Unless you want to be alone."

She shook her head and stayed seated. Her feet were bare. "I suppose if we're going to read, we could combine our candles. It would be easier to see."

A gentleman would leave the room and go blind. "I think that's a sound idea."

He sat on the sofa, close the fire and the windows, perpendicular to her chair. Their candles stood side by side on the table between them. Richard opened his book, content to read while the fire popped in the grate and the squeaky-wheeled taxi went past again.

Amelia's breathing marked her passage in the story as much as the speed with which she flipped the pages.

"I believe your novel is better than mine." *She* was certainly more interesting. He'd read the same page three times. "What's it about?"

"An orphan girl who becomes a governess and goes to work for a mysterious man, teaching his ward." She cast a sideways glance. "And yours?"

"A man who is wrongly sent to a dreadful prison for the remainder of his life and his quest for revenge." Richard closed the book. "Are you nervous about tomorrow?"

Amelia nodded and marked her place. "The circle took a chance on me. I don't want to disappoint them."

"You won't." He wrapped his fingers around her delicate

wrist and gave in to the temptation to stroke her silky skin. "What you have created is as unique as you are. You should be proud to show it off."

"Drake says I should expect questions about our engagement."

Of course her lenders would have questions. She'd just started a business that any marriage would require her to leave, but if she told them the truth in front of Oliver and Thea, there would be hell to pay at home. "We'll deal with it." He knelt in front of her.

"I wish you'd asked me instead of assuming," she said.

Her large blue eyes drew him forward. "I wish you'd trust me to help." Her lavender and geranium scented skirts were soft on his palms as he made room between her thighs.

"Richard." Her gasp caressed his skin as her lashes dropped over her eyes.

The moment their lips joined, his body surged forward, demanding the sweetness on her tongue until she whimpered in need, and then he ate that too, nibbling her lips as he untied her wrapper. "Christ, Amelia." Her neck smelled of flowers and tasted of the fairy floss he'd had once at the fair.

The more he tasted, the more she offered. Her salty collarbone led to her caramel-textured sternum and then to the sinful flavor along the swell of her breast. Amelia arched just enough to put the mound in his hand, and his fingers flexed on instinct, caressing her through the cotton, rolling her nipple until it begged for his mouth and then answering the plea. The starchy fabric was dry against his tongue for a moment, but it was easy to imagine the fruit beneath, especially as the nightshirt fabric softened. Richard pulled away enough to breathe across it and watch her skin draw tighter.

Amelia's nails scraped his scalp, pulling him to her as her heels grazed his spine. Her kiss was as demanding as his had been, and Richard groaned in frustration as his erect shaft grazed the front of her chair. All he had to was shift—

He couldn't take her. She wasn't his. And a child, should there be one… Ignoring every cell in his body, he stopped and looked into her hazy, hungry eyes.

"You can't leave me like this." Her hands slid from his hair, across his shoulders and down his arms, so warm it was easy to imagine he was naked. "Please, Richard."

"You don't know what you're asking, *ma belle*." She couldn't guess how difficult it was to put two rational thoughts together when he was blind with need and drowning in the scent of her.

Her hand left his arm to lay flat on her stomach. "It's like craving strawberries at Christmas."

The insides of her knees were like velvet, and he was losing his mind.

"I won't leave you hungry." Her thighs were like silk. "But you have to be quiet, *chéri*." His thumb brushed her mound and came away wet as she trembled beneath him. On his second pass, he rotated the digit across her bud and watched her eyes fly wide. Leaning as close as he dared in his condition, he sealed his lips over hers and captured her sensitive flesh between a finger and thumb, rolling it as he'd done her nipple.

Amelia came apart beneath him as she groaned against his tongue.

Richard could have stopped there, but when he backed away, she was exposed to him, her sweet body wet from his touch. His mouth watered like a man at an oasis, and he was drinking from her before he knew what had happened, his fingers coaxing her body to give him what he needed, her knees over his shoulders as her heels bruised his back.

He would have felt like a bastard, but every time he moved away, she dragged him back, her fingers in his hair as she arched upward. Her wanton cries vibrated from his palm to his elbow as he fought to keep this their secret.

Eventually, she nudged him away from a body that trembled without his touch. Richard eased her legs from his shoulders and straightened her skirts with shaky fingers. He lifted her into his arms, intending to help her to her feet, but he fell backward against the wall.

"So that's what can happen in ten minutes when we're alone in a library." Amelia's sleepy giggle tickled his chest, and her hair swept across his cheek.

The squeaky hackney had stopped its rounds. Their candles had gone out, leaving them in darkness save for the dim fire and the glow from the streetlamps. Their books had tumbled to the floor.

Richard crossed his arms over Amelia's back to keep her warm, ignoring the mess, the hard floor, and his even harder body. He kissed the top of her head and then rested his cheek over the spot, sealing in the affection.

Maybe, if he was lucky, Oliver would find them like this and force him to marry her.

CHAPTER NINETEEN

AMELIA HAD ENTERED Octavia Foster's home two years ago and been awed by the number of successful women in the room. Now, she was one of them.

"Welcome back, Lady Amelia," the butler said as he took her cloak and hat.

"Thank you, Martin." She resisted the impulse to curtsey to a man more regal than most she'd met in London ballrooms. Instead, she presented him with the bottles she'd carried from Thetford in her luggage, carefully wrapped in her softest clothes. "Would you see these get poured for our meeting today, please?"

"I'll do it personally, miss." He turned to Thea and bowed, coming up with a twinkle in his eye and wide smile. "Your Grace. How lovely to see you again."

Martin always saved his best smiles for Thea.

"Darling girl." Octavia swept through the crowd and took her hands. "You look every inch the happy bride-to-be. Thea wrote me of your news." Her sharp gaze swept the room. "Where is your fiancé? He did accept your invitation?"

In a manner of speaking. Heat flooded Amelia's face, and she masked it by taking a cup of tea from an attentive young maid. The hot, sweet liquid soothed her raw throat even as the lemon juice found the irritated spots. It was just as she liked it. One only had to order tea once in this house.

"He and Lord Rushford are delivering wine and white whiskey to my cousin Jasper in preparation for a party this evening." Amelia searched the crowd herself. "Has Drake arrived?" He had picked up a case of whiskey yesterday afternoon with the plan to sell it to establishments he knew.

"Not yet, but I'm sure he's fine." Octavia sipped her coffee. "You, on the other hand, sound awful. Have you come down with a cold, or is it this dreadful air?"

It came from a night Amelia had thought was a dream when she woke in bed this morning, her book on a nearby table with a lily marking her place, with no recollection of how she'd been transported from the library. It wasn't until her nightshirt brushed against her that she suspected it had been no dream. Finger-shaped bruises in hidden places had confirmed it, as had a throat raw from screaming in pleasure against his salty palm. It had been the most exquisite torture.

"It was a long day yesterday, Octavia. I am well."

Which was a lie. She had hopped from precipice to pinnacle all morning, first pretending over breakfast that her world hadn't shifted. Every time she looked at Richard, she fought the urge to drag him into a corner and kiss him until he gave her something she knew he was withholding but couldn't name. Because all Mother had said was that she should never be alone with a man for fear of something scandalous that would leave her pregnant. If girls fell pregnant from kissing, half the women in society would have been with child by the end of the Season, And that's all Richard had done to her. Essentially. Heat bloomed deep in her belly as she recalled his fingers dipping inside her.

Well, touching didn't leave one pregnant either. And pondering it didn't dispel her other worry.

This was the Circle's first opportunity to see what their risk had produced, to declare whether she was successful and learn what her plans were for the future. None of which she knew without Richard and Drake.

"Amelia, I'd like you to meet someone." Octavia put a hand

on Amelia's shoulder, directing her to a small, thin woman. "Mrs. Reid, this is the young lady I mentioned last week, Amelia Chitester. Amelia, this is Elizabeth Reid."

"It is a pleasure, Mrs. Reid. Are you new to the Circle as well?"

The woman looked up, making Amelia feel like a giant. Her sharp eyes and quick smile contrasted with the gray threading through her hair. "A friend invited me here to meet charitably-minded ladies who would be willing to take a risk on a new venture."

"If they'll take a risk on me, surely they'll consider you," Amelia chuckled. She remembered the looks on the members' faces as a baron's daughter had stood in front of them bragging that she made the most sought-after white whiskey in Norfolk, but she needed funds to expand into aged spirits, and that it would take two years to see any return. She had had her detractors, but the support had been overwhelming. Perhaps she could do the same for Mrs. Reid. "What is your venture?"

"A university for women. I believe it's time England's young ladies learned more than how to be good wives and hostesses, though education makes them better at that as well." She smiled. "No offense, Miss Chitester."

"None taken, and please, call me Amelia." She left Octavia's side to stand next to Mrs. Reid. "You need investors for the university?"

"My late husband left me enough for that, as well as other things." Mrs. Reid faced her. "But the university will not be successful if students aren't prepared to enter, and the current governess system is too unreliable."

Amelia nodded. She'd been lucky to have Graves, whose father had been a professor at Oxford. Margaret Gerard's governess had been more interested in her needlework.

Thinking of Margaret brought all the girls in Thetford to mind. Thea, like Graves, had benefited from her father's conviction that she be educated. In turn, she and Oliver had been insistent that the vicar include village girls in the classroom, though no student learned more than basic skills. Boys like Simon, who would move on to university, were an anomaly. Girls like Florence were unheard of. "Would you take low-born girls?"

"I would take any young lady who could pay tuition and pass the entrance exam, so long as she was truly interested in education," Mrs. Reid said. "The key is preparing students to enter the university, filling the gap between governesses or village schools. I'm here to encourage your members to consider sponsoring preparatory programs."

The door opened, bringing the fall wind in to brush against skirts and shawls. Drake entered with it. His height gave the impression of a heron standing amongst lily pads—if all-black herons existed.

"I would like to visit with you more, Mrs. Reid, but I must speak with Mr. Fletcher." Amelia squeezed the other woman's hand in reassurance. "I am most interested in such a program."

She reached Drake just Thea did.

"You're a mess," Thea said as she pulled him into the drawing room. "Are you well?

Amelia followed. He didn't look unwell. He looked like Richard had done when he'd spun on her in the dark library last night. "You look as though you've seen a ghost."

"You could say that," Drake muttered as he batted Thea's hand from his cravat. "Thank you." He faced the mirror, but talked to them as he righted his hair. "Thea, you have a grasp on your report already." He tightened the knot at his throat before tugging his waistcoat. "Amelia, I reworked your figures in the coach on the way over." He pulled the paper from his breast pocket. "I'll read it because I don't believe you'll get through it with a straight face."

Outside the door, Octavia called the meeting to order.

Drake buttoned his coat and offered each of them an elbow. "Since Oliver and Richard aren't here, shall we?"

They took their places at the boardroom table, and Amelia thrilled at seeing each place set with Richard's wine and her whiskey. Tasting wouldn't be enough. The mere fact that she'd succeeded meant she needed a plan to ensure future success. A plan Richard had promised to help her create, but he wasn't here.

"What am I supposed to say?" she whispered to Drake.

"You don't need anyone to tell you that." He looked down his nose at her, but his eyes were kind. "You know what you're doing, and you know what you want. This is just another negotiation, Amelia. Be direct and be honest."

Reports began on the other side of the room, but Amelia half-listened to stories of paper mills, dressmakers, and sheep farms. That changed when Mrs. Reid took the floor to explain her proposal for expanding women's education.

"We could do that easily," Thea whispered.

"I was thinking the same thing. There's a vacant parcel on the other side of the village, past the print shop and the jeweler." Amelia rubbed her thumb over her betrothal ring, tracing the intricate facets until the large stone was warm. She'd worn it today for luck, and as evidence of her and Richard's solidarity, but was it useful if he wasn't here?

And if her conviction was only based on his presence, was she really convinced?

Thea began her report on the inn's profits, the expansion of her holdings, and the interest garnered on her investments throughout the village. Oliver and Richard slipped into the back of the room while she was speaking. One's pride was just as evident as the other's shock as he took in the number of women at the table.

"Now for Miss Chitester's report," Octavia said. "Which I have saved until last because I wanted to give you a chance to savor the wine at your places—which it appears all of you have." She waited for the laughter to subside. "But now, let us raise our whiskey glasses to our youngest member's first aged batch."

Tentative sips were greeted with smiles and nods. Most then

finished their glasses, though some abstained. Amelia cleared her throat and wished, not for the first time today, that she hadn't screamed so much overnight.

"This is a two-year old wheat whiskey flavored with figs and oranges. While it aged, I continued brewing white whiskey and distributing it to inns and taverns in Norfolk, as well as to some private buyers. To help cover operating expenses, I entered into a distribution agreement with Villa Rosnay, a small winery owned by Richard Ferrand, whereby I retain a portion of the profits and a supply of barrels to use for future whiskey batches."

Drake unfolded his report. "My apologies, but I didn't have time to copy this since I completed Miss Chitester's most recent sales this morning. She has orders for this batch and a waiting list for future ones. The work she has done with Mr. Ferrand has covered her operating expenses as well as added significantly to both their accounts. Net of expenses and the payment she is contracted to make to you today, she has netted close to thirty pounds this month. I see no reason that profit margin won't continue, putting her on track to earn approximately three hundred pounds in the coming year."

Amelia stared at him open-mouthed. *Three* hundred *pounds?*

"Well done," Octavia said from the head of the table. "Questions? Yes, Lady Barber?"

"You are engaged to Mr. Ferrand, are you not?"

"I am." Pride shot through Amelia's chest and down her fingers, where it was anchored by her ring.

"And since he's Canadian, I assume you will reside with him there." Lady Barber addressed the room as a whole. "This is why I was leery of loaning funds to such a young lady for a labor and time intensive venture. She has tired of it in favor of a family and a home."

Richard rose from his chair, but Amelia found her voice first. "Lady Barber, I remember your objections well." She fought her rising temper. "Let me assure each of you. There are two years' worth of barrels aging in Norfolk. If I never brew another batch, or if I have a failed batch, the distillery will continue to pay dividends and support our charitable mission. Should I leave for Canada, or any destination, I have a staff fully capable of bottling my product and distributing it under Mr. Fletcher's direction."

The truth of her statements rang through her as she focused on Richard. She knew what she wanted.

"Mr. Ferrand is a successful businessman in two profitable industries on three separate continents. Should I need an adviser, he will be an asset." Amelia nailed the sour-faced older woman with a glare. "But unless you have sat beside me in the middle of the night while I've filled whiskey barrels, or helped me negotiate a price for wheat, you cannot consider yourself my supervisor. I believe I've proved I don't need one."

⌒

"ARE YOU CERTAIN I can't convince you?" Jasper Warren asked. Smoke from his cigar circled his head before drifting into the night sky. "Oakdale would be the perfect wedding gift."

"It would be," Richard agreed. "But you're setting me up to disappoint her every anniversary for the rest of my life." His dry laugh scratched deeper than his throat.

"Or to escape gifts altogether." Warren's smile was feral in the lamplight. "And think of the honeymoon."

Richard let the risqué comment go. After all, men in glass houses…

"I appreciate the offer, Jasper, but I have my reasons."

The other man extended his hand. "If I had to choose between France and Norfolk, I know which I'd settle on."

Perhaps Warren would take the winery in trade. Though Richard would never sell it now. "Exactly." He shook Warren's hand, sealing his fate. "Thank you for understanding."

They returned to the ballroom, and Richard found Amelia in the crowd. It wasn't just her dress, which she'd worn for their first engagement party. She'd glowed since the end of their meeting today. And justifiably so. She'd succeeded in the face of obstacles her class and her beauty had put in front of her. Now she was excited by the opportunity to help others do the same.

Her smile was blinding as he joined them. "Lord and Lady Althorne, may I present Richard Ferrand. Richard, Lady Althorne is a poet, and Lord Althorne has a shipping business in Paris." She turned to the other man. "Richard has lumber mills in Canada and in Norfolk, and his winery is in Rosnay."

"We've just returned from our home in Bougival," Althorne said. "We traveled through Rosnay on our way from the coast. It's a lovely area."

"It is, thank you. I keep finding reasons to enjoy it." One was that it would give him an excuse to visit England on a regular basis.

"If you'll excuse us." Althorne leaned forward to whisper. "My wife is allergic to cigars. She needs air."

"The nearest terrace attracts the most smokers," Richard warned. "Use the library exit."

The man nodded his thanks as he ushered his wife from the room.

"They are fascinating." Amelia took Richard's arm, her betrothal ring glittering against her white skin. "Thea has the countess's book in the library, and the earl is in trade. I wonder how he managed that."

"Likely the same way a French-Canadian lumberjack managed to escort the most successful business owner in London." He led her onto the dance floor. "I am very proud of you. Have I said that?"

"Not it so many words, but we haven't been alone."

She tilted her chin so she could meet his gaze, exposing most of her neck in the process. If he followed the curve, it went straight down her cleavage. Thank God he was tall enough to see it and that he was the one dancing with her. "We aren't alone now either." It was a reminder to him as much as to her.

"Everyone is alone on a dance floor, Richard."

He couldn't hear her say his name without thinking of their night in the library. Holding her in his arms recalled carrying her to her bedroom and the temptation to crawl onto the mattress beside her. He needed to redirect his thoughts before his cock became their threesome in this waltz. "You stood up for yourself quite well today."

"I shouldn't have lost my temper," she sighed. "For someone in an organization to help women advance their stations, Lady Barber isn't very helpful to younger generations."

"Oliver and I ran into similar obstacles starting out." It hadn't been helped by Oliver's abysmal French. "We used it to fuel our determination on bad days. And then we invited them all for drinks to celebrate our second groundbreaking." He looked down into her smile. "Which is along the lines of what you did." She had also added a few names to her waiting list of buyers.

She'd have to expand before long.

"Foolish girl!" The shout stopped movement on the crowded dance floor so everyone could stare.

At the end of the room, a maid was on her knees scrambling to retrieve ruined food from the floor. An outraged lord leaned over her. "You'd best hope there is no damage…"

Amelia's hand tightened on his arm as she observed the overwrought tableau, her head tilted as though she were studying another barrel in her bottling room. After a moment, her gaze met his before traveling down his torso to the most troublesome part of his anatomy. After a glance at the floor, she giggled softly. "No wonder Jasper hit him."

Richard coughed to hide his chuckle, but her obvious glee ruined his efforts. Hand in hand, they hurried from the room. Once on an empty terrace in the cool air, she dissolved into peals of laughter and dragged him with her.

"Who knew poetry could be so naughty?" She wiped the tears from her eyes.

"Limericks generally are." Richard nudged her into the shadows to prevent discovery, though if the moon hit her hair, they were done for. Because one look at the challenge in her eyes and he was lost.

"There once was a girl from Dumbras." He skimmed his fingers from her shoulders to her wrists. "Who had an incredible ass." His hands flexed on her hips. "Not round firm and pink, like you really might think." He took a handful of her silk-covered behind. "But had long brown ears and ate grass."

Amelia laughed with her whole body, vibrating against his fingers as her breasts jostled against his chest. "I keep imaging bottoms with ears bouncing around a field."

And now, so would he. Richard hauled her against him and sealed his lips over hers, kissing her until he was drunk on her happiness. And drunk, hungry people grew ravenous. He tightened his hold and rocked her against him, tormenting his body even as he reveled in her gasp.

"Ow." She pushed against him enough to get his attention.

He was an arse, and not a happy one bouncing in a field. He released her and stepped back. "I hurt you?"

"It's not bothersome, but you like to grab the same place every time." She rubbed her palm over her behind. "Your finger marks will have finger marks."

The thought of leaving his marks on her body made him harder, hungrier. He was a bastard of the worst kind. "We should go in."

He let her pull him back into the shadows.

"So if I was on my knees like you were last night," she whispered.

He was going to have to talk to her cousin about what he'd put in the punch. "No, Amelia."

"I think I can imagine." Her knee grazed the inside of his thigh—which meant she had that foot off the ground.

A groan crawled up from deep under his ribs. "That's what I'm afraid of."

"Is it like when we kiss with our tongues or is it like a lolli—"

Richard put his hand over her mouth, felt her wicked smirk. She was going to kill him, and she was doing it on purpose. "You are wicked."

Her inhale tickled his palm. The look in her eyes was one he'd seen glinting back at him from the mirrors at some of Quebec's best cabarets as he'd celebrated every profitable year. She wasn't drunk on alcohol. She was high on success.

She lifted his hand from her mouth. "And that's how women's knees get dirty?"

God help him. "One of them." He would not show her any of the others.

She kissed him then, just long enough to tease his lips with her tongue. It ricocheted through his body all the way to his toes. "Shall we get the carriage?"

Richard rested his forehead against her warm one. If it was daylight, he was sure he'd find her blushing. "Let's."

He stopped their charge to the door. They couldn't be seen together with him in this state. "I'll go around the front. You go through the ballroom. I'll come get you."

Once Richard was alone, he adjusted his shaft so he could walk without crippling himself. The breeze cleared the air of Amelia's scent, and the chill helped him rein in his impulses. Still, he went for the carriage, his heart thudding in his ears.

If she barters her virtue for whiskey... Richard's steps slowed. He could have predicted this evening, especially after the last one. He couldn't keep his hands from her, and she showed an amazing lack of self-preservation. Except this wasn't a woman looking for a scandal as an excuse, or even for scandal's sake. She wanted to celebrate her success, her confidence that she'd climbed to the top of the heap and knew she could do it again.

But she didn't know how difficult that could be.

Oliver's driver saw him and began threading the carriage toward the door. Richard went back toward the party, formulating how to keep them both from getting hurt.

One look at Amelia speaking with Jasper told him he didn't

need to bother. Dreading the encounter, Richard still walked to her side. They said their thanks and goodbyes to her cousin and went down the front steps to the carriage without touching.

It was dark in the coach, but the gas lamps fluttered outside, points of golden light so regular he could predict them. *Light. Ten hoofbeats. Light. Ten hoofbeats.* Amelia stared out her window, the light gilding her skin. *Ten hoofbeats.*

"You refused Oakdale," she whispered.

He had, and he should have sworn Warren to secrecy. "Jasper's offer is based on a lie."

"But what if—"

If he married her next week, they'd be in France for their honeymoon and then in Quebec by the end of the year. It would be wonderful, until she grew bored of snow, and trees. And him. "No more pretending, Amelia. We knew going in that this would end. Your life is here, and my life is there. We simply got distracted."

"Is this about you being in trade again? Because I—"

Richard would rather be dragged behind the carriage than in here having this conversation. "This is about either of us being half a world away from a land that is a part of us and businesses that need us," he stated, working to keep his voice level. "You will hate making whiskey in Quebec with ingredients you don't understand, in a city with piped water, and people you don't know."

"I know you."

Her whisper sliced through him. "And if something happens to me? If I go into the woods and a tree falls wrong or a saw comes loose? If you have to stay there alone or come home and start over? Again?"

"I'm stronger than you give me credit for."

She probably was. How many times had she set herself on fire? "I'm not."

The driver slowed on Oliver's street. Richard banged on the carriage ceiling in what he hoped was a universal signal to drive on. The carriage lurched forward. The trees slipped past as he waited for the storm to break across from him.

"So you won't take me with you, but you won't give me my home."

He knew this tone. He'd heard it at the house party when she'd been angry with Ethan Raymond. He could imagine the tears in her eyes. "You began this knowing you'd lose it. You had a plan—"

"I didn't have an option then."

He understood that. He'd never considered her in Quebec until he'd suspected she'd come if he asked.

"You still don't, Amelia." This was the worst sort of negotiation. "Even if I told Jasper I wanted it, I can't deed it to you."

"Drake could—"

"I will not give Oakdale to Fletcher with the hope he stays loyal to you." He suspected Drake would lay down his life for her, but his death would put her at the mercy of strangers.

He knocked on the carriage ceiling again, sending them in another circle.

"Oliver then."

After this, Oliver would never speak to him again. Or he'd send letters every day telling Richard in detail about how she was succeeding without him—to spite him. And, God forbid, she didn't succeed, Oliver would be forced to either shoulder the debt or evict her. "No, Amelia."

Her handkerchief was white in the shadows. Her sniffle echoed.

Richard anchored his back to the seat. If he held her, he'd give in. He'd deed her the moon to make her happy.

She was quiet for a long moment. "That's it then."

Half an hour ago, she'd been tormenting her way into his bed. Now they were separated by a gulf he'd dug in the blink of an eye.

Richard smacked the carriage ceiling and stepped through the door before it was fully stopped. "Take Lady Amelia home," he ordered the driver without looking back. "I'm going for a walk."

I publish the banns of marriage between Richard Pierre Ferrand of this parish, via Quebec, Canada and Rosnay, France and Amelia Christine Chitester, daughter of Baron Kilverstone, of this parish. If any of you know cause or just impediment why these two persons should not be joined together in Holy matrimony, ye are to declare it. This is the third and final time of asking.

CHAPTER TWENTY

"**H**AVE YOU HEARD from Richard, dearest?"

Amelia looked up from her book, marking the spot where Jane got to the altar with Edward before realizing he was a faithless bastard. "He sent me the same note he sent his family. His business in London is taking longer than expected. He'll return soon."

As lies went, it wasn't bad—especially from a man who'd sat across from her and decried lying as a general practice. It had also been enough to satisfy an entire congregation as to why her groom hadn't been here to celebrate clearing their last barrier to marrying at the end of the week.

"He and the Earl of Althorne struck up a fast friendship at Jasper's party. Their estates in France are close to one another. Perhaps they're discussing future opportunities."

Take that. Not a lie.

"It's common for grooms to get cold feet before the wedding, I suppose." Mother went back to her embroidery. "At least that's what your father says."

"Richard hasn't gotten cold feet." Amelia returned to her book to see how Jane coped with *her* wedding becoming a shambles.

Technically true. He'd always *had them.*

Mother nibbled her bottom lip. "As long as you aren't worried."

"I'm sure he's fine."

Liar. When Richard hadn't returned to the townhouse, Amelia hoped he'd found a hole in the river to fill. Now she lay in bed at night and worried he'd walked away from her and into danger on that dark night. He might wish to end their doomed relationship, but he wouldn't abandon his family and his responsibilities.

Which is why she'd sent word to Drake. If anyone could find Richard in London, he could.

Of course, that was assuming Richard was still in London. He might have sailed for Canada and no one had the heart to tell her. Oliver hated to deliver bad news.

Thea would have had the courage to tell her.

"Your father is certain of it as well." Mother kept her eyes on her needlework. "Doctor Anderson says having the wedding to look forward to has made Augustus a better patient. He's following orders so he can be stronger when the time comes to walk you down the aisle.

"I hope he's not pinning all his recovery on my wedding," Amelia said. "It's only one day out of many."

"Perhaps we could bait him with grandchildren next." Mother looked to the door. "While we're alone, should we talk about your…duties?"

Amelia's inhale ended in a cough that threatened to kill her before her nonexistent wedding. "What?"

"They don't have to be dreaded," Mother rushed to continue. "It's actually better if you don't dread them. And if your husband is kind and handsome, like your father, it's actually pleasant. I'm sure Richard will be the same."

What Richard had done to her in London would scoff at *pleasant.* That night had shifted her world on its axis. Amelia found it difficult to sit quietly without remembering it. And as for the encounter on Jasper's terrace—Amelia had never felt more herself than that night in his arms.

It was all she could do to hold onto that feeling.

"Do you have any questions about what should happen?" Mother's face was as pink as the dress Amelia had worn that last night. "Or how things…function?"

She wanted to think about her parents having sex about as much as she wanted to be in an empty bed aching for a man she'd never have. "We have some time yet."

Amelia lifted the pressed lily she now used as a bookmark. Though it was flat, it wasn't yet dried, and the dark, spicy scent still clung to the petals. No wonder it was Richard's favorite flower. Or, at least, she assumed it was.

"I'm going to up to bed." She stopped at Mother's chair and bent to kiss her cheek. "Try not to worry."

Once in her room, Amelia placed the novel on her bedside table before tumbling the sheets in an artful mess that looked like she was having a restless night, which is what everyone expected. Her work clothes went on without unfastening them, and she'd taken to wearing a belt with her braces. Otherwise, her skirt gaped in odd places. Even her hat was too big.

She carried her boots down the stairs to avoid the noise. The cold tile in the servant's hall and the lingering scent of cherry pie had her hurrying to the back door, where she fumbled tying her boots while holding her breath to keep her stomach from curdling.

The modiste said if she lost any more weight they'd have to remake her wedding dress. Mother had marked it up to nerves.

Was it a lie if she just let people believe what they wanted?

She'd eat later. As soon as everything was settled, as soon as she knew Richard was safe. It wouldn't take that long.

Molly heaved a great sigh as Amelia swung the saddle over her back and cinched it. Faithful friend that she was, she lowered her head for the harness without complaint. There wasn't a groom in sight. Amelia couldn't bear to see people. Even if their questions weren't voiced, they were still there.

She stroked the soft gray neck. "I just can't stay in there."

They fell into an easy trot, and once out into the open field,

Amelia coaxed Molly into a canter. The warm horse under her worsened the wind biting her nose and stinging her eyes as they took the shortest route to the distillery.

Her heart stuttered at the sight of a tall shadow waiting at the manger. As she neared, it lifted a lantern. Too tall, too blond, too thin. "Hullo, Ben. Waiting on us?" Dismounting gave her a chance to compose herself.

"Heard you coming, miss." He handed her the lantern before taking Molly's reins. "It's cold out. Why don't you go on to work? I'll get her settled for the night."

Amelia was halfway to the door before she caught the meaning of his words. "You know I'm just—" *Checking on things. Overnight. Every night. Lying.* "Thank you, Ben."

The distillery was warm and dry, and the lantern banished the shadows that always alarmed her this late, aided by a wobbly marmalade cat.

Who was nowhere to be found.

"Caspar?" Amelia called. When he didn't answer with his usual petulant meow, she went from room to room. She returned to the cold paddock. "Ben? Have you seen Caspar?"

"He made a run for the door this morning when Florence got here, as much of a run as he could manage anyway." Ben looked over Molly's back, a brush in his hand. "I'm sure he's around somewhere."

Amelia scanned the trees as she returned to her refuge. No one but Ben knew how much time she'd spent here, raking wheat and stirring mash, letting the scent of raspberries, lemon, and mint rise to the rafters. The downside of all her work was that her stills were full, as were the mash tanks, and the loft creaked under the weight of wet wheat. It only left ledgers, which were much more fun now that they weren't full of red ink.

She settled into the office, reviewing sales and expenses. Father had taught her long ago never to take anyone at their word when it came to money. She was certain Drake knew she checked his figures. He likely found it amusing.

Tonight it was more confusing than funny. Amelia reached into the desk drawer and retrieved the report he'd done in London. The numbers in the ledger were off. Not by much—a few shillings here, a crown there—and not with regularity. Someone was stealing from her.

It couldn't be Drake. If he was stealing, he'd be smart enough to make his numbers match. He'd also be too wise to steal in the first place.

Ben, perhaps. He was new, on the premises alone, and was short on funds. While the Latimer family had always been respected, Ben hadn't been home for quite some time. "Silly," Amelia whispered. "He not stupid enough to risk a roof over his head for two pounds."

Which only left one person. Amelia closed her eyes and rubbed the center of her forehead. Damn. Why did it have to be Florence? And why now? When so many things were in motion.

The gurgle and hiss of the stills, the warmth of the fire, the sputter of the lantern, all coaxed Amelia to keep her eyes closed. No dreams rose up to meet her; her worries subsided.

An unholy screech split the night, jolting her out of her chair. She was still running for the door when a shot rang out.

"Miss," Ben called. "I've found Caspar. Come quickly."

She pulled a towel from the bottling room and ran into the yard. Caspar lay in a bloody orange pile next to a very dead wolf.

"It looks worse than it is." Ben took the towel and swaddled the cat. "I think his drinking thins his blood."

Once inside, Amelia retrieved her meager medical supplies. She and Ben went to work cleaning and bandaging the shivering animal, though Caspar wasn't injured enough to cease hissing and swatting them. Afterward, despite his protests, he leaned his face into her chest. Tears sprang to her eyes as she cuddled him close and let his wheezy purr rattle over her fingers.

This was her fault. If she'd supervised her employees better, there wouldn't be whiskey puddles on the floor, or roast beef temptations. There wouldn't be open doors and missing money.

If she wasn't trying to do everything at the same time, be everywhere she was needed, fulfill everyone's expectations, her cat wouldn't have been lonely enough to go in search of a new home. He wouldn't have been hurt.

If she hadn't come tonight, he'd likely be dead.

"It's going to be okay, Cas." Tears fell from her eyes as she stroked orange fur and imagined inky curls. "I promise."

❧

A LARGE ORANGE cat darted across the street, dodging cart wheels and horse's hooves, and finally Richard's shins, before reaching the alley. Richard looked after it, expecting to see it bathing while perched on refuse or sunning itself on secluded back stairs. It had vanished.

Perhaps it was wishful thinking. More likely it was a result of being drunk for three days.

Maybe it hadn't been here at all. Richard had encountered familiar faces every day in London, only to blink and have them be strangers. Many children in London resembled Simon, and Oliver's gray top hat was apparently in vogue. Richard had even seen Mrs. Bell, the swineherd, and he could've sworn Thea worked at the shipyard ticket office. He'd changed directions more than once to avoid Fletcher look-a-likes.

Amelia was everywhere.

Today was the day he reclaimed his sanity. He had breakfasted on tea and toast, cleaned up after himself, and met Rory Bolding to finalize their deal. He'd exercised with a walk to the shipyard, and a new ticket for Canada was tucked into his breast pocket. He sailed for home tomorrow. He'd go back to the townhouse and write a few letters before—

"Rich—Mr. Ferrand!" Fiona Allen was already crossing the street in his direction. There was no escape.

"Miss Allen." He forced a smile and remembered to lift his

hat in greeting. It had still been in the carriage after Amelia had traveled home. "What brings you to London?"

"I believe the better question is what brings *you* here?" She paused midway to touching his forearm, reversed course, and clasped her parasol. The two-handed grasp made it appear she feared flying away on this non-windy day. "Aren't you to be married at the end of the week?"

"Ah, yes." Because if Amelia had cried off, he would have heard by now. Oliver would have kicked the door in. Surely she wasn't planning to show up at the church and stand at the altar alone. She wouldn't paint him as the cad he actually was. "Business with the Earl of Althorne kept me in town."

It wasn't a lie. He and Rory Bolding had brokered an agreement to export lumber, either from Quebec or Thetford, in exchange for French silk. Richard was sure certain Thea knew a dressmaker who could make use of it.

But they had signed the contract before luncheon the morning after Jasper's party. Richard could have been back in Thetford two days ago.

"I never thanked you." Fiona lowered her voice, but kept to her side of the pavement. "You have always been a gentleman, despite my outlandish behavior."

The young lady in front of him bore little resemblance to the one he'd met aboard ship. "Gentleman is a bit of a stretch."

"Put cheese in front of a mouse and he'll try to eat it, according to my chaperone." Fiona turned to walk, tilting her head in a silent invitation.

Richard went to her side, but left a wide space between them and his hands behind his back, bumping against his waist with each step along the busy path. The chaperone fell into step behind them, making him breathe easier.

"I should explain," Fiona said. "At the beginning of the Season, I met a charming man who said all the right things and promised me the moon." Her smile was sad. "Until he found a larger purse."

"Warren," Richard breathed. Not for the first time since the party, he'd wished he'd just agreed to take Oakdale and worked out the details later.

Fiona shook her head. "Jasper loves nothing more than a good intrigue, especially at house parties. I played along because I enjoyed flaunting an almost marquess in front of the man who ruined my chances."

And though he did try,
His plans went awry.

"Raymond." Richard replayed the house party, seeing it through clearer eyes. "He jilted you to pursue Amelia."

"And Father ordered me to France to ride out the gossip." Amelia slowed to ensure her chaperone stayed nearby. "He'd hoped I would redeem myself by finding a husband in Paris, but I failed."

"And then we met." Richard put his tongue in his cheek.

"Exactly." Fiona sighed. "Which is why I was so hateful to your fiancée. She'd stolen the man I thought I loved and the only man in England who didn't know I had been an idiot."

"People in love do idiotic things," Richard murmured. He'd known that the moment he'd returned from Althorne House that first day and stared into the empty library. Three drunken nights hadn't convinced him otherwise.

"Amelia is a lovely, sweet girl. No one else I know would have been so concerned over me after the way I'd behaved." She laughed. "And I believe she has the mettle to stand up to you."

He chuckled, recalling her on that stool declaring *the world is too tall.* She'd likely knock it down to size soon enough, as she'd done to Mr. Raymond. Or she'd sweep it off its feet when it wasn't looking. "She can be terrifying for such a little thing."

"I'm glad you two have found one another," Fiona said. "It gives me hope."

That was a daunting notion. Also a large responsibility. How would she feel when she read next week's scandal sheets? "How do you know I'm not after her dowry?"

"Experience," she sighed.

"Miss?" The chaperone called out. "We should cross and go back."

They were in front of The White Rose, or at least in front of its iron fence heaped with rose bushes. A few determined white blooms dotted the shrubs. The imposing house sat far enough back that the shadows shrouded guests in secrecy.

"I'll escort you back," Richard said.

"No." Fiona signaled him to stop without touching him. "We should go up the hill alone." She took one last look before they parted. "Whatever is keeping you from her, resolve it and go home, Mr. Ferrand."

Richard watched them go, following their progress up the hill until the chaperone's brown striped skirt vanished from sight.

He'd walked Fiona Allen to a brothel, and she'd run away. Amelia would laugh over that for days.

"Ferrand?" The familiar low growl came from behind him and raised the hair on Richard's neck. He managed to turn halfway 'round before he saw stars.

And then nothing at all.

CHAPTER TWENTY-ONE

"**I**'M HONORED YOU'D ask me to come with you today, ladies," Miss Graves said. "I'm also quite happy Lady Amelia brought the barouche." She tilted her face toward the sunshine and smiled.

"Was that a joke, Miss Graves?" Amelia smiled like she'd practiced in the mirror, though the unseasonably warm day helped add authenticity. She would come out the other side of this a changed person, but she would come out of it.

"I do wish you'd call me Lillian."

"Not until you call me Amelia." Graves had called her *Lady* since their first meeting, as though reinforcing it. Today she was going to learn how little it had helped.

"Which I can do from the start of your wedding breakfast until I leave for Felton House." Graves's smile widened as she looked to Thea. "Though I'm uncertain how I can begin with Lady Carys at this point, I am grateful for the position, Your Grace. I've come to love Norfolk." Her lips quirked. "Just not the horses."

"Given Carys's parentage, I believe the earlier we begin the better." Thea's enviable laugh pealed across the carriage and out into the fields beyond. "But the position is not as her governess."

"With Lord Simon? Are you unhappy with the village school?"

"We would like to start our own school," Thea said. "A private preparatory school for young women."

"A finishing school?" Graves asked, managing to look down her nose at a duchess. "My apologies, Your Grace, but Lady Amelia can tell you how I feel about that *education*."

Amelia almost laughed. Father had mentioned it once, only in passing, and Graves had lectured him like a schoolboy on how it would be a waste of his daughter's intelligence to teach her little more than flower arranging. She'd taken to her bed immediately after, certain she'd be sacked. Father had never mentioned it again.

Graves might rethink the sacking in a few moments.

"Not a finishing school," Amelia said, taking her oldest confidante's hand in the hopes of softening the shock. "Thea and I have met a woman in London who is beginning a proper university for young women. It will be a few years before she takes her first pupils, but you know as well as we do that most young women won't be academically prepared without support."

"For village girls?" Graves's wide stare shot between them as she removed her hand to her lap. "How could they afford school? And preparing them for university only to be turned away because they're common would be cruel." She shook her head. "You cannot—"

"Mrs. Reid has assured us the university will be open to any young woman who can pass the entrance exams and pay tuition," Thea said. "And we've already begun securing scholarship pledges, mostly from our trustees."

They had been overwhelmed by how quickly the women they had approached had agreed to serve as the inaugural board members and how many of them had pledged funds without being asked. Evelyn Bolding, Lady Althorne, had been particularly generous in her response to Amelia's letter. She'd even included a note about how she'd been impressed by Richard.

Blinking into the sun, Amelia put a hand on her hat to keep it from slipping while she gulped until her throat and eyes were dry.

It was one of the more useful skills Graves had taught her.

"I could not possibly prepare a class of girls for that," Graves said. "Perhaps one at a time."

"We don't want you to teach," Amelia said. "We want you to be the matron."

"There will be instructors for each subject, or at least to divide subjects between them at first," Amelia continued in a level tone. She couldn't muster enthusiasm for anything, but right now it was useful. The more serious she sounded, the less Graves would doubt her. "You would be in charge of recruiting and supervising the women—we do hope to have as many women on the faculty as possible. You would also be in charge of the students."

Graves's mouth fell open in a most unladylike way. "This is a huge expense. Are your husbands supportive?"

"Rushford is, yes." She frowned when Amelia stayed silent. "And I believe Mr. Ferrand will be once Amelia outlines it for him. This has come together quite quickly. But we have our own money, Lillian."

"Begging your pardon, but allowances and pin money won't cover this." Graves took Amelia's hand as though to warn her of the foolishness. "This would take everything your mother left you and still require more. And you'll be in Canada."

"There will be plenty of time to settle things." Amelia squeezed her friend's thin fingers in reassurance. "And the duchess and I have six hundred a year, at present."

For she was sure her business would grow. Society ran on whiskey, workers celebrated with it. Drake was already reviewing investment opportunities offered by other circle members. She would have other businesses, other partners.

Graves looked ready to faint. There was no turning back now. Amelia smiled the way she'd practiced. "Lillian, we are going to tell you something that must remain our secret." She drew a deep breath. "I am Eamon Brewer." She fought to keep her grip on the woman beside her. "I was too tired for painting lessons because I'd been up all night bottling whiskey while everyone slept."

"And I own The Galloping Goat." Thea placed her hand on Lillian's knee. "As well as what my husband likes to call the village bank."

"That's…mad," Graves whispered. "How on earth…?"

Thea looked past her before giving a reassuring smile. "We'll explain later. Right now, we have another task."

The carriage stopped in front of a worn gate that bridged a gap-toothed fence. The house beyond it looked equally tired. It had been neat once. Whitewashing was still visible, and the paint on the door was just beginning to peel.

But the flowers were long dead. The vegetable patch, which should have been ready to harvest, was a straggly, withering morass. The sickening smell of rot and waste gave all the women pause.

"I didn't know this was happening," Amelia whispered. She should have. The Beyers were Father's tenants. They were her responsibility, but she'd been too busy with too many things to visit. She'd considered her duty fulfilled because she'd purchased the sharon fruit Florence and her father had carted to the distillery, because she paid Florence a wage.

"Nothing for it now that we're here." Thea stepped down from the carriage. "Let's see what's going on. If this is her father's doing, he won't have a job after today. Which Oliver would say only compounded the problem, but we don't pay our employees so they can drink or gamble their wages away."

If Florence's father had wasted his money on alcohol, Amelia would take her three hundred pounds to the church and join a nunnery. Which might not be a bad idea anyway. She'd heard tales of orders who made alcohol.

The girl came to the door with one child on her hip and two more at her knees. They were all wide-eyed, but they were clean. Florence did her best to curtsey despite her load and her siblings' grip. She was already crying.

"M'lady. Did Mr. Brewer send you? Tell him I'm sorry for not coming to work. My mama is ill. Papa didn't have time to go by the distillery to send word, and I didn't trust the boys on their own."

The boys looked to be four years old. But her father would have passed the distillery on the way to the lumber mill.

"Is your father not here at night?" Thea asked in a voice she'd used long before she was a duchess.

"He's… He's taken another job in town, Your Grace. At the abattoir." Florence's tears grew to a flood. "Please don't be cross with him. We need the meat."

"Of course not." Thea took the toddler from her arms and handed it to Lillian without looking. She offered her hands to the boys and smiled. "Take me to see your mama while your sister speaks with Lady Amelia."

Lillian followed them into the house. "I'll see what's in the kitchen."

Amelia half-dragged Florence from the door, shaking her gently to get her attention. "No one is angry with you. We've come to help." Technically, she'd come to lecture the girl on theft and keeping to her time, but that agenda was no longer appropriate. "How long has your mother been ill?"

"She hurt her back in the garden last summer, but the medicine Doctor Anderson gave her didn't help enough, even though he said she should be better."

Amelia's stomach plummeted. Despite the glitter, the *ton* was full of whispered stories. "So she found something else to help?"

"A man came through Elveden last fall with a tincture he said would cure her pain, but she's still not well." The young girl produced a frayed but clean handkerchief and blotted her eyes. "And it takes more and more to make her comfortable."

Laudanum. It had to be. "Were you stealing from the distillery to buy the drug?"

"No, m'lady." Florence's bottom lip trembled. "Food. Papa's wages take care of it most of the time, and the butcher gives him meat in trade, but the boys needed new winter things this month. They can share most things, but it means they wear out twice as fast. Or that only one of them can work at a time. We need every hand, Papa says. Mama's doctor is costly."

Her mother's doctor was likely no doctor at all.

Florence stared at the square window, where Lillian was visible. "Has she come to take me for thieving? I was going to put it back once Mama got better. I didn't think Mr. Brewer or Mr. Fletcher would miss a few shillings. Not right away, Especially since Mr. Brewer is never there."

She was wrong about Drake, but she was right about Brewer.

Richard had lectured about working when no one was there, about hiring children because they didn't ask questions. He'd been more concerned about danger from outside forces. This incident proved there were threats as dangerous from within. Threats Amelia could have seen if she'd been present. Not to watch her tenants' children—to care for them.

She couldn't do that from Quebec, or even France. She couldn't keep relying on Drake to do it. He was never in one place for long, and these families weren't his responsibility.

They were hers, and she couldn't help them while continuing to keep secrets. Richard had been right.

"I'll take care of it this time." She helped Florence to her feet. "But it can never happen again."

Florence nodded like her head was loose at her neck.

"And you are going to come tell me if your family needs help with anything else while we see about getting your mother well." She led the girl back to the house where Lillian and Thea were waiting. The baby reached for Florence, but Amelia intervened to take her. The boys had gone to chase the only hen in the barnyard.

"Florence, this is Miss Graves. She has been my teacher for a very long time, and my friend for almost as long." Amelia couldn't meet Lillian's gaze. Tears had been too close to the surface for days. Now that she'd accepted the future she'd thought she wanted, grief settled over her like a rain cloud. "She is going to ask you some questions about your lessons, and I want you to pay close attention as you answer."

Lillian tucked the young girl's hand in her arm and headed for the pitiful garden, talking as they walked. Amelia had learned many lessons the same way, in a very different home.

"Our first pupil, I suppose?" Thea asked.

"I hope so." Amelia dashed tears away with her free hand. The baby warmed the other. Someone else's child. She would forever be holding someone else's children. Because she couldn't have Richard's.

"Are you well?" Thea put a hand on her shoulder. "You've not been yourself since London."

"I'm—" Amelia stopped the lie before it passed her lips. This plan—her life—only worked if she was honest, no matter how much she lost. No more hiding in the shadows. "Thea, I have done something incredibly daft."

It all poured out of her like a barrel with the tap left open. Her father's request, her mother's preference of Ethan, Fiona Allen, the limericks…everything but the library and that evening on the terrace. She'd keep those dregs for herself.

"Richard can't cry off first, Amelia," Thea said. "It will ruin your character and, regardless of how you feel about the *ton*, you need that as an asset. You have to do it first."

"You think he's sitting in London *waiting* for me to…" *Lie. Because it would be the worst sort of lie to say she didn't wish to marry him.*

"We don't even know if he's in London. Oliver went to town to find him and warm his bloody feet." Her last words were such an overblown impersonation that Amelia laughed and actually meant it.

"It's a shame, though," Thea said. "I think you two are perfectly matched. And I was looking forward to having a sister I like."

Amelia felt the same, but she was too busy not crying to

agree. "Tell me." The sun was blinding. "How do I break my engagement?"

⌒

"HE WAS IN a goddamn brothel, Oliver."

Richard opened his eyes slowly, as much for fear of being pounced on as that blinking made his head hurt.

"He's been drunk for days," Fletcher bellowed.

Richard wiggled his toes and fingers as much as he dared before checking his knees and elbow, then his neck, and finally his jaw. The click in that joint concerned him, but a quick swipe of his tongue told him all of his teeth were there, were stable enough to stay in place, and he wasn't bleeding.

"There is no way Amelia is marrying him."

"Ye gods," Richard groaned without lifting his head. "Do you only have one volume?" He straightened his arm and raised his middle finger. "I was outside a brothel, not in one." His index finger. "Haven't been in…months." His thumb. "I'm not drunk today." He lifted himself to his elbows. "And of course Amelia isn't marrying me. You've known that since the beginning, Fletcher." He swung over so he could sit on the mattress before cradling his chin and wriggling his jaw in earnest. "Which of you hit me?"

"He did," Oliver grumbled. "But only because he reached you first. And don't change the subject, either of you." He dragged a chair across the floor. "This was a ruse?"

"I didn't know until it was too late to stop them." Drake's chair squeaked as he dropped into it.

Richard swore they were making as much noise as possible to torture him. "I told her to ask you, and she wouldn't do it."

"Because I had enough sense to tell her no." Fletcher squeaked his chair again.

"Because she couldn't afford you." It had been one of the first jokes Amelia made on purpose, but he took pleasure in twisting the knife a bit. Mr. High and Mighty with the Squeaky Chair was an employee. "And I told her no, too."

"And then?" Oliver twitched his fingers like he wanted to pull the story free.

"And then Augustus fell ill, and Ethan Raymond was an arse, and Fiona Allen was a flirt, and Amelia…" He drew a deep breath. Everything stopped at her feet. "Before I knew it, they were reading the banns, and I was turning down a house, and we were…here."

That was as much as he was going to say. No one needed to know about braces, split skirts, and a wicked sense of humor. Or that her taste buds were a wonder and her tongue drove him mad. Or that her heart was as large as her imagination—and her ambition was bigger than the two combined.

Or that he'd never eat another apple again.

"Drake, would you please go tell Jasper we've found Richard and that he's unharmed—mostly?"

The chair protested again when the man stood. "Of course. There's no sense of going to more trouble or expense than he already has."

"God, that man is a prick," Richard groused as the door closed. He didn't care if Fletcher could hear him. "And can't you afford well-made chairs?"

"You only dislike him because Amelia doesn't," Oliver said. "But he seems to have a genuine distrust of you."

"Likely because she threatened to let me ruin her so she could stay on the shelf and make whiskey for the rest of her life."

Oliver's mouth fell open. "That's the daftest thing I've ever heard. Tell me you didn't—"

"I'm engaged, not stupid." Richard looked down his nose. There was no reason for anyone to know how close he'd come. "By the time Augustus, you, and Warren got through with me, there wouldn't have been anything left for Fletcher's axe."

Besides, Amelia would be wasted on a shelf, always on display but never touched.

Oliver snorted an agreement as he rubbed his forehead. "You scared us to death, Rich."

"I told you I was working. I sent you a contract—a damned good one." He rose from the bed, pulling his shirt free as he went. It was torn from where he'd hit the pavement, and it smelled of the street.

"Which took half a day, according to Bolding." Oliver swept his hand toward the door. "I get here to find the house empty, no liquor, no ink, and my library covered in ruined paper. Warren has people walking up and down the Thames looking for your corpse."

"He's likely stopped that since I saw Fiona." He checked his torso in the mirror. He had a few minor scrapes, and he'd likely have some colorful bruises. Especially on his jaw. Other than that, he looked unscathed. "I'm sure—"

"Dammit, Richard! That is not the point. Did you have no consideration for your family?" Oliver banged a cosmetic pot on the dressing table. "That's for your bruises. Thea thought you might have been in a scrape."

"She's very kind, your wife," Richard muttered as he used his reflection to apply the cream as far as he could reach.

"She likes you."

"It's easy to see why you never stopped loving her." Richard winced as he pulled a clean shirt over his head.

"Rich—"

"Every time he calls Thea mother, I think of how much Julia was looking forward to that." He shoved his shirt into his trousers and reached for the buttons. "Do you remember that, Ol?"

"Of course I do."

"Really, because you had *this* life." Richard pointed to the floor. "And then you had *that* life," he said as he gestured toward what he hoped was west. He didn't even know anymore. He'd completely lost direction. "And now you have *this* life again. It's like we were grafted on but didn't take root." He faced his silent friend, his dead sister's husband. "When I'm introduced, people think I'm Thea's brother, did you know that? They don't know anything about Julia. They know Canada. They know Simon. But they don't know her."

Oliver managed to look surprised and sad at the same time, but he stayed quiet. After all, what was there to say?

"Not even Simon." Richard reached for his cravat and paused. He wasn't wearing another one of those until he had to. And that one was bloody anyway. "There's not a portrait of her any-where."

"And you think that's because I don't love her?"

Oliver's quiet question contrasted with his white knuckles. Richard didn't care if he was angry. It was time he heard the truth.

"You didn't even come back to say goodbye," he said. "I was left to tell everyone how you'd met someone and married and were staying in the English countryside on an estate you'd inherited along with a title as long as my arm, which you had claimed you never wanted." By the time his sentence ended, he was shouting.

"My brother died, Richard. My father—"

"So did my sister. Your *wife*, the mother of your child, died."

"I was fucking there, remember?" Oliver's eyes blazed. "Hold-ing a child that looked so much like his mother I couldn't stand to be in the same room with him for a week. Keeping myself going because you kept telling me she wouldn't have wanted me to crawl in the mausoleum next to her and turn to stone. Do you remember *that*?" He sneered. "I guess she just didn't want me to live *this* much?"

"That's not—Do you remember when we started telling fairy stories to Simon and they all had black hair and light eyes, and their laughter was like rain on glass?"

Oliver waited for him to nod, which Richard had to do. Of course he remembered.

"The miniature of Julia from our wedding day is on my dressing table, next to my shaving brush," Oliver continued. "Simon comes in and tells fairy stories every morning. After he leaves for school, Thea puts the miniature back in its place. Because it's the only damned portrait I have of her. You didn't send me a larger one when you packed." He held up a finger to stop Richard's rebuttal. "I know I shouldn't have asked you to do that alone. I should have come home, but Simon...it would have been the Bremen Town Musicians comes to Canada. He refused to leave anything behind, the family finances were a mess, and the business was just starting, and then Thea was increasing and..." He drew a deep breath. "I'm sorry I left you alone to deal with that, but I won't apologize for not giving everyone I meet my personal history. I don't talk about Julia to strangers here because I didn't talk about Thea to strangers in Canada—unless I was drunk in a pub."

Which had stopped when he'd married Julia. Richard dropped into the vacant, squeaky chair. Oliver dragged his across the floor so they could face each other, elbows on knees, hands dangling, just like they'd done for years, whether they were discussing a timber contract or Simon's dinner schedule.

"If the roles were reversed," Oliver said. "If Thea had...died and I had arrived in Quebec with Jamey. If Julia had married me, would you have considered Jamey your family, or would he always have been an outsider?"

Richard wanted to say it was different, that a child needed a mother, that...was exactly what he and Oliver had argued about when Simon became old enough for solid food. As much as he cherished his memories of Simon as their third co-chairman, Simon *the boy* had thrived here. Because he had a mother.

Oliver's mouth tipped up in a wry grin, as it did every time he knew he was right. "You may disagree with me, but I will not tell my seven-year-old son that he had a mother he never knew and a brother he never knew, and an uncle. If he understands it at eight, I'll tell him. But it might be at twelve. Hell, it might take until he's twenty."

Richard chuckled. He knew Oliver was hoping for twenty.

"My life has been shaped by loss," Oliver said. "I will not have it shape my son's. And I won't have it shape yours."

It was too late.

"I'd wager you haven't changed that hideous wallpaper in the foyer." Oliver laughed when Richard wouldn't answer. "We hated that when she chose it, Rich."

Laughing made things better, but also worse. "She's alone, Oliver. She's over there now with no one to—"

"No she isn't. She's in the barn when Simon giggles over feeding that fool pig. And, when he insists on sliding down the banister, she's next to Thea holding her breath." He kicked Richard's foot. "She's here, now, making us face each other when we disagree, just like she always did. And she's taking my side this time."

Richard scrubbed his face, clearing his vision. "How do you figure?"

Oliver hoisted a stack of paper. "You can't finish these. You always stop in the same place." He made a show of reading the line. "I don't want to marry Amelia." He dropped a page. "I don't want to marry—"

"I can't cry off without ruining her."

"You can't cry off because you can't lie." Oliver smirked and held up three slips of paper. "Three passages to Quebec, all on separate days, all missed. Just admit it."

"The business—"

"As much as I love Quebec, it doesn't need us anymore, Richard. It's what we've always wanted—a business that earns us money without taking our time. We get to pick a new trail, plan a new adventure." His partner's eyes sparked. "Who do you want next to you when you do that? Other than me, of course."

God help him, he knew the answer to that all too well. "How is she?"

"Quieter. Thinner." Oliver helped him stand. "She and Thea came back from London set on starting a girls' school and, of course, they already have a board of trustees, most of their funding, and a building site. We're going to be cutting a lot of timber." He went to the door and looked back, waiting.

Richard had a choice. He closed his eyes and heard his sister's voice.

Allez, idiot.

CHAPTER TWENTY-TWO

AMELIA ENTERED THE front door in her work clothes, shrugging the left brace back onto her shoulder because her hands were full. "Simms, is Father in the library?"

The old butler's gaze swept from her hat to her work boots, his brows climbing higher with each item of clothing. "Yes, my lady. He and your mother are meeting with Mr. Warren. If you would like, I can fetch Rose."

"No, thank you." There was no reason to delay and risk losing her nerve. "If you would get the door, please."

Simms paused, his hand on the knob, as though he might deny her entrance. "Are you certain? I heard your cousin say something of Mr. Ferrand. They may be deciding—"

"They won't decide anything without me involved." Amelia's heart climbed to her throat. If Simms didn't open the door, she'd scream as she had as a child. "Let me in, Simms."

All three members of her family stopped talking as she entered; all of them turned. Amelia focused on Jasper's bemused smile. "Have you found him? Is he well?" *Is he coming home?*

"Yes, and yes." His lips quirked. "Are you drinking from worry or did you anticipate celebrating?"

Amelia blinked, breathed, relaxed. The ledger slipped, tipping toward the floor.

Drat. This was already a disaster.

Gathering the poise she'd learned from hours with Lillian and from watching Octavia at the Circle, Amelia placed the whiskey on a table and laid the ledger next to it. Then she removed her hat, smoothed her hair, and claimed the nearest chair, sitting as straight and carefully as if she were in a ball gown.

"Is that skirt split?" Mother's eyebrows had climbed almost to her hairline, carrying her voice with them.

Of all the things to worry over right now. Amelia patted her mother's hand. "It is. I'll explain why in a minute." She looked to Father, who was behind his desk. His cheeks were mottled, which was never a good sign. "Papa?"

"The duke and his man, Mr. Fletcher, found Richard in London. He's been there since you left, chilling his feet, I suppose."

She wouldn't have her father think ill of Richard. This wasn't his fault—at least not all of it. "Richard wouldn't lie, Father. If he said he was doing business, he did it."

"That faith is admirable, dear girl, but I cannot ignore that he has been encamped at Rushford's townhouse while you have worried yourself sick. That's not suitable behavior for a husband."

"What would happen if you arrived in Quebec and he hared off in such a fashion?" Mother put her hand over her chest, her favorite linen handkerchief between her fingers. The lavender lace exactly matched her dress. "You'd be without connection in a strange city. I shudder to think.'

Now or never. "I'm not going to Quebec. I never was." She couldn't breathe for her heart pounding. "And I'm sure Richard has kept his word to me because we had an agreement which he has fulfilled." She looked toward her father's desk, but focused on the sunlight over her shoulder. "I asked him to act as my fiancé so I didn't have to marry Ethan Raymond—or any man for that matter."

"Amelia!" Mother shrieked. "How could you possibly…" Her words were lost in tears and then in her handkerchief.

"Explain yourself, Amelia Christine," Father said. He didn't shout. He never had to.

With her hands and knees shaking, Amelia carried her ledgers and a bottle of aged spirits to her father's desk as though they were an altar offering. "I'm Eamon Brewer, Papa."

"The devil you say," he harrumphed. "If this is a ploy—"

"I *am*," Amelia said, using the same tone he had earlier. The one she'd rehearsed for hours, which she'd used in Octavia's ballroom. "I brew the best whiskey in Norfolk, using Thetford wheat and fruits and flavors from our tenants' farms and village markets." Jasper's open curiosity made it easier to continue. "I've hired their oldest children and pay them a living wage to help their families. And I've just sold my first batch of aged whiskey in London. It was so well received I'll have trouble keeping up with orders."

Mother was weeping. Father was staring like she had two heads. Amelia looked to her cousin. "Tell them. Please."

Jasper uncorked the bottle and poured a shot into Father's glass and then into his. "I've had it, Augustus. Ferrand brought a case for my party."

He sipped as though it was cough syrup. The first time. The second sip was more generous. "Richard helped you do this, then?"

Oh, for goodness sake. "This went into barrels two years ago, Father. He wasn't here to do anything." *And I didn't let him help when he was here.*

Her father swirled the whiskey in his glass. "How?"

"Do you think I toured all those wineries with you and learned nothing?" She knelt beside his chair so she could see his face and he could see her smile. "Or that I hid in the pantry because I liked potatoes? I have given up *everything* for this this, and I can support myself with it."

Jasper leafed through the ledger and gave a low whistle. "Is this a net figure?"

"It is, and before investments. Drake has some he wants me to consider."

"Fletcher?"

Jasper raised an eyebrow, reminding her of Richard and her purpose for doing this in the first place. She stood and looked between her parents. "Richard agreed to help me climb onto the shelf. That's done now. If I cry off first, I can just be heartbroken and not ruined." A lump bloomed in her throat. "I have to keep to our agreement, which precedes the marriage contract." It was easier if it sounded like business.

She pulled the ring box and letter from her pocket and delivered them to Jasper. "Give these to him, please."

THEA GREETED THEM in the stable, Simon's giant dog on her heels. "There you are."

Richard braced himself for a tongue-lashing and received an embrace instead.

"Don't ever do that to us again," she said. "Welcome home."

"Thank you." Richard let himself enjoy the affection, but this wasn't his home. Not yet. "I'm sorry for worrying you. Are the children all right?"

"Simon has declared you each owe him a story." She put a box in his hands. "After you resolve this."

He didn't need to see the box to know it was Amelia's ring. He was more interested in the letter.

Her handwriting was much like her, clear and direct with just enough flourish to make it interesting.

There once was a lass who told lies.

She thought that it proved her quite wise.

But Cupid did dart,

And she gave up her heart

To a man who saw through her disguise.

Dearest Richard, I don't know how to say goodbye, but I promised you I would. Thank you for your help and for encouraging me to take control of my life. You're free.

A~

He looked to his family and was able to see the joy and peace on Oliver's face when he had Thea in his arms. Oliver had worked hard for this reward—twice. Richard had fallen into it on the road when he'd arrived and then thrown it away.

"Go, you idiot." Thea pushed him toward his horse, which was already saddled. "Jasper said he'd delay his trip to London as long as he could."

Oliver nodded his encouragement.

Richard swung into the saddle, and kneed Rabbit into a gallop down the lane. The horse never slowed once they cleared the first fence, then the second and third. The wind skimmed Richard's hair from his face and whipped his jacket open to lash at his waistcoat. His eyes watered, but he could still see Oakdale on the horizon. He flattened his back and leaned into the horse's neck. "Get me to her, boy."

They thundered to the front steps, and a groom ran to catch the horse while Richard took the stairs in two quick leaps. Simms already had the door open. "Mr. Ferrand, I'm not sure—"

Richard clenched his fists to keep from shoving the man aside. At the last moment, Augustus walked into the hallway on his cane. Jasper was at his side.

"Augustus," Richard called from the doorway. There were too many things to say, too many explanations and promises, too many plans and apologies. It all boiled down to one word. "Please."

The old man's glare faded after a few long moments. "She's in the garden."

Richard didn't stop running until he saw her, wearing her work clothes in the middle of the day, her nose in a lily. He closed the distance carefully, and while she didn't turn, she didn't run either. Reaching for her an inch at a time, he put his back to her front, his hand on her stomach, and dropped his head until her hair tickled his nose.

"Oliver says that when one cries off, they're supposed to return everything they've been given. You didn't do that."

Her fingers covered his, but she didn't pull him away. "It was just a dried up old lily, Richard," she whispered. "I didn't think you'd want that."

Her linen shirt had been washed to the softness of silk, but it was warmer than a ball gown. "I don't want my heart back either." Surely she had it. It hadn't beat since he'd left her. "I'm an arse, Amelia. With the floppiest brown ears you have ever seen."

Her sputtered laugh dissolved into a sob that shook through her shoulders and down. Richard turned her into his chest and wrapped his arms around her. She was thinner than in London. "I am so sorry, *ma belle*. I will never do it again."

Richard sat in the nearest chair and cradled her in his lap, whispering about what had driven him from her, his conversation with Fiona Allen, his sister, his fight with Oliver, what he'd learned.

"I wrote you a poem." He took her silence as permission.

"There once was a man from Quebec,

Who took an incredible trek.

In search of a prize

That he found in your eyes,

And it's left him a God-awful wreck."

He ended it by kissing her on the forehead.

"I'm still angry with you," she murmured.

"As you should be." Richard brushed his lips over her skin. "I fell in love with you the moment you knocked Raymond out of the way and led me to Felton House yourself."

"For me, it was that day in the market when you were over-dressed and talking about shipping." Her quick kiss struck the tenderest part of his chin. It was the best thing he'd felt in days.

"There's a naughty line in that poem, isn't there?" she asked in a whisper.

Her smile caught the sunlight. His fiancé loved a good scandal—just not *too* scandalous. He'd spend the rest of his life making sure she smiled like that and she only had shadows under her eyes for the best of reasons.

"I'll tell you on our wedding night." Richard teased her lips with his, letting her control when she opened to him, when their tongues touched, how long. "Marry me, Amelia."

Her dark blue eyes refocused. "I can't go to Quebec," she whispered.

"I am more than content to follow you home, if you'll let me." If she didn't, he'd camp at the gate until she took pity on him.

Amelia's smile widened as she caressed his bruised jaw and played with the curls behind his ear. "You're already there."

⟡

CHAPTER TWENTY-THREE

"**I** WOULD PREFER this section be clearer on the tenants' properties. There shouldn't be any doubt that you aren't responsible." Amelia dipped her quill into the ink pot. "I'm going to write that in."

Jasper chuckled. "Of course you are, cousin." He reclined in her father's chair, which was vacant only because Father insisted on dancing every waltz with Mother, and she insisted every third tune was a waltz. They would likely be responsible for making the dance passé.

"I warned you my wife is the toughest negotiator I've faced."

His wife. She enjoyed that almost as much as "my husband."

Richard was wandering the library, hands behind his back as he scanned the shelves. Occasionally, he looked upward at the shelves overhead as though he was deciding how best to climb them to see what treasures were out of reach. He'd be disappointed to learn Father kept his most boring books up there.

Amelia started to tell him that, but decided he could discover it for himself. She had loved coming in here throughout the week to find him exploring. It wasn't just the books. He asked about every trinket on display, never tiring of stories from her family's travels.

"I cannot help that I was taught by a smuggler," she said. She wouldn't have changed it either. Drake had become one of her most trusted friends, and she was certain he and Richard would be the same one day. They had already had a good start. Drake had offered to deed him her distillery for safekeeping, and Richard had refused.

"Thank God more women don't know of his prowess," Jasper teased as he signed the agreement. "The men in London would find the world on its head."

"It's not such a bad feeling." Richard joined them. He put one hand on her back as he took the quill and signed his name. Then he gave it to her.

By law, it had the same meaning as an inkblot in the margin. For Amelia, it meant everything. After her father's death, she and Richard would own Oakdale together. It would be their home, in name as well as in action. She returned the quill to Jasper. "Grandfather will raise a fuss."

"Which is why I don't plan to tell him." Her cousin blotted the ink, folded the paper, and slid it inside his coat.

Richard's fingers curved to her waist. "The funds should reach your bank—"

"They already have." Jasper took his drink in one hand and offered Richard the other. "It seems odd that I'm the one getting the gift on your wedding day."

"I wouldn't say that." Richard's thumb swept an arc from her spine to her waist, dragging heat in its wake. On the return trip, he flicked the tie at the end of her laces.

"We shouldn't keep you from the dance," Amelia said. "Who knows? You might find a marriage-minded miss of your own."

"Ye gods." Jasper shuddered as he plucked his half-full glass from the desk. "That's a reason to avoid a party if I've ever heard one." He kissed her on the cheek. "I wish you every happiness, Amelia. I cannot think of a better family to care for this lovely home."

He shook Richard's hand again and, though they didn't speak, a long stare and a sharp nod passed between them.

Then Amelia was alone with her husband. "He's really not a

bad sort, but I wish he wouldn't drink so much."

"Says the best distiller in England." Richard brushed his nose along the curve of her ear, and his breath set her aflame.

"He has gin in his hand from breakfast until bedtime. Surely—"

"It isn't gin." His words danced along her shoulder before his tongue chased them away. He pulled her to him, so her back was against his chest. "And I don't wish to talk about your cousin, wife."

His mouth on her skin turned her muscles to water and threatened to char her bones to ash. All week, he'd kissed her senseless, but he'd stopped there. Even when they were alone, he'd stayed his hands. She and Mother had a vague and embarrassing conversation about martial duties which, combined with their tryst in London, had left Amelia more confused than ever.

Thankfully, Lillian Graves had been more direct, though no less embarrassing. *"We will talk about this once, because I don't wish for you to be ignorant or alarmed after your wedding."*

Contrary to those worries, Amelia wasn't alarmed. She couldn't wait for what happened next. "Would you prefer to read?"

Richard froze, his hands on her shoulders. "What?"

She smothered her giggle as best she could. "I noticed you scanning the shelves."

His laughter shook them both as he turned her. "I was trying not to molest you in front of your cousin."

Their kiss at the wedding breakfast had been but a hint of this one. Richard's tongue danced with hers, stroking and retreating in a pattern much more scandalous than a waltz, especially when his body mimicked the movement, pressing into hers. His knee coaxed her thighs apart, and then he was there. Nothing between them but their clothes, his hardness against her stomach.

Other parts of her ached for him, and she took his hips in her hands to move him.

"Christ, Amelia," he groaned. "Stay still, or they'll hear you screaming over the orchestra."

That didn't sound like such a bad thing.

"Honestly, I was hoping for a hidden staircase behind a shelf." Richard looked down at her, both eyebrows raised. "I'd prefer no one see me carrying you upstairs to ravish you."

Beyond the door, the orchestra was playing a lively dance. Everyone would be in a gallopade. "They'll never notice." She took his hand and led him to the door.

They raced down the entry hall to the stairs, him half-pushing and her half-running, careful to keep in his shadows so her gold dress didn't shimmer in the light.

Her heart was pounding as they reached the top of the stairs, and her feet flew down the carpet to their newly redecorated suite of rooms. Richard closed the door behind them and gathered her into his arms, but only to reach for the laces at her back. "Finally."

"Miss?"

The squeaky voice froze them in time. Richard's lips quirked in a most endearing way.

"I have it managed, Rose." His deep voice soaked through Amelia. "Thank you."

The maid might have giggled as she slipped out the door that led to Amelia's sitting room.

"Where were we?" Richard asked as he untied her laces.

Amelia tangled her fingers in his hair and dragged his lips to hers. "Here, I believe." She kissed him the way he'd taught her, her heart swelling as he groaned his approval.

The laces loose, the gown slipped from her shoulders. Her corset followed, and then her chemise, until she was naked in a pile of clothes, like Venus coming out of the sea. She'd seen that painting in Rome and thought—

She couldn't remember what she thought, because her husband was staring at her like she was the painting, his lips slack and his eyes bright. His fingers were a soft brush, like he was the artist himself.

Amelia wanted to see him the same way. Stepping close, she slid her fingers under his jacket and up to his shoulder. Her touch broke the spell, and he shrugged free of the garment. The tint to his cheeks might have been a blush.

"I've never forgotten to get undressed before," he murmured as she undid the knot in his cravat. He undid his waistcoat as she pulled the cloth from his neck.

This time when he kissed her, she curved her hand around his warm, strong neck. His jaw was heavy against her thumb, and the skin under his hair was velvet against her fingertips.

He walked her backward to the bed until her knees hit the mattress. The sheets were cool against her bare bottom as she sat, but the shiver had everything to do with watching the man across from her rid himself of his boots, then his shirt, and finally his trousers.

Richard was magnificent. Long muscles flexed as he joined her on the bed, pushing her backward until his chest hair teased her breasts, his large bare feet against hers as his knee nudged her legs open.

But it was his mouth that stole her breath as he claimed a nipple and sucked it until she was arching into him, like in London on a night that seemed a lifetime ago.

"Put your hands on me, *mon amour*," he whispered as his hands slid down her body.

Amelia was happy to follow his lead, reveling in the play of his back muscles under her hands as his mouth reclaimed her nipple and his hand found the other. Heat pooled as though she were melting in the sunshine.

It wasn't enough. She writhed against him, trying to get closer. Richard rewarded her by dragging one hand down her body and slipping it between them. His fingers stroked her as they had once before. Just like then, her body shimmered to life, drawing her muscles tight as her shoulders bore into the mattress and her toes curled against his knotted calves.

And then his body was where his hands had been, and her

legs were around his hips, making it easier for him. "Look at me, Amelia."

It was difficult to open her eyes because he was still stroking the spot that sent stars across her vision. Her reward was watching his eyes darken as he slid inside her, uniting them in a way she'd never considered possible. It brought tears to her eyes.

Richard stopped. "Am I hurting you?"

Amelia shook her head. His stubbly jaw scratched her thumb. "To think I might have missed this."

His throat bobbed as he nodded. And then he was moving, withdrawing and returning, stoking the fire inside of her until it was unbearable, and then continuing until she was clinging to him, his shoulder solid against her teeth and his skin salty on her tongue. His neck trembled against her lips, and his hips flexed against her ankles. She wasn't satisfied until he poured himself into her and quieted against her, his heart pounding against hers. Even then, when he tried to move away, she held him tight, her hands on his backside.

"I'll crush you," Richard whispered as he wrestled free. "And I have plans for many more nights like this." He kissed her nose. "Years of them, in fact."

The bed chilled when he left it, but the sight of him walking away reminded her of a tiger she'd seen at a zoological exhibit. He was all power and grace, her husband.

He returned with a basin and cloth.

"What's this?" He moved a wrapped box from the bedside table to make room for the basin.

"It's a wedding gift from me." Amelia had forgotten it in her drive to get him naked. Now, after something so sensual, the gift seemed childish. "You don't have to—"

Richard was already unwrapping it. "A book?" He flipped it open, the parchment pages shuffling against each other before thumping against the leather covers. "A diary?"

"I thought you could use it to write your stories with Simon. So you could remember them, and maybe tell them to—" *Our children.* She couldn't bring herself to say the words. After what had just happened between them, her emotions were too close to the surface.

His lashes shaded his eyes for a moment, but when he looked at her, the blue was bright and glassy. It was like looking at a summer sky and seeing forever. "It's a perfect gift, love. Thank you."

He wrung the water from the cloth and smoothed it over her skin, cooling her outside and heating her insides once again. By the time he was finished, his shaft was erect. Amelia gave into her curiosity and closed her fingers around him.

"Oh God, yes," Richard groaned as he curled his hand around hers and showed her how to stroke him. His head fell back while his hips flexed.

"It must be difficult to ride like this," Amelia said. Richard's laughter made her want to suck the words back onto her tongue. "I just mean…is it like this all the time?"

"Only when I'm with you." Richard wrapped his fingers around hers and coaxed her to return to her task. "And, yes, sometimes it makes riding difficult."

His flesh grew hot. Harder. "Then we shall take a lot of walks."

"When I don't have you on your back." Richard rolled onto the mattress and pulled Amelia over him, using their hands to guide him back inside her. "Or you have me on mine."

It was Amelia's turn to throw her head back in a cry, which doubled as his hands closed over her breasts and his hips thrust upward, driving him deeper. Still, when he crashed down, she rode him into the mattress. Again and again, until his thumb found the place where they were joined, that magic spot between her thighs…

In search of a prize, that he found…

Her eyes flew open, and her smile curved as she met his laughing gaze. He was a naughty man, her husband.

And she loved him for it.

ABOUT THE AUTHOR

Peri Maxwell has lost herself in reading romances all her life. She began writing as a challenge to herself and wrote her first historical romance on a dare, and now she's hooked. She prefers to write heroines who can stand toe-to-toe with a hero, challenge society's rules for good reasons, and find love with heroes who admire an equal (even if it's a little reluctantly).

She enjoys history, humor, and a good mystery. An armchair historian, she also has a background in women's studies.

Peri lives in Arkansas with her husband and the two cats who rescued them. When she's not writing or reading, she's working her day job or spending time with her family and friends (the same ones who dared her to write a historical romance).

www.ingramcontent.com/pod-product-compliance
Lightning Source LLC
Chambersburg PA
CBHW071230210726
48293CB00002B/643

9 781960 184696